Jake Me

Jake, Book 2

SABRINA STARK

CHAPTER 1

What was it with me and lamps? As the miniature table-lamp whizzed by my head, I whirled toward the crazed brunette who'd just hurled it.

Ignoring the hammering of my heart, I gave her my snottiest smile. "Missed me."

Inside Jake's penthouse, Bianca was still glaring at me. "You are so immature. You *do* realize that, don't you?"

"Me?" I said, glancing toward the destruction. I spotted bits of glass, a crumpled lamp-shade, and chunks of a blue ceramic vase that had somehow gotten caught in the crossfire. "You've got to be joking."

I had known this morning would be bad. But just how bad, well, that was definitely a surprise.

Near the penthouse double-doors, my suitcases were old, half-crushed, and mostly empty. But on the bright side, I'd had waffles for breakfast, so things couldn't be all bad.

Right?

Who was I kidding?

It wasn't even noon, and already this day was scoring double-digits on the suck-o-meter, and not only because of flying housewares.

I sucked in a deep breath and faced the lamp-thrower head on. Bianca was gorgeous in that classic sort of way, with long brunette hair and even longer legs. This morning, she was decked out in a form-fitting mint-green dress with matching heels. Her hair was sleek, and her makeup was perfect. If someone told me she pooped diamonds and rubies, I wouldn't have been surprised.

As for me, I was wearing black yoga pants and an oversized sweatshirt that I'd yanked out of my largest suitcase. My hair was in a loose ponytail, and I'd skipped the makeup in hopes of saving time – time that Bianca was costing me with this impromptu tantrum.

All things considered, shouldn't I be throwing lamps at her?

I took a deep breath and tried to keep my voice level. "Why are you here, anyway?"

"As I've already told you," she said, "I'm here to pick up my things."

"Yes. And as I've already told *you*, you'll have to wait until Jake's here."

It was *his* penthouse, after all. At the thought of Jake, my stomach clenched. By the time he returned, I was planning to be long gone. But the clock was ticking. I needed to leave *now* – for his sake as well as mine.

It wasn't a goodbye, not really, but I hated the thought of it just the same.

Across the room, Bianca's eyes narrowed to slits. "We've already had this conversation," she said.

"Yeah, and a lot of good *that* did."

Her eyebrows lifted. "Excuse me?"

"Look," I told her, trying to sound reasonable, "you can't just come in here and start loading up on stuff. I don't even know what's yours."

"But *I* know," she said, "and that's all that matters."

I couldn't believe I had to spell things out. Again. Just a couple nights earlier, she had tried a similar stunt. If it didn't work on Saturday night, why would she try it a second time? And more to the point, why hadn't she grabbed her stuff on Sunday, when Jake had actually been home?

Again, I wondered what kind of stuff she was talking about. Bianca was Jake's former event-planner, not his ex-girlfriend, not technically anyway. Was she here to pick up paperwork? Or panties?

"You need to leave," I told her.

She crossed her arms. "I'm not leaving without my things."

I wasn't stupid. I knew that Bianca's timing was no accident. There was probably a darn good reason she kept showing up when Jake was gone. Either she was trying to drive me nuts, or she took me for an easy sell.

Whatever the reason, I didn't have time for this. My gaze shifted to the door. Tick Tock.

"And besides," Bianca reminded me, "you're the one who let me in."

"No," I said. "You're the one who *barged* in when I opened the door to head out." I glanced at the suitcases. They contained only the clothes I'd brought with me, and none of the beautiful things that I'd received from Jake. I don't know why, but it seemed important to leave mostly the way I'd come.

Following my gaze, Bianca stopped short, as if noticing my suitcases for the first time. She froze, staring at them with more than casual interest. After a long moment, her lips formed the barest hint of a smirk.

Oh crap.

Slowly, she turned toward me. "Going someplace?" she asked.

It was a big question, filled with all kinds of implications that were mostly true. Yes, I was leaving. Yes, things had gone off the deep end. And yes, I was on my way out with no guarantee that Jake would ever welcome me back.

But none of that was any of her business.

If I had my way, I wouldn't be the only person going someplace. I pointed to the door. "I don't know about *me*, but *you* are."

She cocked her head to the side and studied my face for an uncomfortably long time. As the silence stretched out, my cheeks grew warm, and my spine turned twitchy. If she didn't leave soon, my plan was toast.

It was Bianca who broke the silence. "On second thought," she said, "I think I *will* come back later." She smiled, more to herself than to me, and I could practically see the wheels in her head turning. If she showed up tonight buck-naked, I wouldn't be surprised.

Of course, I wouldn't be here to find out. Would I? Something in my heart twisted. If Bianca did show up tonight, would Jake let her in? Would they take up wherever they had left off? Would she be handling more than his public relations?

Looking for something – anything – to wipe that smile off her face, I pointed to the broken lamp. "You're gonna have to replace that," I told her.

"Why?" she said. "That wasn't my fault."

"You threw it across the room." My voice rose. "At me."

"Oh, get real," she said. "If I really wanted to hit you, I'd have gone for the vase." Bianca gave an elegant little shrug. "And besides, you provoked me. If it's anyone's fault, it's yours."

Okay, so I might have provoked her the teeniest bit, but she totally had it coming. I had known Bianca for just a few days. In that short timeframe, she'd tricked me into wearing the ugliest dress of the century, convinced me that Jake paid for sexual favors, and had done everything in her power to make me feel like I didn't belong here.

I swallowed. *Did* I belong here? I had to face facts. No. I didn't. At least not under the current arrangement. And that –

not anything to do with Bianca – was the reason I had to leave.

But not before she did.

"Forget it," I muttered. "Just go."

"Hey," she said, tossing back her hair, "you don't have to ask *me* twice."

Liar. I'd asked her a dozen times, maybe more. But I didn't have time to nitpick. I marched to the door and wrenched it open. I turned toward Bianca and waited, not bothering to hide my impatience.

Taking her sweet time, Bianca picked her way through the rubble and finally strolled past me into the lobby beyond.

I stood, watching from the penthouse doorway, until the elevator came and went, taking Bianca out of my sight, but not out of my thoughts. She'd be back. I just knew it.

As I shut the penthouse door, my gaze drifted to my suitcases. And what about me? After I left, would I be back?

I straightened my spine. Yes. I'd be back. Or at least, that was the idea.

I looked around, taking in the expensive furniture, the stylish décor, and the Detroit riverfront view, visible through Jake's floor-to-ceiling panoramic windows.

Three days. Was that really how long I'd been here?

The place was a palace. Jake had come a long way from the dump he'd grown up in. But that wasn't why I'd fallen for him. And it certainly wasn't why I was determined to make my way back here someday, hopefully someday soon.

Fearful of losing my nerve, I left my suitcases by the front door to make one final sweep of the place. Looking for anything I might have forgotten, I found my toothbrush in the master bathroom and a black lacy bra – mine, thank God – under his bed.

I dashed back to my suitcases. I opened the largest one and tossed the forgotten things inside. I grabbed the handles of both suitcases, and then hesitated.

What about the mess? I turned around to eye the destruction. I winced. It looked like the remnants of a robbery gone bad. Damn it. I couldn't leave it like this.

Cursing, I dashed to the kitchen in search of a broom and dustpan. Stupid Bianca. Aside from the time she'd already wasted, I was now cleaning up her messes too.

My mental clock was ticking like a time-bomb. Somewhere on the street below, my brothers were waiting. And worse, Jake would be back within the hour.

I had ten minutes, fifteen tops.

I had just ducked into his kitchen pantry when I heard a telltale click – the sound of a key card in the front entryway.

Oh crap. Make that *zero* minutes.

Jake. It had to be. And unless I was mistaken, things were about to go boom.

CHAPTER 2

Standing in the pantry, I froze, dreading the scene I'd been hoping to avoid. I heard the penthouse door open, followed by a pause and then hard footsteps.

I closed my eyes, trying to decide how to play this. Should I simply announce that I was leaving? Or play it cool and duck out tomorrow, when Jake wasn't around to say I couldn't go?

I was still thinking when those footsteps grew closer. I opened my eyes, and there he was, Jake, standing in the doorway a few feet away.

He had dark hair, dark eyes, and a body to die for. He wore jeans and a thin, white T-shirt, giving me the barest glimpse of that muscular chest, his washboard abs, and those all-too familiar tattoos. Last night, I'd traced the patterns of those tattoos, first with my fingers and then with my lips.

But that was then. This was now. His face was ashen as he stared into the quiet space. His gaze slid from my head to my toes and back up again. "You're okay?"

I tried to smile. "Of course I'm okay." Physically, anyway.

In front of me, his shoulders eased, and he blew out a long, unsteady breath.

I shook my head. "What's wrong?"

He glanced toward the living area.

"Oh." I winced. "Yeah. The lamp."

"Screw the lamp." He strode forward to gather me in his arms. "When I saw that...I just." He squeezed me tighter. "Never mind. Sure you're alright?"

I forced out a weak laugh. "Yeah, but don't you want to know what happened?"

He pulled back to study my face. "You wanna tell me?"

"Not particularly."

Caressing my waist, he flashed me that grin of his, the one that made my heart melt and knees go wobbly. "Wild party, huh?"

"Oh please," I said. "You were gone like forty minutes." I tried to say it like it was a good thing. Of all the times for him to be early, why now?

Plus, looking at him, having him near me, and seeing that smile of his — it made everything that much harder. I didn't want to leave. But for his sake as much as mine, I had to. It was the only way.

If I didn't leave now, I sure as hell wouldn't have the willpower tomorrow.

"Jake?" I said.

"Yeah?"

"I'm leaving."

On my waist, his hands froze in mid-motion. His smile disappeared, but he didn't let go.

"Aren't you going to say something?" I asked.

After a long moment, he dropped his hands. "Alright." He took a step backward. "No."

I stared up at him. "No?"

"No," he repeated, crossing his arms. "You can't leave." He leaned sideways against the door frame and gave me a long, penetrating look. "Not yet."

I felt my temper rise. "That's what *you* think."

"Wrong," he said. "That's what I *know*."

I knew something too. I was getting pretty darn tired of being bossed around, even if it was supposedly for my own safety.

"Tell me something," I said. "Who am I to you?"

"You *know* who you are."

The girl he loved? That's what he told me last night, among other things — things that weren't quite so pretty.

"I mean," I said, "am I your prisoner?"

His body stiffened. His voice, normally so strong, was very soft in the quiet space. "Is that what you think?"

Was it? Honestly, I didn't know. Just a few days earlier, he'd barged into my dump of an apartment and practically dragged me out of there. He'd hauled me across town and settled me into his penthouse, supposedly for just a week or two. He'd quit both of my jobs and burned a lot of my bridges.

Was it to seal off my escape routes?

Other than vague warnings of unseen danger, it occurred to me that his explanations on that front had been pretty skimpy, all things considered. "I don't know what to think," I admitted. "And you wanna know why?"

His voice was a monotone. "Why?"

"Because you haven't told me squat."

His gaze bored into mine. He said nothing.

"So," I said, pressing the issue, "why, exactly, can't I leave?" It was ironic, really. Just last night, he'd made it perfectly clear that I couldn't stay forever. Once the danger had passed, he said, I needed to go — for my sake, not his. His words from the previous night came flooding back to me.

I hope to God that you never love me back.

I ruin everything I touch. And I don't wanna ruin you.

Jake pushed away from the door frame and moved toward me.

I held up a hand, stopping him just beyond arm's reach. "Unless you're planning give me a good explanation, just stay where you are, alright?"

It wasn't that I didn't want him near me. Foolish or not, I trusted him. And I wanted him. I wanted to throw myself into his arms and never let go. But I'd spent too long working up the willpower to do this, and I couldn't have my shaky resolve shattered by the temptation of pretending that everything was okay.

It wasn't okay. There were too many things I didn't know. But one way or another, I was determined to find out. "So, answer the question," I said.

He stared at me without expression. "What question?"

Steeling myself, I gave him a hard look. "For starters, am I your prisoner?"

"No. You're my guest."

"Is that so?" I glanced toward the main living area. "So if I want to walk out your door, you're not gonna stop me?"

Jake said nothing.

"Well?" I said.

Our conversation – if you could call it that – was interrupted by the sound of a loud knock, coming from the main penthouse door. Jake turned his head toward the sound. "You expecting someone?"

"Me?" I said. "It's *your* place." I tried to laugh. "It's probably Bianca again."

"She was here?" he said. "What happened?"

"Well, I didn't throw a lamp at *her*, if that's what you're asking."

"She was throwing stuff at you?" His jaw tightened. "You serious?"

Again, there was a knock at the door, louder this time. Soon, I heard a familiar male voice call out, "Hey! What the hell? Open up!"

I stifled a groan. Well, at least it wasn't Bianca. But in that moment, I almost wished it were. ☐

CHAPTER 3

Standing just inside the penthouse entrance, I gave my brothers an exasperated look. "You were supposed to wait outside," I told them.

"Yeah," Steve said. "And *you* were supposed to be down there already. We've been circling the block for like an hour."

My gaze shifted to Jake, who stood just a few feet away, watching us in stone-cold silence.

I returned my attention to Steve. "It hasn't been *that* long," I said.

Anthony spoke up. "It hasn't been that short neither."

At twenty-one and nineteen, my brothers were younger than I was, but not much. Both were tall and lean, but that's where the similarities ended. Steve, the older of the two, resembled our mom, a blue-eyed blonde, while Anthony had my dad's olive-skin, dark hair, and dark eyes.

At the moment, I didn't give a flying flip how old they were or what they looked like. They were supposed to be part of the solution. Instead, they were just adding to my problems.

Anthony glanced at the suitcases. "Those yours?" he asked. "Want me to grab 'em?"

I glanced at Jake. He was eying the suitcases like he wanted to crush them with a bulldozer and mangle the scraps with his bare hands.

Suddenly, it felt like things were moving way too fast. I edged toward my brothers to ask, "Can you give us a minute?"

Steve gave a noncommittal shrug.

I waited.

Neither of my brothers moved.

I gave them a what-the-hell look. "Maybe you guys can wait in the hall?"

"No way," Steve said, glancing over at Jake. "He looks pissed off."

Reluctantly, I turned to see for myself. Jake stood utterly still, eyeing my brothers with an expression that should've scared the crap out of them. The phrase "pissed off" just might be an understatement.

So much for a drama-free departure.

I turned back to Steve. "It's fine," I said. "Just go outside. I'll be out in a minute, alright?"

Steve and Anthony shared a look. They still didn't move.

With a sound of frustration, I leaned toward Jake and asked, "Can we talk in your bedroom a minute?"

After a long, unsettling look at my brothers, Jake turned away to stalk toward the back of the penthouse. Following after him, I called to my brothers over my shoulder, "Wait by the door. I'll be right back."

On Jake's heels, I strode down the hall and into the master bedroom. Taking a deep breath, I shut the door behind us. Slowly, he turned around to face me. He crossed his arms and waited.

I cleared my throat. "The thing is, you told me to leave. Remember?"

He didn't move, and he didn't speak. His biceps were bulging, and his jaw was set. His breathing, low and ragged, seemed to fill the whole room.

"Oh come on," I said, "don't look at me like that."

He made a sound like a laugh.

I gazed into his dark eyes and saw no trace of humor. "What is it?" I asked.

"Nothing." He glanced toward the bedroom door. "So, what was the plan?"

I shook my head. "What plan?"

He shrugged.

There was a plan, actually. I was going to stay with my brothers for a week or two, get my life back on track, and then, well, the details were a little fuzzy. But I did know one thing. This wasn't the end. Or at least, it wasn't meant to be.

Somewhere in my loosely drawn plans, I returned here and dealt with Jake as an equal, not some girl to be protected, whether it was from an ex-boyfriend or some unknown bogeyman.

"I'm still working on it," I admitted.

"The way it looks to me," Jake said, "the plan was to duck out without so much as a goodbye."

"There was a goodbye." I bit my lip. "Sort of."

He gave me a dubious look. "Right."

"There was," I insisted. I pointed to his king-sized bed, where a small white envelope rested on the nearest pillow. "I, uh, left a note."

In the note, I'd explained my reasons for leaving and promised to return once things were more settled – for a talk if nothing else.

Jake spared the envelope half a glance. He said nothing, and his silence hung thick in the air.

I gave the envelope another look. In truth, it did look kind of pathetic. But I had my reasons. "You want the truth? I was worried you'd try to stop me."

"Uh-huh. Because you're my 'prisoner'?" His gaze hardened. "I guess that makes me what? Your jailer?"

"Oh come on," I said. "I didn't mean it that way."

"Didn't you?" He glanced toward the bedroom door. "So what are my choices?" He made a sound of disgust. "Let you walk out of here, or kick your brothers' asses?"

From somewhere just outside the bedroom, Steve's voice rang out. "Bring it on, tough guy!"

What the hell? I whirled toward the sound. "Hey! You were supposed to wait by the door. Remember?"

"I *am* by the door," Steve called back.

I let out a sigh of frustration. "I meant the *front* door, asswipe!"

"Hey! Moonpie!" Steve called through the door. "I wasn't the one who called *you*, begging for a ride and a place to hide out. So *excuse* me if we're being careful out here."

Careful? My brothers? If I weren't so stressed out, I might have laughed. "I wasn't begging," I called back. "Now, go on. Wait by my suitcases, will ya? Please?"

When he didn't answer, I turned again toward Jake. His body was rigid, and his eyes were flat. At something in his expression, I wanted to run. To him? Or away from him? I still wasn't sure.

I flicked my gaze to the bedroom door and mumbled, "Sorry about that."

His voice was quiet. "You were begging?"

"Oh come on," I said. "You know how my brothers are."

"No," he said. "I don't."

I crossed my arms and threw out the best defense I had. "Well, maybe there are things *I* don't know either."

"Like?"

"Like why I'm *supposedly* in danger and why I *supposedly* can't go anywhere."

When he spoke, his voice was clipped. "Supposedly?"

"Well, what am I supposed to think?"

"Tell me something," he said. "Why?"

"Why what?" I asked.

His jaw clenched. "Why now?"

The answer was too complicated for words. He was my dream guy. I'd adored him for years. Over the last couple of days, he had made nearly all of my fantasies come true. If I didn't have the strength to leave now, how on Earth would I find the strength to leave in a week or two?

But that wasn't his problem. It was mine. So I squared my shoulders and said, "Because I don't want to be your responsibility."

His gaze darkened. "You're a hell of a lot more than that, and you know it."

"Yeah," I said, "but for how long?"

He moved forward until our bodies nearly touched. His chest rose and fell with his controlled breathing, and I fought two competing urges – to back away, or to throw myself into his arms. Frozen by indecision, I did neither.

"For always," he said

CHAPTER 4

My breath caught, and my palms tingled. I gazed up at him, wondering if the longing in his eyes matched the longing in my own. "Jake—"

But then, as if wrenched away by some unseen demon, he pulled back and said, "But that doesn't change anything."

I shook myself out of the trance. "What?"

"How I feel..." He shook his head. "None of that matters, and I'm not gonna do this."

"Do *what*?" I asked.

He glanced toward the door. "When you take off, leave the book. I'll handle it."

What the hell? The whiplash of emotions was almost too much. "I don't care about the book," I said. "I care about *you*." I swallowed. "And us."

In spite of my jumbled thoughts, I knew exactly which book he meant. A couple of months earlier, I'd swiped a little black book from Rango, my turd of an ex-boyfriend. For a couple of insane weeks, I had used Rango's scribbled passwords to wreak some justified chaos on the guy's social media accounts.

The short-term satisfaction was *so* not worth it. In the end, Rango had trashed my furniture, stolen my clothes, and cost me my perfect little apartment – not that I could prove any of it.

But all of that – all of the inconvenience, all of the anger, all of the frustration – that was nothing. Or at least, it was nothing compared to what I was feeling now.

I gave Jake a pleading look. "Why won't you talk to me?"

His mouth tightened. "Your ride's waiting."

"Look, I'm sorry, okay?"

"Yeah. Me too," he said. "You got the book?"

Glaring at him, I pulled Rango's black book from the front pocket of my oversized sweatshirt. I held it out to Jake. "You want it? Fine by me."

Jake took the thing from my outstretched hand. He shoved it into his back pocket, and said, "See you around."

"See you around?" I stared at him. "Is that all you have to say?"

His voice held no trace of warmth. "What do you want me to say?"

"I don't know," I said. "But you don't have to act so funny about it." I softened my tone. "Come on. We don't have to do this on bad terms, right?"

"The way I see it," he said, "we don't have to do this at all. But hey, it's your choice, right? You do what you gotta do."

I gave him a good, long look. His jaw was set, and his muscles were tight. Apparently, this was my cue to leave.

But I couldn't. Not yet. Because amidst everything – the tension, the confusion, the awkwardness – a new question was rattling around in my brain. And stupid or not, I was determined to ask it.

"Jake," I said, "answer me *something* at least."

His voice was clipped. "What?"

"Why is it that I couldn't go just a few minutes earlier? And now, all of a sudden, you're alright with it?"

He looked at me like I was insane. "You serious?"

"Yeah. Of course I'm serious."

From outside the bedroom door, I heard Anthony say, "Five

bucks he doesn't answer."

Oh for God's sake. I whirled toward the sound and hollered out, "Will you guys shut up! As a matter of fact, go outside! Pull up the car or something. Alright? Jeez!"

"No way," Anthony called back. "And besides, I wasn't talking to you. I was talking to Steve."

"Yeah!" Steve called. "Rude much?"

With a sound of frustration, I grabbed Jake's hand and tugged him toward the master bath. I slammed the door behind us and whirled to face him. "Just answer the question," I said. "Why is it you wouldn't let me leave before, and now it's all fine?"

He made a sound like a laugh. "Fine? Is that what you think?" He shook his head. "What is it you want from me, Luna?"

I didn't know what to say. What *did* I want from him? He was tough as nails, and sweet as a daydream. He made me laugh, and he made me quiver. I loved him, even if I knew I'd be an idiot to say so. The things I wanted from him had nothing to do with what was going on now.

"I don't know," I admitted, "but not this."

"What is it?" he said. "If I make you stay, I'm an asshole? And if I let you go, I'm a *bigger* asshole?"

My mouth opened, but nothing useful came out.

Jake glanced toward the closed bathroom door. "You want me to march out there and tell your brothers to get the hell out? You want me to tell them you're staying? Against your will?" He leaned closer, and his voice became eerily quiet. "You want me to stop them when they put up a fight?" He gave me a long, serious look. "You ready for that?"

Somehow, it felt like all the air had just been sucked out of the room. I felt like crying. It wasn't supposed to be like this.

I gave him a pleading look. "Oh come on. That's not what I want, and you know it." I swallowed. "I mean, I just figured we could be civilized about it, you know?"

"Yeah. And I'm working like hell to be 'civilized.' So if you wanna go, go. The other stuff? I'll work it out, like I said. So don't worry about it." He looked at me with dead eyes. "It'll be 'fine.' Just like I said."

"Jake—"

"Like I said, your ride's waiting." And with that, he turned and wrenched open the bathroom door, strode through it, and disappeared from my sight.

I stood in stunned silence, trying to figure out what had just happened. Before I'd even begun to gather my thoughts, I heard the penthouse door open hard and slam shut.

Somehow, I knew it wasn't my brothers who had just left.

It was Jake. □

CHAPTER 5

"Man, you pissed *him* off," Steve said from behind the wheel.

We were in the Moon Construction pickup truck, heading across the city. On the wide bench seat, I was crammed in tight between my two brothers amidst piles of discarded fast food wrappers and crumpled soda cans.

I buried my face in my hands. "Oh shut up."

So far, the drive had been mostly silent, on my part anyway. I'd spent the last half-hour sulking while my brothers went back and forth about the reason they were staying in Detroit rather than in our hometown, two hours north.

It had to do with some big construction project that had them staying in town for at least a few days, maybe longer. Lucky for me – or so I'd thought at the time – this gave me a place to stay until things were settled. Now, after the ugly scene at Jake's penthouse, this whole thing was feeling like one giant mistake.

Bleary eyed, I looked up, giving Steve a murderous glare. "By the way," I said, "you guys were totally rude. Maybe *you* were the ones who pissed him off."

On my other side, Anthony spoke up. "Nah. I'm pretty sure it was you."

With a sigh, I turned my attention to the road ahead. "Yeah, I know." I rubbed at my eyes. They felt hot and tired, like I'd spent all night crying. I hadn't. But I doubted that I would be so lucky tonight. "It was just wishful thinking, you know?"

"Wanna know what I'm wishing for?" Steve asked.

I didn't even look. "What?"

"A cheeseburger."

I turned toward him. "Seriously? Is that all you care about?"

"Hey," he said, "driving makes me hungry."

"Yeah," I muttered, "because everything makes you hungry." As for me, my stomach was still in knots. None of this was going like I'd planned. Thinking of Jake, I blinked long and hard. "He hates me."

And could I really blame him? He'd rescued me from a terrible situation with my roommate. He'd given me the best weekend of my life. He'd vowed to protect me no matter what. He had loved me – physically, emotionally, and yeah, even verbally.

I love you, he had said. And if he'd been telling the truth, I had been the only girl he'd said that to in his whole life.

And what did I do? I tried to skip out on him the very next day.

It was official. I was the worst person, ever.

But what should have I done? Wait around until Jake gave *me* the proverbial boot? At least this way, we might stand a chance for something more. Or at least, that had been the plan.

In hindsight, my plan sucked.

From the front pocket of my sweatshirt, I pulled my cell phone. I stared at the thing. Maybe I should call him. I wanted to. But then what? Would we just end up right back where we started?

"Nah," Anthony said. "He doesn't hate you."

"Yeah, right," I said. "I'll probably never see him again."

On the other side of me, Steve laughed.

I jerked sideways in the seat to face him. "What's so funny?"

He grinned. "Ten bucks."

I shook my head. "What?"

"Ten bucks says you see him again." He leaned back in the driver's seat. "Twenty bucks says it's today."

I recalled the look in Jake's eyes just before he walked away. If I *did* see him again, it wouldn't be any time soon. But cashing in on that sad reality seemed wrong on so many levels. "I don't feel like betting," I said.

"Why not?" Steve gave me a sideways glance. "You chicken?"

"No," I said. "I just don't want your money." I sank down in the seat as another depressing reality hit home. "Besides, I don't have any money to bet."

On my other side, Anthony spoke up. "No shit? But the dude's super-rich. How'd you end up with no cash?"

I whirled toward him. "Just what do you think was going on between us?"

"Uh." He glanced away. "Never mind."

"What'd you think?" I persisted. "That I got paid for 'services rendered'?"

At the memory of those particular services, I felt just a little more forlorn. Jake, with his hot body and sizzling sexual prowess, had rocked my world in *and* out of the bedroom. When it came to services rendered, I probably owed *him*.

"Jeez," Anthony said, "like I think my sister's a big ho-bag. Get your mind out of the gutter, will ya?"

I gave him an annoyed look. "Then what were you talking about?"

"I saw you in that video," Anthony said, "where Jake fought that linebacker dude. You're telling me you didn't get a cut of the action?"

As I'd learned just a few days earlier, Jake was some sort of internet superstar with twelve million subscribers worldwide and a rabid fan base of frat boys, groupies, and mixed-martial arts fans. By pure chance, I'd appeared in a recent viral video where Jake had mixed it up with some linebacker nicknamed The

Chainsaw.

As for me, I played the part of the panic-stricken girly-girl who had no clue what was really happening.

"I didn't get paid for that," I told Anthony.

"Why not?" he asked.

I cleared my throat. "Well, because I wasn't acting."

"No shit?" Anthony laughed. "You really had no idea what was going on?"

"Not really." When it came to Jake, it seemed, I'd been embarrassingly clueless.

Steve leaned forward to ask Anthony. "How about you? You want the bet?"

"Yeah, right," Anthony said. "Like I don't see what you see."

I looked over at Anthony. "What do you mean?" I asked. "See what?"

Anthony glanced in the side-view mirror. "I see Jake." □

CHAPTER 6

Inside the pickup, I did a double-take. "What?"

"Yeah," Anthony said. "He's been following us since Chatham."

I twisted in my seat to look out the pickup's rear window. Scanning the city traffic. I saw lots of vehicles, but none I recognized. An embarrassing wave of disappointment coursed through me. "Very funny," I muttered.

"If you say so," Steve said.

Unwilling to turn away, I kept looking. Soon, a couple of blocks behind us, a big white van changed lanes. I sucked in a breath. There it was, Jake's car – red, exotic, and beyond expensive. I'd never seen another one like it.

The last time I'd seen it, the rear end had suffered some major damage. Squinting at the car, I couldn't see any damage now, at least not from this vantage point. Still, it had to be his.

I yanked my gaze back to Anthony. "Since Chatham? But that's like a block from Jake's building."

"Yeah. I know," Anthony said. "Crazy, huh?"

I whirled back toward Steve. "You *knew* he was following us the whole time, and you didn't say anything?"

Steve glanced in the rear-view mirror. "I *did* say something. The bet. Remember?"

"Gee thanks," I said, twisting around to look. Jake's car was still there. He was so achingly near that I could hardly contain myself. I turned to Steve. "Pull over."

"Why?" Steve asked. "If the dude wanted to catch us, he would've already."

"You don't know that," I said.

Steve gave me a dismissive look. "The hell I don't. You see his car? That thing does zero to sixty in like two seconds. Besides, we're almost there. Why stop now?"

"Oh come on!" If I were standing, I might have stomped my foot. "And seriously, why didn't you tell me earlier?"

"Because, you'd have told me to stop," he said, "and I'm late already."

"For what?"

"Lunch."

"God, you are such an ass," I said.

"Hey, I'm hungry. So sue me."

I turned toward Anthony. "And what about you?" I asked. "Why didn't *you* say something? Wait. Let me guess. You're hungry too?"

"Well, yeah," Anthony said, "but that's not the reason." He shrugged. "I knew what would happen. That's why."

"Oh yeah?" I said. "What?"

Anthony glanced backward toward Jake's car. "You'd tell Steve to pull over. He'd say no. And then you'd spend the whole time yelling at him. Screw *that* noise."

"Oh, whatever." I turned back to Steve. "Seriously, stop the truck."

He held up a hand. "Just a couple more blocks."

"No!" I yelled. "Now!"

"See?" Anthony said. "Yelling." He leaned back in his seat. "Sucks to be right."

Ignoring Anthony, I leaned in close to Steve's ear. "I'm not kidding," I said. "If you don't stop, like *now*, I'm crawling out that back window." My jaw clenched. "And don't think I won't."

"Be my guest," Steve said. "But just so you know, the pickup bed's full of shit."

I twisted around to look. Inside the open cargo area, I saw my two suitcases, along with some motor-looking thingy and a bunch of oversized flexible tubing. "So? I'll just crawl over that stuff. What's the big deal?"

"And then what?" Steve said. "You're gonna jump into traffic? Jeez, chill, will ya?"

"Hey Luna," Anthony said.

I whirled toward him. "What?"

"Just so you know, when he says shit, he means shit. For real."

"Huh?"

"Yeah," Anthony said. "There's this dive-bar a couple miles from here. Anyway, last night, it had this bigtime sewer backup. I'm talking explosive." He grimaced. "Literally. You don't wanna know."

I stared at him. He was right. I didn't want to know. But it actually made sense. They *were* sewer contractors after all. Again, I turned to look at all that stuff in the pickup bed. I frowned. Some of that stuff was mine.

"Oh my God," I said. "And you threw my suitcases back there?"

"No room up front," Anthony said. "Sorry."

Well, this was just great.

Shuddering, I turned back to Steve. I gave him the look of death. "Pull. Over. *Now.*"

To my utter amazement, this time, he didn't argue. Instead, he eased off the gas-pedal, and navigated a right turn, onto a side-street that was only slightly less busy.

I looked around, hoping to find a good parking spot. To our

left was a tall, stately hotel, at least a dozen stories high. To our right was a sprawling, active construction site. The site was surrounded by a tall, chain-link fence, topped with razor wire. In front of the fence was a diagonal parking area littered with orange construction cones.

I pointed to a gap in the cones. "There."

Steve laughed.

"What's so funny now?" I asked.

"You," he said, pulling up where I'd indicated. He shifted the truck into park and turned to face me. "Well? You got what you wanted. Now what?"

"Um, actually ..." I looked around. "I'm not sure yet."

"You know what you're like?" Steve said. "You're like the dog who finally catches the car. It's like, yeah, you got what you were barking for, but what the hell do you do now?" He leaned forward and said to Anthony. "Am I right?"

Ignoring Steve's idiotic dog-theory, I twisted in my seat to watch for Jake's car. Almost instantly, I spotted it, rounding the same corner behind us. A moment later, it pulled off to the side, parking maybe five or six spaces away.

Feeling my heart rate quicken, I squinted at it through the glass. It was definitely Jake behind the wheel. I felt my brow wrinkle. But he wasn't getting out. He wasn't even looking at us. Instead, he was turned sideways, leaning toward something on the passenger's seat.

"What's he doing?" I asked.

Steve spoke up. "Hiding his dead hooker?"

"Hey!" I whirled toward him. "Stop being an ass, alright? He's actually a really nice guy."

On the other side of me, Anthony snorted. "You mean he's fuckin' nuts."

I turned to give him an annoyed look. "He is not."

Anthony held up his hands. "Hey, I'm a fan. Honest. But

nice? Get real."

"You guy stay here," I said. "I'm gonna see what he wants."

A few seconds later, my feet hit the sidewalk, and I began walking. As I moved, I took deep, steadying breaths, trying to decipher what exactly I was feeling. Happiness that he was here? Anger that he'd followed after us? My steps faltered. Concern that I might smell like crap?

I stopped in my tracks. Trying to be subtle, I turned my head and sniffed the shoulder of my sweatshirt. It smelled the same as always, like soap and fabric softener. I snuck a quick glance at my suitcases. No way I'd be sniffing *those* any time soon.

Pushing the suitcases from my thoughts, I strode forward, keeping an eye on Jake's silhouette as I moved toward him. He was still facing the passenger's seat. He was still looking down. In spite of everything, I almost smiled. In spite of everything, he was still the guy I loved.

When I reached the front of his car, he finally looked up. Through the glass, our gazes locked, and I almost forgot to breathe. My heart raced forward, but my feet stopped moving.

At the sight of me standing there, Jake became eerily still. I stood, frozen, watching him watch me through the front windshield. Suddenly, all of my conflicting emotions meshed into one solid sensation – utter relief.

He was here. And so was I.

It didn't guarantee anything, but it was a start, right?

Throwing caution to the wind, I dashed forward, making for the driver's side window. The glass slid down, leaving us face-to-face. His dark gaze met mine, and I felt that familiar tug of whatever it was that made me so damn crazy about him.

He was so rugged. And so beautiful. And so crazy sometimes that I could almost strangle him. But now, all I wanted to do was crawl through the car-window and wipe away the darkness that was haunting his features.

I summoned up a shaky smile. "Long time, no see, huh?"

His eyes looked hollow, and his mouth was tight. He didn't smile back.

But could I really blame him? I tried to put myself in his shoes. How would I feel if he had run off, leaving nothing but a note?

I knew exactly how I'd feel.

Like crap.

Finally, he spoke. "Luna—"

"Wait," I said. "Let me go first, okay?" He'd done the driving. The least I could do was meet him halfway.

"Listen," I said in a rush, "I am *so* sorry. About the thing this morning, you were right. It was a crappy thing to do." I rolled my eyes in self-mockery. "Jeez. I mean, who leaves a note? Dear Jake?" I forced out a shaky laugh. "Good thing your name's not John, huh?"

As I spoke, Jake had no reaction. No smile. No twitch. No sign that he was hearing me at all. If it weren't for his eyes, trained so eerily on my own, I might have felt invisible.

I cleared my throat. "You know? John? Like a 'Dear John' letter?" I waved away my lame attempt at humor. "Never mind. Stupid joke. Really, I just want you to know something."

His voice was a dull monotone. "What's that?'

I stared into his eyes, trying to make him understand. "Earlier, at your place, that wasn't a kiss-off." My voice softened. "I didn't plan on being gone forever."

Still sitting in the driver's seat, Jake turned his head to gaze out the front windshield. He said nothing.

Confused, I looked toward front of his car, trying to see what he was seeing. Ahead of us, inside the construction area, I spotted a dump truck rumbling along just inside the fence. As it drove past, Jake had no reaction. Was he seeing anything? Was he hearing anything?

I tried again. "Just so you know, the thing with my brothers, it wasn't like I'd been planning it all weekend or anything."

He stared straight ahead. "Don't worry about it."

"I'm not *worried.* I just want you to understand." I took a deep breath. "By some weird chance, I learned Steve and Anthony were in town. One thing led to another, and I figured I'd crash with them a while. Get some space, you know?"

"Yeah. I know."

I studied him in profile, wondering what exactly was going through his head. Whatever it was, it was making me nervous.

At last, he turned to face me. "Luna?"

Something about his expression filled me with dread. "What?"

"I'm sorry."

"For what?"

"For not stopping you."

Something tugged at my heartstrings. "From leaving?"

"No," he said. "From talking."

CHAPTER 7

I drew back. "What's *that* supposed to mean?"

He shrugged.

"Tell me." My face was flaming now. "What exactly are you getting at?"

"Nothing." He looked away. "I'm an asshole."

"Oh shut up," I said. "You are not."

"I know what I am."

"So why'd you follow us?" Suddenly, I felt like a giant fool. "To spy on me? To embarrass me?" My voice rose. "To see if I'd make an idiot of myself? I guess it worked, huh? Well, goodie for you."

His tone was softer now. "Luna…"

"Don't Luna me," I said. "I hate that name." Yes, I *was* being childish, but I couldn't bring myself to care. "Tomorrow, I'm gonna pick a new one. Something nice and normal."

"Don't."

"Why not?"

"Because your name's perfect." On his face, I saw the whisper of a smile that didn't quite meet his eyes. "Like you."

"Thanks for the flattery," I said. "But next time, do me a favor, alright? Just tell me to shut up from the get-go."

"I should've. But I couldn't."

"Why?" My tone grew snotty. "Because you're too polite?"

"The truth?" He shook his head. "Because I wanted to hear your voice."

My anger fizzled like flat ginger-ale. "Really?"

"—which makes me a selfish bastard."

"Jake—"

"Whatever you're gonna say, don't. I don't deserve it." He reached over to the passenger's seat. From somewhere near the floor mat, he grabbed something that I instantly recognized – my favorite purse, my *only* purse now, actually.

"Here." He held it out the car-window. "You forgot this."

I looked down at the thing. "Oh." With a shaky hand, I reached out to take it. "Thanks. I, uh, thought I had it already."

"No. It was in the car."

"*This* car?" I said. "But we took the other one last."

"Yeah. We did."

At the recollection, I almost wanted to look away. Fueled by raw lust, I'd been in a massive hurry to get Jake alone. At the time, I might've forgotten my own name. Suddenly, that seemed like another lifetime.

Desperate to keep the conversation going, I asked, "So that's where you found it? In the other car?"

"Does it matter?" he asked.

"No. I was just wondering. That's all."

He said nothing, and the sounds of traffic grated on my already shaky nerves. I wanted to climb into his car and shut out the world – the cars, the horns, the lost sensation that was growing with every minute.

Stalling for time, I reached into the front pocket of my oversized sweatshirt and felt around for my phone. Sure enough, it was still there. The phone was my lifeline. My purse – filled with almost no money and one useless debit card – was mostly dead weight. Lust aside, no wonder I'd forgotten the thing.

Still, I should feel thrilled to have it back, if only for my driver's license. Except I didn't feel thrilled. Clutching the purse, I tried to ignore the sinking sensation in my stomach. "So *this* was the reason you followed us?"

I held my breath. Was it the only reason?

Jake flicked his head toward the purse. "You wanna check, make sure everything's there?"

"I don't know." I tried to smile. "Did you steal anything?"

"No."

"Then I don't need to look, do I?"

"Yeah. You do." He glanced toward the passenger's side floor. "It slid off the seat. Some stuff fell out. I think I got it all, but..." He gave a small shrug. "If something's missing, now is the time to get it."

Now? As in now or never? With my mind running on overdrive, I opened the purse and gave a half-hearted look. I spotted my hairbrush, my wallet, and a few other incidentals.

"Yeah," I said. "It's all here."

Was that true? I had no idea.

"Good." Jake looked away and reached for the key in the ignition.

"Listen," I said, "about this morning—"

"Forget it."

I gave him a pleading look. "What if I don't want to forget it?"

"Too late for that," he said.

"Why?"

"Because you were right." He glanced away. "Better to get it over with."

I shook my head. "It?"

"This. The goodbye."

"So this is goodbye?" I blinked hard. "You don't mean for good?"

"Good?" He made a scoffing sound. "There's nothing *good* about this."

"Just stop it," I said. "What is it? You think you're doing me some kind of favor?"

His jaw clenched. "I know damn well I haven't done you any favors."

"That's not true."

In front of me, Jake's gaze shifted to something past my right hip. Whatever he saw, he obviously didn't like it.

I turned around and stifled a groan. Parked on the other side of the busy street was a familiar beat-up yellow sports car. And in the driver's seat was the car's owner – Maddie, my skank of a former roommate.

Worse, she was looking straight at us

CHAPTER 8

As I watched, Maddie jumped out of her car and slammed the door. She balled her fists, took one step toward us, and nearly got squashed by a red pizza-delivery truck. Turning to lift her arms high and wide, Maddie flipped the truck the double-bird and yelled out after it, "Deliver *this*, asshole!"

On the sidewalk in front of the hotel, a couple of businessmen stopped to gawk at her. As if sensing their gazes, Maddie whirled toward them and hollered out, "What are *you* lookin' at, baldy?"

The two men exchanged a look. Technically, neither one of them was bald. They glanced around, as if looking for the unknown hairless guy. Spotting no one by that description, they hurried into the hotel and disappeared from sight.

With a look of triumph, Maddie whirled again to face us. Her face was flushed, and her long red hair was a wild tangle of loose curls. She wore a black spandex micro-skirt, thigh-high black boots, and a tight white T-shirt emblazoned with the name of the city's raunchiest strip club.

Funny, I had a T-shirt just like it, but only because Maddie had given me the thing a couple weeks earlier, not as a gift, but as a sorry-ass substitute for her portion of the electric bill.

"You!" she called out, as she began stalking across the street, heading straight for us.

I felt my brow wrinkle. Me? Or Jake? I slid my gaze to Jake, trying to gauge his reaction.

"Get in the car," he told me.

"Why?" I asked.

"Just do it."

I lifted my chin. "I'm not afraid of Maddie."

"Then move," he said.

"Where?"

"Out of the way." He cracked open his car door, nudging it against my hips. "I'm getting out."

"Oh fine," I muttered, edging back to give him some room. "But just so you know, if she takes off her clothes, it's your fault, not mine."

The possibility wasn't exactly far-fetched. The last time I'd seen Maddie, she'd been nearly naked as she chased me and Jake into the parking lot.

Jake got out of his car and shut the driver's side door behind him. He moved to claim the spot in front of me, acting as a barrier between me and my psychotic former roommate. With a sigh, I edged forward to stand by his side.

Together, we watched Maddie dodging cars with blind stupidity as she charged toward us. A couple moments later, she stopped within arm's reach, out of traffic, but too close for comfort. "You!" she said again.

"Uh, me?" I flicked my head toward Jake. "Or him?"

She looked from me to Jake. Her gaze narrowed. "Both of you."

Jake spoke in a low, calm voice. "What do you want, Maddie?"

Her eyes were blazing. "You know damn well what I want."

If Jake didn't, I did. She wanted *him*.

I felt a twinge of guilt when I considered that she and Jake had actually dated, if you could call it that. But all too soon, the guilt evaporated when I recalled the other stuff – the money she still owed me, the awful lies she'd been telling behind my back, and the fact that she'd given me absolutely no warning when she thought that Jake was one of my ex-boyfriends, looking to do me harm.

"And *you*." She whirled toward me. "You owe me, sister."

"I owe *you*?" I said. "You're kidding, right?"

"Oh, I never kid about money." It was true. Maddie was a stripper. If the stories were true, she'd once had a guy's arm broken for copping a feel and refusing to pay up.

Jake stepped forward. "Listen," he told her, "you're done dealing with Luna. If there's a problem, you deal with me, okay?"

Maddie gave a hard laugh. "Well aren't you the knight in shining armor?"

I grabbed Jake's elbow. "Jake, I can handle this, alright?" After all, she was *my* former roommate.

He turned toward me. "Baby—" Instantly, his lips slammed shut, and his face froze. I knew exactly what he was thinking – the same thing I was thinking. The term of endearment was horribly outdated, given the fact we were done, over, finished.

Shoving aside the heartache, I turned to Maddie. "You know," I told her, "you've got a lot of nerve asking *me* for money, since you still owe me like two-hundred bucks."

"I owe *you*? Get real." Her tone grew snotty. "Aren't you forgetting something?"

"Yeah," I said, looking at her wrist. "Apparently, my lucky bracelet."

It wasn't like the piece was expensive. It was just some chunky red plastic thing that I'd won at the hometown corn festival of all places. But I *had* wondered when it went missing a few weeks earlier. Come to think of it, my luck *had* gotten noticeably worse since its disappearance.

Maddie raised her hands wide. "You want it? Come and get it."

I gave the bracelet a speculative look. Was it really worth a hair-pulling street-side spectacle? "Nah, you keep it," I said. "Ever since

Leon barfed on it..." Shuddering, I made a face. "Well, you know."

The story wasn't quite as far-fetched as it sounded. Leon, who lived one floor above Maddie, was a notorious barfer, especially on Saturday nights.

Maddie gave me the squinty eye. "You're just trying to gross me out."

"Don't blame me," I said. "Blame Leon."

"Oh yeah?" She tugged the bracelet off her wrist. "Well, blame *this*, hoochie mama!" She hurled it onto the pavement, where it bounced once and rolled past my feet to settle somewhere under Jake's car.

"Gee, thanks," I said.

"Gee," she mocked, "you're not welcome."

"I uh, pretty much figured that."

Next to me, Jake spoke. "Maddie—"

I whirled toward him. "It's fine," I said. "Really. I can handle this."

Maddie gave a hard laugh and mimicked me, school-kid style. "It's fine. I can handle this."

One thing about Maddie, she had this way of making me feel almost mature. Almost, but not quite. "You forgot the word 'really'," I told her.

"Listen, whatever-your-name-is," she said, "my apartment was trashed because of you. I don't know who did it, but I'm damn sure it's your fault."

"Look," I told Maddie, "I don't know what happened at your place, but since you kicked me out – with no notice, by the way – I'm having a hard time seeing how any of this is my responsibility."

"Screw you!" she hollered. "I want my money!"

Next to me, Jake spoke again. "Luna, get in the car. Alright?"

I gave him an irritated look. "No. I *said* can handle this."

"No," he said in a scarily calm voice. "*I'll* handle this."

"Hey!" Maddie hollered.

In unison, Jake and I turned to look.

With both hands, Maddie reached up to cup her breasts. She pushed them freakishly high and gave them an angry jiggle toward Jake. "Handle *these*, asshole!"

I looked to Jake, who looked anything but eager.

Suddenly, a wolf-whistle sounded somewhere behind us. I turned to look. At least a dozen construction workers were jostled shoulder-to-shoulder, with their faces pressed up against the chain-link fence. They were watching us with undisguised delight.

"Hey Red!" One of them hollered out toward Maddie, "If *he* won't, I will!" A chorus of male laughter echoed out from the rest of the group.

Maddie dropped her boobs and glared at the guy. "Dream on, pervert!"

"Don't you know it!" he called back.

With a little huff, Maddie turned back to me. "About our apartment," she hissed, "don't bother playing dumb, because I know you got my voicemail."

Oh, I'd gotten it, alright. That message was still burned into my brain. As Maddie continued to foam at the mouth, I stopped listening while snippets of that godawful voicemail skittered across my brain.

I don't know what shit you're into, but I sure as hell don't appreciate you dragging me into it.

Someone broke in. They trashed the place. They ripped up Monica's – or should I say your – room.

Everything's destroyed, even the furniture, and I'm sure as hell not paying for it.

And if that weren't bad enough, she'd ended the message by calling me a whore.

Pot, meet kettle. Except I wasn't the one who gave out nooners on Tuesdays for the low, low price of ninety-nine bucks.

"Are you listening to me?" she said.

Beside me, Jake spoke. "Maddie, she's done listening to you."

CHAPTER 9

I turned to give Jake a look. There he was again, trying to fight my battles. On any other day, it might have been sweet. But today, given everything else that had happened, it was leaving only a sour taste in my mouth.

Frustration made me blunt. "Jake, butt out. Seriously, okay?"

He looked at me with a stony expression.

Maddie laughed. "What's the matter? Trouble in paradise?"

I whirled toward her. "Just shut up, okay?"

"I'll shut up when you give me my money." She leaned closer. "Two-thousand. Like I said on the phone."

"Two-thousand?" I had to laugh. "Dollars?" Our place had been a dump, with faded carpet, paper-thin walls and cheap second-hand furniture. Two-thousand pennies was more like it. Did she think I was stupid?

Apparently, she did, because she held out her hand, palm up. "Now fork it over."

I looked down at her hand. Even if I *were* that stupid, did she really think I had a couple thousand dollars tucked away in my wallet? How clueless was this girl, anyway?

"Maddie," Jake said, "if you're looking for restitution, you take it up with me. Not her."

I heard myself sigh. "Jake, I already said—"

His voice was low. "I don't care what you said. And I'm not

gonna 'butt out', so just deal with it, okay?"

I glared up at him. "No."

He glared down at me. He said nothing.

Maddie elbowed her way between us and looked up at Jake. "Restitution, huh? Is that a fancy way of saying *you're* the one paying her bills now?" Maddie looked over her shoulder to give me a sneer. "So, I guess you *are* his whore."

Behind Maddie, Jake froze. His face grew white, and his body went rigid.

Before he could say – or do – anything, I gave him a pleading look. "Jake, seriously, stay out of this, alright?"

"Yeah *Jake*," Maddie said, turning back to him. "Don't worry about *her*. Because you and me? We're gonna be talking later." She tossed back her hair. "Nobody blows *me* off and gets away with it."

"Hey!" I said. "Are you threatening him?"

"Butt out, sister," she said over her shoulder. "He's a big boy. He can handle himself just fine."

On this, Maddie was right. From what I'd seen, Jake could handle just about anything. I'd watched nearly all of his fights on the internet. Some of the footage was nearly barbaric, with blood-spattered fighting that almost hurt just to watch. No matter how insane things got, Jake never backed down.

But those were guys. A screaming hoochie was another matter.

If this kept up, we'd be drawing an even bigger crowd, or worse, the attention of the police. I looked toward my brothers' truck and felt my eyebrows furrow. In it, I saw only one silhouette – Steve in the driver's seat.

Where the hell was Anthony?

I shook off the distraction and edged around Maddie to stand once more by Jake's side. Facing Maddie, I lifted my purse. "I'll make you a deal," I told her. "Leave now, and I'll give you all the cash I have on me."

Next to me, Jake spoke. "Luna, don't."

I turned to give him an annoyed look. "I got this. Alright?"

What Maddie didn't know was that I had like three dollars to my name – in quarters no less, not even dollar bills. It would totally be worth it to make my point. Cheaper than a latte and twice as delicious, right?

Maddie looked down at the purse. "You think I'm stupid? You've probably got like five bucks in there." She gave me a smirk. "Sorry, no deal."

I gave her an odd look. She had just told me to pay up. Why would she say that if she knew how broke I was? But of course, I knew the answer to that. The money was supposed to come out of Jake's wallet, not mine. But first, he was supposed to pay *me*, not her directly -- so I'd be the "whore," just like she said.

With an effort, I tried to look unconcerned. "Fine." I pulled the purse closer to my body. "It's your loss."

Her gaze narrowed. "You think I won't take it. Don't you?"

I shrugged.

"Luna," Jake said, glancing down at the purse, "you don't owe her anything."

I held up a hand. "This is between me and Maddie, alright?"

Jake's jaw clenched. "You're not giving her your money."

I let out a sigh. This was so ridiculous. I had no money. That was the whole point. If Jake kept interrupting, he'd totally ruin it.

In front of me, Maddie was giving Jake a speculative look. I could practically see the dollar signs form in her eyes. Her assumption was obvious. He was rich. We'd had sex. Thus, I just might have plenty of cash after all.

Jeez, did everyone think Jake paid me for 'services rendered'?

"On second thought," Maddie said, "it's a deal." She made a grab for my purse.

I yanked it away from her bony clutches. "Not so fast," I

said. "If anyone's pawing through my stuff, it's me."

"Why?" she demanded. "So you can pull a fast one?"

"No," I said. "So you don't swipe my hairbrush. Again."

"Whatever," she said. "Count up, or shut up."

Smiling to myself, I opened the purse and reached for my wallet.

Beside me, I heard Jake suck in a breath. I snuck a quick glance at him. He was eyeing the wallet with a pained expression. I glanced down at it, wondering if he knew something that I didn't.

Stalling, I glanced around and felt my eyes grow wide. "Oh my God," I said.

Maddie glared at me. "What?"

I pointed. "Your car."

She made a sound of annoyance. "What about it?"

"It's gone."

"Nice try," she said.

"I'm serious," I told her.

Rolling her eyes, Maddie let out an exaggerated sigh and turned to look. That's when she saw exactly what I saw. I hadn't been kidding. Her car was definitely gone.

And, if I wasn't mistaken, I knew exactly who had taken it.□

CHAPTER 10

Through the ongoing traffic, Maddie stared at the spot where her car used to be. She contorted her face and hollered out, "What. The. Hell!"

For once, I agreed with Maddie. With growing trepidation, I looked toward my brothers' pickup. The driver's side door opened, and Steve got out. He began strolling toward us.

Maddie had never met my brothers. Come to think of it, she probably didn't even realize I had brothers. When we'd been roommates, it's not like we spent a lot of time talking about me.

I glanced at Jake. He was scanning the street, as if searching for the same person I was searching for.

I leaned toward him and lowered my voice. "You should go."

"Not gonna happen," he said.

Next to us, Maddie was still ranting. And I couldn't exactly blame her. It totally sucked to have your car stolen. And this, I knew from recent experience.

Maddie thrust a hand in my direction. "Gimme your phone."

"Why?" I asked.

"So I can call the police, dumb-ass."

"Sorry," I said. "It's out of order."

"Sorry my ass," she said, turning to Jake. "Gimme yours then."

Jake gave her a deadpan look. He said nothing.

From the sidewalk a few feet away, Steve called out toward

Maddie. "Hey, Miss! Was that your car?"

Miss? I gave Maddie a good, long look. In that getup, she wasn't so much a miss as a madam – or maybe someone who worked for one.

Maddie whirled to face him. "Yeah," she said. "A yellow one? Did you see something?"

"Yeah, a big-ass tow-truck," Steve said. "You didn't see it? It hauled your car away like five minutes ago."

Maddie looked toward the now-empty spot across the street. Her gaze stopped at the no-parking sign. "Son of a bitch," she said. "Not again."

"You need a lift?" Steve asked.

Maddie looked around. "In what?"

He pointed to the pickup. "That."

Maddie eyed the truck. She squinted at the Moon Construction logo, with the words Sewer Contractor emblazoned in neon-green letters. "Get real," she said, flicking her head toward Jake. "I'm going with *him*."

Jake gave her a cold look. He said nothing.

I made a scoffing sound.

"What?" Maddie said. "I need a ride."

"Yeah, I just bet," I told her.

She glared at me. "Well, I'm sure as shit not gonna ride around in some sewer truck."

"Right," I said. "Because you have such high standards."

"Damn straight," she said.

I glanced at Steve. For someone who'd just been insulted, he looked pretty darn chipper. He was up to something. I just knew it.

"And besides," Maddie said, glancing again at Jake. "He knows the way."

"You've got your ride," Jake said, flicking his head toward Steve. "So take it. Or walk. Not my problem."

Maddie looked longingly at Jake's car, all sleek lines and shiny paint. She glanced briefly at Steve's pickup, with its muddy tires and crap piled in the back. She gave Jake a pleading look. "Oh come on!"

It was almost funny. Maddie lived in a dump. She worked in a dump. She drove a dump. Then again, the vehicle itself wasn't really the issue, was it? I knew how Maddie operated. She wanted a ride, alright. The hot, naked kind.

I slid my gaze toward Jake. As I watched, he leaned his backside against his car. He was tall, with dark hair and even darker eyes. He was still wearing those jeans and plain white T-shirt, except on Jake, there was nothing plain about it. Whether he realized it or not, the white cotton served only as a blank canvas to showcase the glorious lines of that amazing body underneath.

His shirt wasn't even tight. It was just that it didn't hide anything – not his finely cut shoulders, not his bulging biceps, and not those perfect pecs of sculpted muscle. My gaze drifted lower, and I felt myself swallow. And it certainly didn't hide those washboard abs, all ridges and valleys of hard perfection.

Jake crossed his arms and gave Maddie a bored look. Damn it. The guy looked like something straight out of a movie poster. In his side-view mirror, I tried to catch my reflection. The angle was off, giving me nothing but a glimpse of cars still buzzing by.

Maybe that was a good thing, because I sure as hell didn't look like a movie poster – unless it was a comedy starring a quirky cat lady who'd fallen on hard times.

"Luna!" Maddie barked out.

I jumped. "What?"

She pointed to Jake and gritted out, "Tell him to give me a ride."

"Yeah, right," I said.

"Oh fine, whatever." With a long-suffering sigh, Maddie turned to Steve. "I *guess* I'll go with you."

"Good," he said. "But it'll cost ya."

She did a double-take. "What?"

"Yeah," he said. "Lunch."

She made a face. "I'm not having lunch with you."

"Jeez, get over yourself," Steve said. "I'm not asking you on a date." He grinned. "I'm hungry. We'll hit a drive-thru. Your treat."

"Son of a bitch," Maddie muttered. She turned to me and held out her hand, palm up. "Gimme the money."

I drew back. "What?"

"Yeah, open the purse, and gimme me the money. Just like you said."

From a few feet away, Jake spoke. "Five hundred bucks," he told her. "From me. Now. Take it or leave it."

I whirled to face him. "Jake, seriously, you don't have to—"

"This is between me and Maddie." He gave me a stiff smile. "So butt out."

I squinted over at him. "Did you just tell me to butt out?"

"You don't like it?" he said. "Yeah, I know the feeling."

Maddie spoke up. "Deal."

Still leaning against his car, Jake gave her a hard look. "It's only a 'deal' if you stop bothering Luna."

I gave him pleading look. "You don't have to do this."

Ignoring me, Jake pushed away from his car. He reached into his back pocket and pulled out his wallet. He peeled off five hundreds and held them out in Maddie's direction. She snatched them from his fingers without so much as a thanks.

I made a sound of frustration. "Jake?"

"It's done," he said.

Maddie turned to Steve. "Let's get this shit over with." Without waiting for a response, she began stomping toward the pickup.

With a chuckle, Steve turned to follow.

"Wait!" I said, lunging for Steve's arm.

He turned to face me. "What?"

"Where's Anthony?" I hissed.

"A couple miles up the road." Steve pointed. "That way."

I glanced at the spot where Maddie's car used to be. "He didn't." I bit my lip. "Did he?"

"Later," Steve said. "You want a cheeseburger or something?"

"No," I said in a hushed tone. "What I *want*, is to know what's going on."

Halfway to the pickup, Maddie stopped. She turned toward us and hollered out, "Hey! Lunch-Boy, what's the holdup?"

"Zip it, hoochie!' he called back. To me, he said, "I'll be back in a few."

"Wait!" I said again. "You can't leave me here."

"Why not?"

"Because," I said, "I'm staying with you, remember? You're supposed to be taking me there."

"Yeah," he said. "And we're here. Trip's over."

Confused, I looked around. My gaze stopped across the street. "You're staying at the hotel?" The place looked nice, too nice, in fact. How on Earth could they afford it?

Steve laughed. "I wish." He flicked his head toward the construction area. "We're staying *there*."

I turned to look. All I saw was a chaotic mess of machinery and men, including the same guys who'd been watching us earlier. A few of them had opened up their lunch buckets and were watching us while they ate.

Great. Now, they were getting lunch *and* a show.

I turned to back to Steve. "Very funny."

"I'm not joking." Steve pointed deep into the construction area. "See?"

I took another look. Through the construction and

commotion, I spotted something that filled me with dread. "Oh my God," I said. "You're staying in the *job-trailer*?" □

CHAPTER 11

Five minutes later, I was standing on the sidewalk with a suitcase on either side of me. Steve and Maddie were long gone, but I wasn't completely alone. A certain someone had flat-out refused to leave my side.

I looked up at Jake. "It's fine. Really." I glanced toward the construction area. "I'll just lug. my stuff into the trailer, and, uh…" Then what? Hell if I knew.

I turned to look over at the job trailer. In the distance, it looked even smaller than I remembered.

Growing up, I'd seen enough construction sites to know that our trailer wasn't exactly like the others. Most job-trailers looked like rectangular metal offices on wheels. In contrast, ours was a vintage, bubble-shaped camper that might have slept four sometime in the 1950s.

It still slept four. Sort of.

Jake glanced toward the construction area. "You're not staying there."

Silently, I ran through my other options. I could call my sister, but she was two hours away in our hometown. Even worse, she was engaged to Jake's brother. I knew for a fact that he stayed at her place all the time. The last thing I needed was to shack up with one of Jake's siblings.

Hell, I didn't even want to shack up with my own siblings — at least, not in a tiny tin can.

But what were my other choices? My parents? No way. My mom would say, "I told you so." My dad? Hardly. He owned the small sewer contracting company. Thus, he was the proud owner of the aforementioned job-trailer – or as I called it, the canned ham on wheels. The trailer was older than my dad and twice as messy. But for whatever reason, he loved that crazy thing.

Next to me, Jake spoke. "You heard me, right?"

I surveyed the construction site. "Actually, I'm pretty sure we're not allowed to stay there. I mean, those trailers, they're supposed to be mobile offices, not mobile homes." I tried to sound convincing. "I'm sure my brothers were joking."

His voice was flat. "Are you?"

Actually, I wasn't. But the longer he lingered, the worse I felt. Embarrassment aside, none of this was his problem. It was mine. I picked up the suitcases and mumbled, "Well, I guess this is goodbye."

"Guess again," he said.

I turned toward him, fighting the urge to fall into his arms and pretend that everything was okay. "Guess again? What do you mean by that?"

"I mean there's no fucking way I'm leaving you alone at some construction site." He glanced at the suitcases. "I'll get those."

I yanked the cases backward. "Why?"

"Because we're going back to my place."

If only I could. The job-trailer was a tin can on wheels. Jake's penthouse was an oasis of sky-high luxury. But that's not why I longed to return. I gazed up at him, waiting for him to tell me that we stood a chance, that he'd at least consider the possibility that he deserved a slice of happiness in this world.

In front of me, he said nothing.

I let out a long, weary breath. "Jake, let's be realistic. What's changed since this morning? Or, since before Maddie showed up, in fact?" I fought against the tide of despair. "Nothing." I swallowed and forced myself to continue. "Nothing has changed."

"You serious?" His jaw clenched. "An hour ago, you told me you had a safe place to stay." He glanced toward the construction site. "You think *that's* safe?"

Even as a kid, I'd been on a ton of construction sites, but never for any length of time. And I sure as hell never slept there. No one did, really. Maybe my brothers *were* joking. I squared my shoulders. And if they weren't, so what?

I'd met more than my share of construction workers over the years. Usually, they were pretty nice guys. A few gals too. Sure, they might get rowdy every once in a while, but who didn't?

About the equipment, well, that was safe too – unless I happened to jump out in front of something, and I had no plans of doing that any time soon.

I wasn't afraid to stay there. Mostly, I was just grossed out.

That stupid job-trailer didn't even have a bathroom. My gaze drifted to the row of orange porta-potties just inside the fence. I stifled a shudder.

Still, I made myself say, "Yeah, of course it's safe. And in case you didn't notice, I was doing just fine before you showed up."

He gave me a deadpan look. "Were you?"

"I didn't mean here," I clarified. "I meant at Maddie's place."

"You think that was any better?"

"Okay," I said. "Yeah, my place was a dump. And yeah, my roommate wasn't exactly a nice person. And yeah, my jobs kind of sucked. But I would've figured it out. And I will this time, too." My voice rose. "So if you're just hanging around, because you feel sorry for me—"

"That's not it."

"Okay, whatever," I said. "Because you're worried about me? Forget it. I'm fine. This is fine. Everything's fine."

What a crock. It wasn't fine. *I* wasn't fine. And if he stuck around much longer, neither one of us would be fine, because I was in serious danger of losing it. I flicked my head toward his car. "So just go. Okay?"

"No," he said. "Here's what we're gonna do—"

"*We're* not going to do anything," I told him. "*You're* going to get into your car and drive away."

"The hell I am."

"And *I'm* going to throw my stuff in the trailer and wait for my brothers." I took a deep breath and tried to rein in my emotions. "Let's just stop this, okay? You made it pretty clear that we don't belong together. So why wait? Why draw this out any longer than we have to?"

"Luna—"

"You *told* me this was goodbye."

"I'm not leaving you like this. If anything ever happened to you—"

"Nothing's going to happen to me."

"Listen," he said, "come back to my place—"

"No!" I glared up at him. My mouth was dry, and my hands were damp. My shoulders were tight from holding those stupid suitcases. But I couldn't set them down. Because if I did, Jake would surely swoop them up, and I'd lose what little control I had in this sorry situation.

He held up his hands. "Just hear me out. Okay?"

Gripping the suitcase handles tighter, I gave him the briefest of nods.

"This is what we'll do," he said. "We'll head back to my place, get you settled, and then, if you want, *I'll* leave."

I gave a quick shake of my head. "What?"

"Stay as long as you want. Invite your brothers too,

whatever."

"I'm not kicking you out of your own place."

You're not kicking me out. I'm offering. Big difference, okay?"

I gave him a dubious look. "Offering? Or making the choice for me?"

"What?"

"What happens if I say 'no'?"

"Why would you?" he asked.

"Oh my God. Do I really need to spell this out?" I glanced away. "You know what? Just forget it." I hoisted the suitcases higher and turned to go.

I felt his hand on my elbow. "Hang on."

With a sigh, I turned around. "What?"

"Yes."

"Yes, what?"

"Yes, you need to explain it."

"It's just wrong," I said. "And weird."

"Weirder than sleeping here? In a construction zone?"

"Yes, actually."

He reached for the suitcases. "Lemme me get those."

I yanked the cases away. "No."

His muscles grew rigid. "Why not?"

"Because you'll throw them in your car, and then I'll be screwed."

"Baby, come on," he said. "I feel like an asshole standing here while you carry those." He reached for them again.

Again, I yanked them away, only to feel the smaller one slip from my damp fingers and go flying. With a sad, hollow sound, it landed on the sidewalk, popped open, and toppled over, ejecting panties and bras onto the dirty concrete.

"Son of a bitch," I groaned. "Not again." I dropped the larger suitcase and dashed toward the mess. Frantically, I began plucking undergarments off the grubby sidewalk.

Instantly, Jake was crouched beside me. "Let me get those."

I whirled toward him. "Just stop, okay?"

A wolf whistle sounded in the distance. I turned to look. A few construction workers had remained at the fence. One of them was giving me the thumbs-up. I looked down at my hands. I was clutching a lacy red bra. I flung it to the sidewalk and screamed out, "You want it? Come and get it!"

Next to me, Jake's voice was soft. "Baby—"

I whirled toward him. "Stop! Just go away, alright?"

He reached for me. "No. Not like this."

"Like what then?" I gave a choked half-laugh, half-sob. I glanced down at the sidewalk, still littered with my stuff. Screw it. I didn't have a washing machine anyway.

Unless I wanted to wash that stuff in the porta-potties, I was totally screwed, short-term anyway. In fit of pique, I dove down onto the concrete and swooped up everything, dirt and all. I stood and marched toward the nearest trash can.

I felt a hand on my elbow. "Luna," Jake said. "Come on."

I yanked out of his grip and kept on going. With a sound of defiance, I flung everything into the trash can – all my underpants, all my bras, and apparently, all my dignity, because the construction workers let out a rowdy cheer.

Just shoot me now.

I whirled toward the guys. "You want 'em?" I yelled. "They're all yours!"

From behind me, I felt familiar arms close around my waist. The arms were strong, but the embrace was gentle. I turned and buried my face against his chest, giving in to the flood of emotions that threatened to wash me away.

I felt his hands in my hair and voice in my ear. "Shhhh…It's okay."

It wasn't okay. It was crap. Still, in spite of my outburst, I knew it wasn't really Jake's fault. Bleary eyed, I pulled back to look at him. "Can you do me a favor?" I asked.

He looked nearly desperate. "Anything."

"Just help me get my stuff into the trailer." I gave him a pleading look. "And then leave. Okay?"

CHAPTER 12

Alone in the trailer, I woke with a start to the sounds of my brothers' voices. I sat up in the top bunk, only to slam my head, hard, into the sloped metal roof. "Damn it," I groaned.

"Uh, good morning?" Steve said.

I flopped back down on the bunk and closed my eyes. "Oh shut up. It's not morning." The trailer had only a few tiny windows, covered in faded blue checkered curtains. Through the gaps in the fabric, I could see plain as day that it was still early afternoon.

Probably, they'd been gone less than an hour.

Sunlight aside, the rumble of construction equipment was a painful reminder that the day was far from over – and I was a long, long way from Jake's place.

At the thought of Jake, I turned my head into the pillow – which had no pillow case, by the way – and tried to imagine myself somewhere else.

Tahiti. That would be nice.

"Are you okay?" Anthony asked.

With a weary sigh, I turned toward them. Reluctantly, I opened my eyes. My brothers were sitting on opposite sides of the trailer's only table. On it, I spotted a large takeout bag from a local drive-thru burger joint. Next to the bag were three takeout drinks.

I pointed. "Are one of those for me?"

Anthony lifted the only drink that was missing a straw. "Coke, right?" He dug into the takeout bag and pulled out a wrapped something-or-other. He set it on the table's edge. "Got you a burger, too."

"Actually," Steve said, "Maddie got the burger. I tried for sundaes too, but…" He shrugged. "Eh, she got all funny about it."

"By funny," I said, "do you mean flipped out and called you a bunch of names?"

"Pretty much," Steve said.

With a sigh, I climbed down from the bunk. I crossed the small metallic space, and squeezed myself in on Anthony's side of the small booth. I turned to him and said, "Speaking of which, *please* tell me you didn't steal Maddie's car."

My brothers loved cars – really, really loved cars. In the summers, they both practically lived at the local racetrack, where Steve was the semi-psychotic driver of car number sixty-three. As for Anthony, he did more driving off the track, sometimes with cars that weren't technically his own.

"Hey, I've never stolen a car in my life," Anthony said.

Technically, this was true. Of all the cars they'd 'borrowed' over the years, I'd never heard of them actually keeping one. But it made me incredibly nervous just the same.

"Let me guess," I said. "You 'borrowed' it?"

Anthony shrugged. "Call it a test drive."

"Meaning," I said, "that you 'test-drove' it to the burger place and waited for Steve and Maddie to show up and buy you lunch?"

"Oh, sure," Anthony said, "because that wouldn't have been obvious at all." He grinned. "Nah, I parked it the next street up. You know, *past* the burger place."

Steve was laughing now. "You should've seen that roommate of yours. After we hit the drive-through, I just 'happen' to hit the street where her car is parked, and she's all like, 'Stop the fucking car!', which by the way, is pretty stupid, because we're driving a truck, right? And I'm acting all dumb like 'What? Why?' And she's like, 'Because that's my car, dumb-ass!'" Steve lifted his drink to take a long, noisy slurp. "Which I *also* think is funny, because she's no genius herself, you know?"

I was almost afraid to ask. "So then what?"

"So then," Steve continued, "I stop the truck, and she jumps out, leaves her burger and everything, sitting right there on the dashboard–"

In spite of everything, I almost laughed. "Did you eat it?"

"Hell yeah, I ate it," he said. "It was still in the wrapper."

"I got the fries," Anthony said.

"Anyway," Steve continued, "she gets to her car, and surprise, surprise, the keys are sitting right there in the ignition. So get this. She flips me bird, starts the thing, and takes off without so much as a thanks for the ride."

"Gee," I said, "how rude of her."

"You're telling me," Steve said. "So anyway, I wait 'til she's out of sight and double back to get Anthony." He lifted his burger. "And here we are."

I shook my head. "And you did *all* this just to get a free lunch?"

"Hardly." Steve shoved the burger into his face and took a huge bite. With his mouth full, he said, "She was mean to you."

I stared at him. "*Mean* to me?"

"Hell yeah," Steve said. "We heard her yelling at you from like a mile away. And we're getting all pissed about it. But she's a girl, so we can't exactly get out and kick her ass. So Anthony says, 'I know. Let's take her car, give her something else to bitch about.'"

I turned toward Anthony. "Really?"

"Sure," Anthony said. "We had to do *something* to get that chick away from you."

"Yeah," Steve added. "That one? She's like a big-ass bag of crazy just waiting to pop."

I wasn't quite sure what he meant by that, but I definitely got his point. In spite of everything, I felt the hint of a real smile. "So you guys did all of that for me? Seriously?"

Steve lifted his burger in a mock toast. "Hey, no one messes with my sister." He grinned. "Well, except for me."

"I hate to sound ungrateful," I said, "but seriously, don't do that again, okay? You guys need to be more careful."

Steve snorted. "Says the girl who's dating a psycho."

At the thought of Jake, my heart sank. "He's not a psycho." I sighed. "And we're not dating."

"Could've fooled me," Steve said.

"Yeah," Anthony said. "The way he talks, he's got a serious thing for you."

I gave my brothers a perplexed look. "The way he talks? What do you mean?"

"He stopped us on the way in," Steve said.

I shook my head. "The way in to where? His penthouse?"

"No," Steve said. "Here." He pointed vaguely toward the street just outside the construction area. "He was standing over there, on the other side of the fence."

I swear, my heart stopped beating. "Doing what?"

"The way it looked," Steve said, "watching you." □

CHAPTER 13

Jake was watching me? With a pang, I recalled our sad goodbye just an hour earlier. Silently, he'd carried my suitcases to the job-trailer. Together, we'd ignored the commotion around us – the rumbling of machinery, the stares of construction workers, and whatever heartache either one of us might have been feeling as we reached the end our sorry journey.

At my request, Jake had handed over my suitcases and left me alone at the trailer's entrance – or so I'd thought.

Sitting at the table, I looked from Steve to Anthony. "Really? He's here? Now?"

I scrambled out of my seat and dove for the nearest window. I nudged aside the curtains and searched the street-side parking area for Jake's car.

It was gone.

I turned to my brothers. "Very funny."

"Actually," Steve said, "it *was* kind of funny. The guy looked ready to explode."

Now, I *knew* they were joking. After my crazy outburst at the trash can, Jake had been the poster-child for self-control. In truth, he'd been so calm, it was almost scary.

"It's no joke," Steve said. "The guy stopped us on the way in, told us that if anything happened to you, he was holding *us* responsible."

"Yeah," Anthony added. "He's all like 'You keep an eye on her.

Or else.'"

"Or else what?" I asked.

Anthony shrugged. "Eh, whatever it was, it didn't sound good."

On the other side of me, Steve said, "So, you gonna tell us what happened, or what?"

"With what?" I asked.

"With you and the psycho."

"For the last time," I said, "he's not a psycho. In fact, he's really nice. So stop talking crap about him, okay?"

"Chill," Steve said. "I meant it as a compliment."

"Yeah," Anthony said. "We're fans. Bigtime."

"Never mind," I said. "So when he said that, what'd you guys tell him?"

"We told him the truth," Steve said. "This is like the safest place in the city."

I gave Steve a dubious look. "Is that so?"

"Shit yeah," Steve said. "You've got this big-ass fence surrounding the whole thing, some security guy roaming the perimeter, and after dark, you need a code just to get in and out."

"A code?" I asked.

"Yeah," Steve said. "The site has two entrances, right? One for trucks, and one for people, workers, I mean. After dark, it's like a damn fortress. Without the code, you're not going nowhere."

Confused, I shook my head. "Like a password or something?"

"No," he said, "like a lock-combination. We're sewer guys, not secret agents."

Anthony was nodding. "Still, pretty sweet setup, huh?"

I let my gaze drift around the trailer. The place was old and tiny, with a weird musty smell that gave me the sniffles. Strewn across the floor were fast-food bags and empty pizza boxes. Or at least, I hoped the boxes were empty. With my brothers, I could never be too sure.

I tried to not to sound as disturbed as I felt. "But you're not seriously staying here?"

"Why wouldn't we?" Steve said. "It's the bomb."

I looked around. The bomb? Or like a bomb exploded? My heart sank. "But when we talked, you said you had a place."

"Yeah," Steve said. "This is it."

"I meant a place with a bathroom."

"There's bathrooms," he said.

I gave him a look. "You mean the porta-potties?"

"Well, yeah, those," he said, "but sometimes, we hit the hotel across the street. Sneak in when they're not looking."

"Sneak into what?" I asked. "A hotel room?"

"Oh get real," he said. "I mean the lobby. Or their fitness center."

"Except now," Anthony added, "they're getting all funny about it, like they don't want us to use them no more."

From what I had noticed earlier, the hotel looked pretty upscale. It wasn't surprising at all that they'd balk at having hundreds of construction workers tromping in and out all day. But that was beside the point. "Seriously," I said, "we can't stay here."

"Why not?" Anthony asked.

"Well, for one thing," I said, "it can't be legal. Can it?"

"Hell if I know," Anthony said.

I gave him a pleading look. "But they can't *really* want you camping out here."

"Who says they know?" Anthony said.

Well, this was just great. "You mean you're staying here in secret?"

"It's more of a 'don't ask, don't tell,'" Anthony said. "It's not like we sit around roasting marshmallows outside or anything."

"But where do you shower?" I gave them a good, long look. "You do shower, right?"

"Well that's where it gets tricky," Anthony said.

I didn't probe him for details, because at this point, I didn't really want to know. So instead, I finished my lunch and spent the rest of the day hunkered down in the top bunk, using my smart phone to look for a new job.

The way it looked, I needed money. And fast.

CHAPTER 14

Early the next morning, I picked my way through the outskirts of the construction zone, trying to keep a low profile. The effort was probably a total waste. Not only did I look nothing like your average construction worker, but at least half the guys probably recognized me from yesterday's spectacle.

Images from the previous afternoon flashed across my brain. In my memories, I saw Maddie, then Jake, and then, for a grand finale, my underpants strewn across the pavement. I lifted my gaze to the far-off trash can, where those items probably remained.

Stupidly, I never had the heart – or the stomach – to retrieve them. So now, on top of all my other problems, I was seriously short of undergarments, among other things.

Like clean bathrooms.

And my sanity.

Moving faster, I kept my head down as I made a beeline toward the sidewalk just outside the construction area. I was dressed in the nicest clothes I had – the same black skirt and white blouse I'd been wearing Saturday morning when Jake had swooped me up from Maddie's apartment.

I needed a bathroom in the worst possible way, and there was no way in hell that I was braving those porta-potties again.

Exiting the fenced construction area, I walked casually along the sidewalk, waiting for a gap in the traffic. At the first opportunity, I made a quick dash across the street, heading toward the hotel's main entrance. Once there, I took a deep breath and strolled through the glass double doors, trying like hell to look like I belonged there.

Manning the front desk was a severe-looking woman around my mom's age. She wore dark-rimmed spectacles and a tan blazer. Her shiny blond hair was pulled back in a bun so tight it looked nearly painful.

I gave her a casual wave as I made my way toward the rear of the lobby, searching for the hallway that my brothers had described. At the snack machines, I stopped, perplexed to find myself at a dead-end. There was supposed to be a door. Where on Earth was it?

Behind me, I heard a crisp female voice, laced with an upscale accent, say, "Can I help you?"

I whirled around, and there she was, the lady from the front desk. She was standing within arm's reach, giving me the hairy eyeball.

"Uh, yes," I said. "Could you point me to the restrooms?"

She crossed her arms. "Sorry, they're for customers only."

I stared at her. "Well maybe I am a customer."

"Or maybe," she said, glancing toward the construction zone, "you snuck in from across the street and thought I wouldn't see you."

Color flooded my face. "Oh come on. Do I *look* like a construction worker?"

"Maybe you're a secretary," she said. "I don't know, and I don't care." Her lips pursed. "Trust me. I've seen it all by now."

From the look on her face, some of those things weren't exactly pleasant. I didn't bother asking for details. I'd seen firsthand what my brothers could do to a bathroom.

"I don't work there," I told her. "And that's the truth."

"Then why were you there?"

Was that really any of her business? Part of me wanted to slink off and never come back. The other part was way too stubborn to give her the satisfaction.

"Actually," I said, "I was looking for a job." It wasn't even a lie. Looking to hammer the point home, I added, "I don't suppose *you're* hiring?"

She eyed me up and down. "You ever work in a hotel before?"

An hour later, I had not only restroom access, but a brand new job. Even more surprising, they wanted me to start immediately – that very night, in fact.

Officially, I was newest member of the hotel's night shift front-desk team. Unofficially, I was a sacred guardian of the hotel's pristine facilities, which as it turned out, had been under siege since the start of construction across the street.

With my new-employee packet tucked under my arm, I stood, gazing around the hotel lobby, shocked at my sudden change of luck. It wasn't the job of my dreams, but it was definitely a step in the right direction.

Even the clerk, whose name I learned was Suzanne, wasn't nearly as frightening as I first thought. The way it sounded, she was mostly just stressed out about the restrooms.

Maybe, just maybe, things were looking up – or at least that's what I thought until I spotted a familiar figure pushing her way through the hotel's glass double doors.

It was Bianca, my least-favorite lamp-thrower. And from the look on her face, she was ready to start throwing things again.

CHAPTER 15

Bianca pushed through the glass doors and into the hotel lobby. At the sight of me standing near the front desk, she stopped short. "You!" she said.

I looked around. It was mid-morning, and the lobby was nearly empty. Other than the uniformed man servicing the snack machines, it was just me and Suzanne.

Behind the front desk, Suzanne frowned. "Me?"

Ignoring the question, Bianca marched up to the desk and announced, "I'm here to see Jake Bishop. And don't tell me he's not here, because I know better."

I heard a soft thud near my feet. I looked down and spotted my employee packet lying on the tile floor. Too stunned to pick it up, I stared down at the thing while my thoughts churned. Jake couldn't be staying here. Could he?

With a sound of annoyance, Bianca stepped toward me. Her gaze drifted down to the packet. "If you're waiting for me to pick that up, you obviously don't know who you're dealing with."

She was wrong. I knew exactly who I was dealing with. I just didn't know *what* I was dealing with. Was Jake really here? Desperate for more information, I looked to Suzanne.

She was giving Bianca the same icy look she'd used on me earlier. "I'm sorry, ma'am," Suzanne said, "but we're not allowed to release the names of our guests."

"I don't need his name," Bianca said. "I *have* his name. What I *don't* have is his room number."

Suzanne gave Bianca a stiff smile. "We don't release names *or* room numbers."

With little huff, Bianca reached into her handbag. She pulled out a twenty-dollar bill and slapped it on the counter. "Maybe this will improve your memory?"

Suzanne eyed the bill. After a long pause, she looked up. "There *is* one thing I remember."

Bianca leaned forward. "Yes?"

"I remember," Suzanne said, "that accepting bribes is also against hotel policy."

I stifled a laugh. Both women turned to face me.

"Uh, sorry," I said, coughing into my hand. "Allergies."

With an epic eye-roll, Bianca turned back to Suzanne and said, "It's not a bribe. It's a tip."

Standing there, I wanted to give Bianca a tip of my own, something along the lines of, "Stay away from Jake, or I'll shove that twenty up your butt."

But that would be pointless. As much as it pained me, Jake was free to see whoever he wanted. Besides, even if I *did* have a twenty, I wouldn't waste it on Bianca. I'd use it to buy new underpants.

Money-aside, I was treading on some very shaky ground here. I literally had just been hired. No way I'd risk a new job just to argue with Bianca.

Bianca shoved the money closer to Suzanne. "You *have* seen a tip before, haven't you?"

"Yes," Suzanne said, pointing at the bill. "Unfortunately, that, ma'am, is not a tip. That is a bribe, which is strictly against hotel policy."

With a sound of annoyance, Bianca snatched the bill off the counter. She shoved it back into her purse and whirled toward me. "This is *your* doing, isn't it?"

"Me?" I said.

"Don't play all innocent," Bianca said. "You told her not to tell me, didn't you?"

The idea was so ridiculous, I almost laughed. "I'm sorry, but I have no idea what you're talking about." Technically, this was only half true. Was I clueless? Yes. Was I sorry? Not hardly.

"Whatever," Bianca said, turning back to Suzanne. "How much did she pay you? Whatever it is, I'll double it. No. Triple it."

Suzanne's brow wrinkled. "Who are you talking about?" Suzanne glanced in my direction. "Laura?"

"Who on Earth is Laura?" Bianca asked.

I cleared my throat. "That's me, actually."

Bianca whirled to face me. "I thought your name was Luna."

Sure, legally it was. I had even used the name Luna on my employment paperwork. But now, after years of practice, I had a system for making sure that no one actually called me that.

"Well yeah, that's my birth name," I said. "But everyone calls me Laura, so…" I shrugged and let the implication speak for itself.

"No one calls you Laura," Bianca said.

"Actually," I said, "Suzanne did. Just now. Remember?"

Bianca looked ready to go insane. "Who's Suzanne?"

Behind Bianca, Suzanne said. "That would be me." She crossed her arms. "The person you're trying to bribe."

Bianca whirled to face her. Through clenched teeth, she said, "It's not a bribe. It's a tip."

As I watched, Bianca launched into another round of bargaining, threats, and general irritation. As far as I could tell, it wasn't doing an ounce of good. The longer Bianca talked, the less cooperative Suzanne was looking.

As the debate raged on, I caught movement just outside the hotel's main entrance. A burly man in a red hard-hat was hustling through the glass double doors. He had a rolled-up magazine tucked under his left arm and a thermos tucked under his right. Sneaking a quick glance at the front desk, the guy scurried toward the far end of the lobby and disappeared toward the restrooms.

I returned my attention to the front desk, where Bianca was

still raging.

"Fine," she was saying. "If you won't give me the number, at least pick up the phone and dial his room." Bianca straightened. "Tell him I'm here." She gritted her teeth. "Please."

"Ma'am," Suzanne said. "I'm going to have to ask you to leave."

"Why?" Bianca demanded, flicking her head in my direction. "You're not asking *her* to leave."

"That's because she works here," Suzanne said.

Bianca turned to face me. Her gaze narrowed. "Oh, *now*, I get it."

Well, that made one of us.

Bianca whirled back to Suzanne. "You want me to leave?" Bianca said. "Fine. I'll leave. But mark my words, I'll be back. And next time, I'll be bringing my boss. Let's see you say no to *him*." And with that, Bianca turned and stalked out of the hotel.

Suzanne stared after her. She let out a long, weary sigh. "That's the third one since yesterday," she said.

"The third what?" I asked.

"The third girl who's come in asking for him."

I swallowed. "Him?"

Glancing around, Suzanne lowered her voice. "Sometimes, we get celebrities here. And when we do…" She looked heavenward. "Well, let's just say it brings out the crazies."

"So there's a celebrity staying here?" I tried to keep my tone casual. "Do you mean the Jake person she was talking about?"

"Oh, you've heard of him?" she said.

Heard of him? Wow, that was an understatement. I'd held him. I'd kissed him. For one glorious weekend, I'd been his girl, utterly and completely. I ignored all that and said, "He's a fighter, right?"

"Oh, he's a lot more than that," Suzanne said. "The way I hear it, he's a huge internet star." She gave a dreamy-looking smile. "Yesterday, I actually saw him." Her voice became husky. "In the flesh."

I stared at her. I didn't like the way she said that. If anyone had a right to drool over Jake's flesh, it was me.

My heart sank. Except, I didn't really have that right, did I? No, I didn't. Not anymore.

"Oh, don't look at me like that," Suzanne said. "I was the epitome of professionalism." Her smile faded. "And if you don't want trouble, you'd better be too." She lowered her voice. "The night manager? He's a real piece of work."

Looking past me, her eyes suddenly widened. "Hey!" she called out across the lobby.

I turned to look. The construction worker was making a mad dash for the exit. I glanced back to Suzanne. She skirted the front desk and sprinted after him. She was surprisingly fast, but the guy had a huge head start. By the time Suzanne reached those glass double-doors, the guy was long-gone.

But, as Suzanne told me a few minutes later, somewhere in the men's restroom, his essence lingered.

Somehow, I couldn't bring myself to care. I wanted to hear more about Jake. Was he really staying here? And if so, why? But no matter how many times I tried to tell myself otherwise, I could only think of one reason.

Because of me.▢

CHAPTER 16

I turned to my brothers. "Hey, can I borrow some money?"

It was nearly noon, and I was huddled in the job-trailer, trying to get everything in order for my new job. I still didn't know what to make of everything, especially the thing with Jake.

But if I thought about him now, I'd go crazy, so I was working hard to focus on more practical matters, like my serious lack of necessities.

"What do you need money for?" Anthony asked.

It was lunchtime, and my brothers had just ducked inside to scarf down some of last night's leftover pizza. I glanced at the open pizza box. At least, I sure hoped it was from last night. There were so many boxes lying around, it was hard to be sure.

"I just need to pick up a few clothes," I said. Mostly underclothes. But there was no way I'd be sharing that little detail with them. If either of my brothers learned that nearly all of my undergarments had ended up in a nearby trash can, I'd never hear the end of it.

Steve took a huge bite of pizza. "So buy some clothes."

"That's the point," I said. "I'm planning to, but I'm a little short of cash."

Okay, *a lot* short of cash.

"Your ass," Steve said.

If he meant my bare ass, he'd soon have a point. I had only one spare pair of panties left and no washing machine. I also had no sink, no detergent, and no intention of flashing my goodies to random hotel guests.

I gave Steve an annoyed look. "Hey, if you're worried I won't pay you back, don't be. I've got a job now. Remember?"

"What happened to the money in your purse?" he asked.

"What money?" I said. "I've got like three bucks in change."

"Not anymore," Anthony said.

I shook my head. "What do you mean?"

Anthony glanced at my purse, sitting atop a nearby pizza box. "The quarters?" Anthony said. "We borrowed 'em last night."

"When last night?" I asked.

"When you hit the porta-potties," Anthony said.

I shuddered at the memory. The porta-potties were cold, dirty, and seriously lacking in decent toilet paper. "Well, that's just great," I said. "I'm gone like ten minutes, and you go through my purse?"

"Sorry," Anthony said. "We needed tip money."

I gave him a look. "You had pizza delivered here? At the job-trailer?"

"I met him at the fence," Anthony said.

Steve chimed in. "And you ate like three slices, so I don't know why you're griping about it."

"It's not that I don't want to chip in," I explained. "It's just that, well, that was the only money I had."

Anthony gave me an odd look. "What happened to the rest of it?"

"There *is* no rest of it," I said. "That's the point."

"Oh get real," Steve said, flicking his gaze toward my purse. "I bet you've got a thousand bucks in there."

I tried to laugh. "I wish."

Steve glanced at the purse. His eyebrows furrowed.

I turned to study the thing. I had barely touched it since leaving Jake's. I opened it up and peered inside. I saw just the usual stuff — my wallet, a hairbrush and a few incidentals.

As far as the wallet, I knew for sure *that* was empty, well of cash at least. While applying for that job, I'd had to pull out my driver's license, so I was sadly familiar with its contents. The only other thing in there was an expired debit card. I couldn't exactly shop with that, could I?

I tossed my purse back onto the pizza box. "Very funny." I turned back to my brothers. "Come on. Just twenty bucks. I'll pay you back with my first check, alright?"

Steve gave me look. "Twenty, huh?" He stood and plucked my purse off the pizza box. He opened it up and unzipped the inside front pocket. He peered inside. "Damn," he said.

"What?" I asked.

He pulled out a wad of cash and began rifling through it. "All I got are hundreds." ☐

CHAPTER 17

I scurried across the darkened construction area, praying that no one spotted me before I made it to the chain-link fence. Supposedly, a security guard made the rounds at least once an hour. In reality, I still hadn't seen the guy.

In my book, that was a good thing.

No matter what my brothers had claimed, I was certain we weren't supposed to be staying on the job site. How they'd gotten away with it so far, I had no idea. It shouldn't have been surprising though. Even when my brothers were kids, they had this uncanny knack for getting away with just about anything.

Me, not so much.

It was half past ten, and my shift started at eleven. But I wanted to get there early, if only for the chance to freshen up beforehand. Plus, I'd used my dad's mailing address on my employment paperwork for a specific reason. The hotel management had no idea where I was staying, and I was determined to keep it that way.

Sticking to the shadows, I skirted a dump truck and edged around a giant pile of gravel. Still moving, I looked toward the narrow metal gate that allowed construction workers to enter and exit on foot. Making a beeline toward it, I kept repeating the lock-combination in my head.

If I forgot it, I was screwed.

I was half-way there when I heard the sounds of scuffling somewhere behind me.

I turned to look. Squinting into the darkness, I saw nothing, only the shadows and outlines of equipment and supplies. But something had made that noise. What was it? A raccoon? The security guy? I swallowed. Or worse?

Oh stop it, I told myself. If anything, it was only my brothers messing with me. Annoyed by my own skittishness, I whirled back around, only to collide with a shadowed figure that hadn't been there a moment earlier.

I stifled a gasp. The figure was warm and solid, and utterly familiar.

Jake.

I lost my footing, and his arms closed tight around me. For the briefest of moments, my eyelids drifted shut. Oh God, the feel of him, the scent of him, the nearness of him. It was pure heaven.

And pure hell.

Regaining my balance, along with a shred of dignity, I pushed away and said, "Jeez, you scared the crap out of me."

His voice was hard. "Good."

"Oh, that's nice."

"No," he said. "It's not. But if being a dick is what it takes, hey, whatever."

I drew back. He *was* being a dick, in fact. But why?

"In that case," I said, "you're doing a fine job of it." I looked around. "What are you doing here, anyway?"

"What are *you* doing here?" His voice rose. "Alone. In the dark. In the middle of fuckin' Detroit."

I drew back, surprised by his reaction. "It's hardly the middle."

Actually, I had no idea where this place was on a map. But I did know one thing. Compared to other areas of the city, this section was actually pretty nice.

His eyebrows furrowed. "It's almost midnight. What the hell are you thinking?"

All day, I'd been longing to see him, to talk with him, to get some answers. But nowhere in my thoughts did he jump out of the dark to read me the riot act. And now, he wanted to know what *I* was thinking?

I glanced toward the hotel. "I'm *thinking* that I've got to get to work."

He looked toward the hotel. "You work there? Since when?"

"Since tonight, assuming I don't get fired for tardiness." Okay, so technically, I was running early, but I knew how this went. If I wasn't careful, I'd go from a half-hour early to a half-hour late. And I needed that job.

Besides, as far as the Jake situation, I had tried all day to reach him, not that it did any good. And *now*, he wanted to talk?

"You know what?" I said. "I've really gotta go." I sidestepped to move past him.

"Wait," he said. "Why didn't you tell me?"

"Tell you what?" I said. "That I got a job there? Gee, I don't know. Maybe because you wouldn't take my calls?"

Since finding that cash in my purse, I had tried Jake's cell phone at least ten times. He hadn't answered. He hadn't called me back. He hadn't even given me the chance to say thank you.

I bit my lip. Actually, the plan was to say "no thank you" in the nicest possible way. As much as I appreciated the gesture, there was no way I could accept that kind of money.

So instead, I had borrowed a twenty from my brothers, bought only the bare minimum, and put Jake's money aside, with plans to return it at the first opportunity.

Unfortunately, that opportunity wasn't now, because I didn't have it on me.

In front of me, Jake said, "Maybe I didn't like your reason for calling."

"How would *you* know my reason?" I asked.

"Because you mentioned the purse."

"So?"

"So, from the way you sounded, I knew damn well what you

were gonna say."

"Oh yeah?" I said. "What's that?"

"That you couldn't accept the money."

"Oh."

"So I was right," he said.

This totally sucked. I desperately wanted to have this conversation. But now wasn't the time. "Jake," I said. "Seriously, I've gotta go. If I call you tomorrow, will you *please* answer?"

He looked toward the hotel. "You really got a job there?"

I gave a hollow laugh.

"What?" he said.

I mimicked his own question. "You really got a *room* there?"

He froze. "What?"

"Oh my God. You did. Didn't you?"

"Forget that," he said. "Where's your damn brothers?"

"They're in the trailer. And quit changing the subject."

He made a sound of disgust.

"What?" I asked.

"They swore they'd keep an eye on you."

My jaw dropped. Talk about insulting. "Keep an eye on me?" I said. "Seriously? I'm older than they are. And a ton more responsible. Maybe *I* need to keep an eye on *them*."

From somewhere behind me, I heard Steve say, "In your dreams."

I whirled around. I saw nothing except the same construction equipment as before. I squinted deeper into the darkness and finally made out the silhouettes of my brothers, leaning up against some heavy machinery.

"Oh for crying out loud," I said. "What are you guys doing out here?"

"Walking you to work," Steve said.

Through gritted teeth, I said, "I told you that you didn't have to."

It's not that I didn't appreciate the gesture. But I had been determined to avoid attracting attention. One thing about my brothers, they weren't exactly the quiet types.

"Yeah, we heard you," Steve said, "which is why we're doing the secret-agent thing."

I glanced over at Jake. The way it looked, there was a lot of that going around.

Jake called out to my brothers. "Go on. I've got this." Turning back to me, he said, "Come on. I'll walk you."

"Well, you'd better walk fast," I told him, "because I heard the night manager's a real stickler."

"That's one name for him," Jake said.

"What do you mean by that?" I asked.

"You keep that job, and you'll find out fast."

With a resigned sigh, I gave my brothers a quick wave and turned around, heading again toward the gate. With long, easy strides, Jake walked alongside me, saying nothing as we went. At the gate, he grabbed the lock and began working the dial. A moment later, it opened.

"How'd you get the combination?" I asked.

"I have my sources."

"Yeah, I just bet," I said, wondering if his so-called sources just happened to be two guys related to me.

When we reached the sidewalk across from the hotel, I stopped to look up at him. I really didn't have time for this, but what if it was my only chance? "About the money—"

"Don't," he said.

"Don't what?"

"Don't tell me you can't take it."

"It's not that I don't appreciate it," I said, "but—"

"Luna," he said.

"What?"

"I've been thinking."

I cringed. That was never a good sign. Still, I made myself ask, "About what?"

His voice was quieter now. "You." □

CHAPTER 18

Somehow, that wasn't the answer I'd been expecting. Through my lashes, I looked up at him. "Really?" A reluctant smile tugged at my lips. "What about me?"

He glanced toward the hotel. "Screw that job."

I shook my head. "What?"

"Come back."

I studied his face. Something about his expression didn't quite match his words. Fearful of assuming too much, I looked toward the hotel and said, "Do you mean, uh, to your hotel room?"

His mouth was tight. "No."

Was I relieved? Or disappointed? Sure, I wanted like hell to be with him. But the whole come-back-to-my hotel thing wasn't exactly what I had in mind. At least, it wasn't the *only* thing I had in mind.

"I'm not following," I said. "You mean come back to your penthouse?"

"No." He glanced away. "The office."

At the memory of my first and only visit to his office suite, my face grew warm. Jake and I had done some delicious things in there. Was he suggesting a repeat-performance? And if so, was that *all* he was suggesting?

Into my silence, he said, "Quit tonight, start tomorrow."

My eyebrows furrowed. "Start what?"

"The job. Like we talked about."

Confused, I searched my memories. At last, reality slapped me in the face, and I drew back. "Let me get this straight," I said. "When you say 'come back,' what you mean is come back to *work* for you?"

Technically, I had never worked for him. But a couple days earlier, he *had* offered me a job. I'd declined, and I couldn't exactly regret it. The job had once been Bianca's. No matter how this thing with Jake played out, I refused to step into her shoes.

Jake flicked his head toward the hotel. "All you have to do is walk in and quit. Right now."

"Oh," I said. "Is that all?"

"Or don't show up," he said. "They'll figure it out."

Stunned, I stared up at him. "God, you are such a jerk."

"Call me what you want. Just do it." At something in my expression, his voice softened. "Alright?"

I let out a long sigh. "I *so* don't have time for this."

He glanced toward the hotel. "That job's trouble."

"How would *you* know?"

"Not hard to figure out."

I crossed my arms. "Is that so?"

"Hell yeah. You can do better."

"Really?" I said. "Because I have a college degree?" My voice rose. "Well, guess what? The job market sucks. Do you know what a miracle it was that I got this job at all?"

"It's no miracle."

"Wanna bet?" I said. "For your information, I was hired on the spot. In my book, that's a pretty big miracle."

"Or," he said, "you were hired because two people quit last night. With no notice."

"What?" I felt my shoulders sag. So I'd been hired out of desperation? "And you know this, how?"

He shrugged.

"Oh, that's right." I gave a bark of laughter. "I almost forgot." I gestured toward the hotel. "Because you're staying there." When he didn't deny it, I added, "And why is that, exactly?"

"I've got my reasons."

"Yeah, I just bet. Like your 'reasons' for offering me a job?"

"It's a real offer," he said.

"Because of pity?" I said. "Or because you want to keep an eye on me?"

"Because you're qualified."

I gave him a dubious look. "Uh-huh."

"You've got the same degree as Bianca," he said. "Or at least, close enough."

My degree was in hospitality management. About Bianca's degree, I had no idea. But I knew she had a ton more experience, and not just with event-planning.

Suddenly, it felt like we'd been having the same conversation over and over again. I looked toward the hotel. "If you really want to help me, wanna know what you'll do?"

"What?"

"Butt out."

His voice was flat. "Butt out?"

Okay, so I'd said it before, but some things were definitely worth repeating, especially when someone refused to listen.

"Yes, butt out," I said. "Because I'm not coming to work for you." I took a deep, steadying breath. "And if you ever cared about me at all—"

"I do." His eyes met mine. "You *know* I do."

"Good. Then you won't mess this up for me."

His gaze slid to the hotel. He said nothing.

"So here's what you're *not* going to do." I counted off on my fingers. "You *not* going to quit this job on my behalf. You're *not* going to do something crazy to get me fired." My teeth clenched. "And you're not going to be hanging around the front desk like a walking menace, because I seriously need this job."

"No. You don't."

"Jeez," I said. "What's your problem? I've already lost *two* jobs because of you. I can't afford to lose another."

"Luna—"

I gave him a warning look. "Don't say it."

"Don't say what?" he asked.

"Don't say, 'then come work for me,' because I've already said no. And I'm going to *keep* saying no." I leaned in close and lowered my voice. "And you wanna know why? Because I know darn well this has nothing to do with my qualifications."

His jaw clenched. "That's not true."

"Well here's my truth," I said. "I've got to get to work. And I swear to God, if you interfere with this job in any way, I will never forgive you."

And with that, I turned and walked away. □

CHAPTER 19

From behind the front desk, the gangly, pinched-faced man greeted me with only two words. "You're late."

I glanced up at the oversized clock, hanging on the wall just over the guy's left shoulder. According to the clock, I'd arrived with ten minutes to spare – unless, had I gotten my details wrong?

"Sorry," I said, "I thought my shift started at eleven. Did I miss something?"

He looked away and mumbled something that sounded suspiciously like, "Just the chance to make a good impression."

"Excuse me?" I said.

"Forget it. Go ahead, clock in. I'll wait."

"Sure," I said, glancing around for a time clock. Unfortunately, I didn't see one. "If you could just point me in the right direction…"

Silently, he pointed to the large wooden door, situated just behind the front desk. I'd been through that door once before, earlier today in fact, when I'd filled out all the employment paperwork. The door led to a small, cluttered office suite that served as the hotel's center of operations.

Without commentary, I skirted the front desk, brushed past him, and made my way toward the door. I reached out and twisted the knob. It didn't budge.

I turned to give the guy an apologetic look. "I think it's locked."

"You *think*?" he said. "Or you *know*?"

Well, I knew one thing for sure. The guy was a total ass.

Biting my tongue, I turned to give the knob another twist. It still didn't budge. I turned back to the guy and said, "It's definitely locked."

"Yes, it is." He pulled a key card from his pocket. "Consider that your first lesson. After dark, there's only one person with that key." He puffed out his narrow chest. "And that person is the assistant deputy night manager. Me."

I glanced at his nametag. Apparently, that person was also named Rupert, not that he'd bothered to introduce himself.

"Oh," I said, glancing at the key card. "Well, then can I borrow it?"

"No." He smirked. "But you can ask me to open the door for you."

Or, I could ask him to bite me.

My eyebrows furrowed. I was a girl. Did that sentiment even apply?

His mouth pursed. "Is there a problem?"

I snapped back to reality. "No. No problem at all." With the most pleasant expression I could muster, I pointed to the door and asked, "So, could you please open that for me?"

He crossed his arms and gave a slow nod. "You and me, we're gonna get along just fine."

I seriously doubted that.

But I was darned determined to try.

For the first hour, Rupert watched over my shoulder as I dealt with the usual things – greeting guests as they returned for the night, fulfilling requests for extra towels, and in one case, running a travel toothbrush up to someone who had forgotten theirs.

Since most of my responsibilities were practically the same as at my previous job, right down to using the same reservation system, it all seemed pretty straight-forward. There was only one thing that confused me.

During my job-interview, I'd been told that the night shift always had at least three people working. But all I saw was Rupert. Maybe the third person was on break?

A little after midnight, when no third person had appeared, I finally asked Rupert about it.

"Forget him," Rupert said. "The guy's a no-show."

"Oh," I said. "That's too bad."

"Too bad for *him*, you mean." Rupert straightened his tie. "If he *does* show up, he's getting fired, courtesy of yours truly."

"Good for you," I said.

"Yeah." Rupert gave a slow nod. "I run a tight ship around here. Ask anyone. They'll tell you."

I looked around. There was no one to ask, probably because they had all quit.

Even so, I still didn't get it. Sure, Rupert was annoying, but in this job market, it would take a lot more than a crappy manager to make me walk out. Of course, I'd only been working with this guy for an hour. Who knew how I'd feel in a week?

We were pretty busy until nearly two o'clock in the morning, when the number of guests slowed to a mere trickle.

"Well, that's it," Rupert announced. "Paperwork time. I'm heading to the back office. If you need something, give me a shout."

"You're leaving me alone?"

He frowned. "Is that a problem?"

"No, of course not." I summoned up a smile. "It's just that you know, since I'm new…"

"You'll be fine," he said. "You'll probably get a few drunks at closing time, and yeah, maybe a few crazies here and there, but mostly, you just stand there and deal with whatever comes." He looked toward the office. "And, if you've got a question, I'm right behind that door."

"So, it'll be unlocked?" I asked.

"No. But you *do* know how to knock. Don't you?"

"Sure. I was just asking, that's all."

Although I'd worked in hotels before, I had never worked the night shift. But I'd heard stories from former co-workers. The way it sounded, I'd spend half the night running my ass off and the other half bored out of my mind.

I could deal with that.

Or so I thought – right up until three o'clock in the morning, when a large, noisy group of trendy people around my own age stumbled through the doors, led by someone all too familiar – Rango, the ex-boyfriend from hell.

CHAPTER 20

Rango's dark spiky hair was in its usual stylish disarray, and he wore the same kind of clothes he always wore, flashy and expensive. Behind him were four other people – two guys and two girls – all dressed for a night on the town.

From the looks of them, they'd been drinking. A lot.

"Oh crap," I muttered under my breath. I knew exactly how they'd ended up here. Bianca had gone blabbing, that's how, because there was no conceivable way that Rango would have found out where I worked otherwise.

"Hey babe!" Rango called over to me. "You got room for a party?"

Behind him, his entourage laughed like he'd just told the funniest fart-joke, ever. I recognized both of the guys, Brody and Chet. Even when Rango and I had been dating, I had never been overly fond of them.

With Rango leading the pack, the group stumbled toward the front desk, laughing and jostling each other along the way. When they reached the place where I stood, Rango leaned across the high counter and said, "You got anything with a hot tub?"

Behind him, one of the girls giggled.

I gave Rango an irritated look. "Was that a serious question?"

"Hell yeah!" Rango said. "We wanna keep this party goin'!" Turning toward his companions, he raised both fists high in the air and called out, "Who's with me?"

Surprise, surprise, they all were.

How nice.

Laughing, Rango put a hand to his ear and roared out, rock-star style, "I can't hear you!"

Like the idiots they were, the group let out another nerve-jangling mix of roars and squeals.

Wincing, I turned toward the office door, located just a few feet behind me. Rupert *had* to be hearing this, right?

Sure, I knew some of these people, but I wasn't so naïve as to think I could handle them alone.

I zoomed in on the doorknob, waiting for it to turn.

It didn't.

Damn it.

My gaze was still trained on the door when I heard a slap against the counter. I whirled to see Rango's palms pressed flat against the high countertop. He loomed toward me and said, "So, who are you looking for? Your boyfriend?"

"No." I lowered my voice. "And what are you doing here, anyway?"

He gave me a sloppy grin. "This *is* a hotel, right?"

"Obviously."

"Then I want a room, just like I said." He straightened. "You got a problem with that?"

Working hard to keep my cool, I spoke slowly and precisely. "We don't have any rooms with hot tubs."

From a few feet away, Chet called out, "You give us the tub. We'll make it hot."

I squinted at him. What did that even mean?

As I watched, Chet draped an arm over the shoulder of the curvy blond standing next to him. Reaching around just a little bit further, he lowered a meaty hand to her breast. He smiled and gave it a squishy squeeze.

As for the blond, she was either too dense to notice or, more likely, too drunk to mind. Either way, judging from her unsteady posture, the girl was obviously under the influence or something. Vaguely, I wondered if mopping up puke was in my job-description.

I gave Rango a pleading look. "This really isn't a party type of place."

Rango grinned. "It is now, babe."

"Oh come on," I said. "Seriously, look around. The lounge isn't even open."

It was true. The hotel catered to long-term business people, mostly auto executives and part-suppliers. The place wasn't exactly party-central. Besides, it was a weeknight. Didn't these idiots have jobs?

But of course, I knew the answer to that. I'd spent a couple of crazy months running with Rango's crowd. Almost none of them worked, at least not at normal jobs like most people had.

Even Rango. Technically, he was a D.J. of sorts, a smalltime celebrity with a big local following. But as far as I could tell, that gig was mostly for kicks.

Rango had money, lots of money. The club where he worked? He owned it, along with a couple of restaurants in Troy and some title-loan place that I refused to think about.

But as far as I knew, Rango didn't really manage anything personally. Like the rest of his crowd, he wouldn't know hard work if it bit him on the ass.

In fact, I wished something would bite him on the ass — anything to make him leave.

"Who needs a lounge?" Rango said. "That's for old people."

"Yeah," said the other girl, a cute brunette in a skin-tight black dress. "Old people. Like fuddy-duddies."

Rango rewarded the girl with a big, raucous laugh. "You got that right."

With his gaze still on me, he eased over to the girl and wrapped an arm around her waist. He pulled her close to his side and said, "We can make our own lounge." He ducked his head to give the girl's cleavage a long, stupid look. "Am I right, Jilly babe?"

Her lips formed a pout. "It's *Julie*. Remember?"

"Whatever, Jules," he said, pulling her tighter. "You still wanna party, right?"

She melted herself against him and planted a loud, smoochy kiss on the side of his face. "If you're paying, I'm playing."

Rango frowned.

I couldn't help it. I laughed.

Rango pushed away from the girl and turned back to me. "Something funny?" he asked.

I shook my head. "Nope."

"Aw come on," he said, "share the joke."

When I still didn't answer, he called over his shoulder. "We like a good joke. Don't we, guys?"

"Hell yeah!" Brody hollered out, turning to leer at me. "Make us laugh, pretty girl."

Eauw.

Rango spread his arms wide. "You heard 'em. Gimme your best shot."

What on Earth did he mean by that? Honestly, I had no idea. I lowered my voice. "Or maybe, you could just go home and sleep it off."

"Yeah?" He gave me an open-mouthed grin with the barest hint of tongue. "You comin' with me?"

I drew back. "No."

"Fine," he said. "If you're staying, we're staying."

I blew out a long breath. "Oh come on. You can't really want a room." I scanned his group. "For *five* people?"

"Why the hell not?" Rango laughed. "It's not like we plan on sleeping."

"Well, maybe *you* don't," I said, "but the other guests do. In fact, most of them are sleeping *now*. Or trying to, anyway." Hint, hint.

"Fuck 'em," Rango said. "If they get pissy about it, we'll invite 'em to the party."

"They're not here to party," I said. "They're here to work. They've got to get up in the morning."

Rango glanced at the clock. He grinned. "Looks like morning to me."

Oh screw it. Obviously, the guy couldn't take a hint. "You need to leave," I told him.

He eyed me with disapproval. "Damn, were you always this prissy?"

"I don't know," I said. "Were you always this dicky?"

His gaze narrowed. He leaned in close, and I felt his hot breath in my face. "Wanna know what I think?"

I didn't bother to hide my annoyance. "What?"

"I think," he said, "that you've got something of mine. And I'm not leaving 'til I get it."□

CHAPTER 21

I stared at Rango. "So *that's* why you're here? Because of that stupid book?"

After our breakup, I'd lifted the thing from his nightstand. Most of the pages were empty, but for whatever reason, Rango had been obsessed with the thing.

I still couldn't see the appeal. But on the inside front cover, I found something totally worth using – the passwords to all of Rango's social media accounts.

For a few crazy days, I had used those passwords to post some pretty ridiculous things online. It was nothing personal, just stupid stuff mostly.

Mature? No. Satisfying? Totally. Short-term anyway.

But in the end, my furniture was trashed, my clothes were stolen, and my perfect little apartment was a no-go zone, after my sudden eviction for all the weirdness. I couldn't prove anything, but I just knew Rango was behind it.

And now, here he was again, dogging me at my new job.

I glanced out across the hotel lobby. Chet and blondie had stumbled to a nearby seating area and were sprawled out on the largest sofa. As I watched, Chet pulled out a silver flask and took a good, long swig before passing it to his companion.

The blond took a big, sloppy drink and flopped back against the sofa cushions. "Hey, you! Hotel Girl" she slurred out in my direction. "Crank up the music, will ya?"

I squinted at her. There was no music. And there wasn't going to be any either.

In front of me, Rango crossed his arms. "You want us to go? Gimme the book."

I crossed my arms too. "I'd love to," I said. "Just gimme the car."

"What car?" he asked.

"Oh for crying out loud," I said. "How could you not know? *My* car? Remember?"

Rango looked down to study his fingernails. "I've got my own cars to worry about." He shrugged. "Your car, your problem."

"A problem *you* caused," I reminded him.

Before Rango and I had begun dating, I needed some money fast. As a so-called favor, Rango had hooked me up with a short-term title loan through that place he owned. In the end, it was no favor.

In front of me, Rango looked up. "*I* caused it? How?"

Like he didn't know. "Remember?" I said. "The title loan?"

As part of the deal, I'd stupidly signed over my car title. The arrangement was mostly fine, right up until our breakup. The very next day, I had no title *and* no car, even though my loan was nearly paid off.

Lounging against the front desk, Rango gave me his sad face. "Sorry babe. Not ringing a bell."

"You are such a liar," I said.

Behind Rango, Brody called out. "Hey, I remember that car." He laughed. "Oh man, that was so awesome."

I leaned around Rango to give Brody a dubious look. Sure, *I* loved that car, but it was nothing a guy like him would go for.

"Oh, give it up," I told him. "You don't even know what car I'm talking about."

"Wanna bet?" he said. "Silver Ford, right?"

Surprised, I studied Brody with renewed interest. "Um, yeah," I said. "A Focus. You know where it is?"

Brody burst out laughing. "Not anymore."

I turned to Rango. "What does he mean? Where is it?"

Rango reached up to rub the back of his neck. "I dunno," he said. "Gone?"

"Yeah, I *know* it's gone," I said. "That's the problem. I need it back."

Behind Rango, Brody gave a little snicker.

I glared over at him. "Why is that funny?"

"Because," Brody said, "when he says gone, he means gone baby, gone." Brody lifted his big hands to squash an imaginary bug between his beefy palms.

"Oh my God." I turned to Rango. "You crashed my car?"

For whatever reason, Brody thought this was absolutely hilarious. Through loud guffaws, he called out, "Nah, he didn't *crash* it. He *crushed* it." Catching his breath, he managed to choke out, "Had this big party after. It was fuckin' awesome!"

I looked from Brody to Rango. "Is that true?" I was having a hard time catching my breath. "You *crushed* my car?"

"Screw the car," Rango said. "Gimme the book. I'll get you a new one."

"I don't want a new one," I said. "I want *that* one."

"Why?" Rango gave a weak little laugh. "Be a little hard to drive *now*. Don't you think?"

At the image of my car – the only one I had never owned – crushed for no good reason, I felt my eyes grow glassy. It wasn't like I really expected to get the car back. But nowhere in my wildest imaginations had it ended up squashed for some idiot's entertainment.

I pointed to the door. "Get out."

"Hey, we're customers," Rango said.

"You're not customers," I told him. "You're assholes."

Behind him, I heard more laughter. Apparently, in their world, this was considered some sort of compliment.

"Hey, shit happens," Rango said. "Gimme the book, I'll make

it up to you, alright?"

"No, it's not alright," I said. "And besides, the book's not even yours." Or at least, that's what Jake had told me.

Rango looked unimpressed. "It's more mine than yours, babe."

I stared at him. What had I ever seen in the guy? Of course, he hadn't always acted like this, or I wouldn't have dated him in the first place. "If you call me babe one more time," I said, "I'm going to barf all over you."

Behind Rango, Julie wrinkled her nose. She called over to the blond. "If she starts barfing, we're outta here."

How stupid could she get? From the looks of it, the blond was ten times more likely to barf than I was.

I gave Rango a hard look. "You want the book?" I said. "Fine. Twenty-thousand dollars."

His mouth fell open. "What?"

"Twenty thousand, and it's yours."

He snorted. "Twenty grand? You're shitting me, right?"

Was I? I gave it some serious thought. The guy had crushed my car. I needed a new one, and there was no way in hell I'd trust any replacement he offered.

"Take it or leave it," I said.

"Screw you," he said. "I'll leave it."

"Fine." I pointed to the door. "There's the exit."

Again, he leaned in close. "Oh, I'm not going anywhere, *babe.*"

"Oh yes you are." Enough was enough. Whether I knew these idiots or not, it was getting painfully obvious that I needed help getting rid of them.

It was time to get the manager.

I turned and walked to the office door. I raised my knuckles and knocked.

Nothing happened.

Behind me, I heard a snicker. Rango? Or someone else?

Screw it. I knocked again.

Nothing.

From Rango's friends, I heard muffled laughter. I didn't even bother to turn around. Instead, I cupped my hands around my mouth hollered out through the door. "Rupert? Are you in there?"

No answer.

Damn it.

I leaned in close and listened hard. Other than the laughter behind me, I heard nothing. But I swear, I smelled something. Popcorn? I shook my head. No. That couldn't be right.

From behind me, I heard Rango say, "Looks like Rupert's not home."

I whirled toward Rango. "That doesn't change anything."

Ignoring the hammering of my heart, I turned and stalked around the desk. With my head held high, I marched across the lobby to the double doors. I pulled the unlocked door open and held it wide.

I looked toward the group. "Get out. Or I'm calling the police." □

CHAPTER 22

Around me, the lobby fell silent. Finally, after a long, tense moment, Chet pushed himself off the sofa. He reached for blondie's hand. "Come on," he said, tugging the girl to her feet. "You heard her."

Watching, I breathed a sigh of relief. I had never liked Chet, but at the moment, I could have kissed the guy. If he and blondie walked out now, the others would likely follow. One thing about Rango's friends, they weren't exactly known for their original thinking.

From my doorway vantage point, I glanced toward the front desk. Rango still hadn't budged. Instead, he stood, watching me with a set jaw and slitted eyes. I'd seen that look before, and it filled me with dread.

Damn it.

I stiffened my spine. So what? Without a crowd, I could handle Rango just fine. It wouldn't be the first time, after all. And maybe if I got really lucky, Rupert might wander out of his private sanctuary and actually help me out here.

Directly in front of me, Chet sauntered forward with an arm wrapped around the blond's waist. He leaned over to whisper something into the girl's ear. She giggled and shoved against him. "You are so bad," she slurred.

He gave her a demonic grin. "Come on, babe. You know you want to."

Her gaze slid to me, and I felt myself swallow. Whatever the thing was, I prayed they'd be doing it somewhere else. To let them pass, I held the door open wider and breathed a sigh of relief as Julie joined in the exodus.

Outside, it was drizzling now. An icy breeze hit my back, and I felt the chill of freezing raindrops pummeling my hair and clothes. I stifled a shiver and counted the seconds until these losers were gone already.

When Chet and the blond finally made it to the doorway, I stepped back to give them more room.

As it turned out, that was a huge mistake.

The moment the girl made it to the open doorway, she lunged forward and gave me a shove with both hands. Caught off guard, I stumbled backward. The metal door handle slipped from my grip, and my ass hit the wet pavement, hard.

Sprawled on the sidewalk, I looked up just in time to see the whole idiotic group of them, laughing from inside the hotel. With a string of curses, I pushed myself off the sidewalk and lunged for the door handle. I pulled. Nothing happened. And I knew exactly why.

Those fuckers had locked me out.

I pounded against the glass and screamed out, "Hey! Open up!"

Inside, Chet and the rest of them were laughing like idiots. Through the glass door, Chet called out, "Sorry lady, we're closed!"

Desperately, I looked toward the front desk. I saw Brody standing just in front of it, but where on Earth was Rango?

A moment later, he popped up *behind* the front desk, exactly where I had been standing moments earlier. In Rango's hands was something all too familiar – my purse. I watched in stunned disbelief as he opened it up and dumped out all of the contents, including my cell phone, onto the front desk.

Meanwhile, the rest of them were still howling like drunken monkeys as they watched me through the glass.

I slapped my wet palms against the door. "You assholes!" I

yelled. "Open up! I mean it!"

From somewhere behind me, I heard an unfamiliar male voice say, "What the hell?"

I turned to see an attractive man, maybe in his fifties, standing on the sidewalk. In one hand, he held an overnight case. In the other, he held the curved handle of a big black umbrella, which was open to shelter him from the drizzle.

He glanced at the hotel. "So is it, uh, closed or something?"

Just great. A hotel guest. As if this couldn't get any more humiliating.

I gave him a pleading look. "Do you have a cell phone?"

With a perplexed look, he handed over his umbrella and reached into the pocket of his wool coat. He was just pulling out his cell phone when I caught new movement from inside the hotel.

Jake. ☐

CHAPTER 23

I looked around. Where had he come from? The elevators? The restrooms? The stairwell?

Ignoring the idiots in the lobby, Jake was stalking toward the front entrance with his gaze firmly on me. His eyes were blazing, and his mouth was set. He wore jeans and a thin gray T-shirt emblazoned with the name of a local gym. I wanted to cry with relief.

Next to me, I heard a croaking sound. The stranger grabbed my elbow. "Come on," he urged. "Let's go."

I was only half listening. "Huh?"

"Come on!" The guy gave a little yank. "You see that guy?" His voice rose. "He's coming straight for us."

As I watched, a half-crazed sound escaped my lips. "Oh, I see him, alright."

Even in nondescript clothing, Jake looked larger than life and dangerous as hell. If I didn't know him, I might run too.

Unfortunately, the stranger and I weren't the only ones tracking Jake's movements. As Jake passed the front desk, Brody lunged forward. He raised a meaty fist and hit Jake, hard, in the side of the face. With barely a pause, Jake elbowed Brody in the neck and kept on going.

Brody staggered backward, clutching at his neck like he was choking half to death. He slammed sideways against a tall decorative table, sending the table, along with an oversized flower arrangement crashing to the floor. The vase exploded into a million pieces, sending flowers and water cascading across the glossy tile.

Standing behind the desk, Rango froze in obvious shock. His gaze slid to me, and I saw raw panic darken his features. He glanced around, as if looking for an easy out.

Brody pushed himself up from the wet floor and staggered to his feet. His pants were soaked, and his shirt wasn't much better. He looked wildly around and spotted Jake, who by now, had nearly reached the door. Baring his teeth, Brody dove for a nearby Ficus tree. Wrapping his beefy arms around the oversized pot, he lifted the thing high over his head. He hurled it, plant and all, straight in Jake's direction.

But by the time it got there, Jake was already gone. The plant missed Jake by several feet and crashed into a glass coffee table. The table collapsed, sending broken glass everywhere and magazines fluttering to the floor. The plastic tree, now loose from its pot, skidded through the debris before finally coming to a stop near a brown armchair.

In front of me, Chet and the blond now had their backs to the door, with Jake heading straight for them. Like a giant rabid squirrel, Chet took a flying leap in Jake's direction. Without breaking his stride, Jake raised a forearm. Chet crashed into the arm, bounced off it, and staggered into a nearby sofa. The sofa toppled over, taking Chet with it.

Poking out from under the overturned sofa, I saw a foot, a hand, and I swear, Chet's flask, sloshing liquid onto the tile floor in a slow, steady stream.

In front of me, Jake plowed past the blond to reach for the door. He shoved at the door handle, and the door flew open.

Beside me, the stranger gave a little squeak. His hand dropped from my elbow, but he held his ground and said, "Run!"

I didn't run. Instead, I lunged forward, meeting Jake in the open doorway. Jake reached for me, pulling me inside the building and into his arms.

I heard his voice, rough in my ear. "You okay?"

I nodded against him. "Yeah. It's fine. I just got locked out, that's all."

His voice was deadpan. "That's all?"

I tried to laugh. "Oh shut up."

I told myself it wasn't a big deal. I was fine. Jake was fine. So why was I still clinging to him? It's not like we were together anymore. But I couldn't help it. He felt way too good, and I couldn't seem to make myself let go. With my cheek pressed against his hard chest, I turned to look at Rango.

His face was pale, and his eyes were wide. He glanced over at Brody, who sometime in the last minute had scooted around the front desk to join Rango behind it.

Against me, I felt Jake's muscles tighten. He gave Rango a long look and said, "You've got one minute to get the fuck out."

Rango bared his teeth. "We're done anyway." He flicked his head toward the rest of group. "Come on," he told them. "We're outta here."

I heard a thud and turned to look. Apparently, Chet was still underneath the fallen sofa. "Hey!" he called out, giving the sofa another kick. "Get this thing off me, will ya?"

Under any other circumstance, I might have laughed. There was a good reason the sofa was too heavy to lift. The blonde was leaning with her backside against it. Her eyes were bright, and her lips were parted. She was gazing at Jake like he was the tastiest morsel she'd seen in forever.

When Chet kicked the sofa again, the blonde sighed and moved forward. Chet gave another kick, and maybe a shove. The sofa toppled over onto its other side, leaving Chet exposed, sprawled in a puddle of his own booze. Slowly, he got to his feet. Standing in the soggy mess, he turned to give Rango a dirty look. "Some party, asshole."

"Quit your bitching," Rango said. "Not my fault you're a lightweight."

Muttering, Chet stooped to retrieve his fallen flask. With a look of defiance, he threw back his head, opened his mouth, and lifted the flask high above his parted lips. He tipped the flask upside-down and waited.

Nothing happened.

The blond giggled.

With a string of curses, Chet hurled the empty flask across the lobby.

Behind the front desk, Rango turned to Brody. "Come on," Rango said. "Party at my place."

Together, the two guys sauntered out from behind the counter. When they reached Chet, he turned to shuffle after them.

Jake and I were still by the door. I held my breath. The guys were heading straight for us. Around me, Jake's arms were steady and rock-hard. He didn't move a muscle as the three guys brushed past us and walked into the rain.

I breathed a sigh of relief. Finally.

But then, something odd occurred to me. Neither of the girls had moved.

And I had a pretty good idea why.

CHAPTER 24

From a few feet away, Julie was staring at Jake. "You're that Jake guy. Aren't you?" She looked around the lobby. "So, where's the camera?" With a nervous laugh, she reached up to smooth her hair. "Is this going on your channel or something?"

I glanced at Jake. Judging from the look on his face, the girl was more likely to get a kick in the pants than a featured spot in one of his videos.

The blond sidled next to her friend. "Heeeey," she slurred. "I saw him first." She turned to give Jake a long, lingering look. "So, uh, you wanna get out of here?"

Jake eyed her with disgust. "No."

She frowned. "Why not?"

I couldn't let that go. "You've *got* to be kidding," I told her. "Why would he go anywhere with you?"

She gave a drunken little giggle. "Sweetie, if I've got to explain it—"

"You don't," I said.

Beside me, Jake spoke. "You wanna know what I want?"

The girl batted her eyelashes up at him. "What?"

"For you to get the hell out."

Her face froze. "Jeez, you don't have to be so mean about it."

I snorted. "Says the girl who pushed me out the door."

"Naw, that was Chet," she said, "because he told me to."

Oh great. Drunk logic. My favorite. "So if Chet told you to

jump off a bridge—" I rolled my eyes. "You know what? Never mind."

Behind the blond, Julie had turned to study her reflection in the hotel window. "How's my hair?" she asked. "It looks good, right?"

I pointed to the door. "Get out. Both of you."

The blonde made another pouty face. "But it's raining out there."

"Good." I turned to look outside and stifled a gasp. The hotel guest. He was still standing on the sidewalk, hunkered down under his umbrella as he stared at us through the glass. Oh crap. I'd completely forgotten about him.

Reluctantly, I turned back to the girls. They needed to leave, like yesterday.

I pointed to the hotel's royal blue welcome mat, emblazoned with its ornate company logo. "Hey, could you two stand on that rug for a second?"

Julie's gaze narrowed. "Why should we?"

Glancing toward the ceiling, I said in a hushed voice, "Better camera angle."

"Oh," Julie whispered. "Got it." She scampered toward the rug, with the blond right on her heels. They stopped, turned around, and struck a pose.

"Hang on," I said. "Just one more thing." Stepping forward, I reached behind them to prop open the glass door. "Alright," I said. "Smile!"

When they did, I reached out and gave them both a shove. Squealing in surprise, they stumbled backward through the open door. I lunged for the door handle and yanked it shut. And then, I twisted the lock until it clicked.

Outside, the rain had picked up. Standing in the downpour, the girls stared at me in open-mouthed fury.

"You bitch!" yelled the blond.

"My hair!" screamed Julie.

A moment later, a big, dark Lexxus sport utility vehicle raced up to the curb. The driver's side window slid down. Chet popped his head out to yell, "You bitches comin' or what?"

Cupping her hands protectively above her head, Julie turned and made a mad dash for the Lexxus. She wrenched open the backseat and tumbled inside, crawling over Brody, who – the way it looked – was refusing to give up his window seat.

With a final, murderous glare, the blond turned to stumble and splash her way toward her friends. A moment later, she was safely inside. The Lexxus roared away from the curb, leaving nothing but sloshing rainwater in its wake.

Standing on the sidewalk, the man with the umbrella stared after them. After they rounded the nearest corner, he turned his gaze back to the hotel. And me.

I unlocked the door and pushed it open to let him in. "So," I said with a shaky smile, "are you checking in?" □

CHAPTER 25

His name was Jonas Clark, and his flight had been delayed six hours in Atlanta, which explained why he was checking in at nearly four o'clock in the morning.

From behind the front desk, I finished the check-in process. "And here's your room key," I said, handing over the key card in its small cream-colored sleeve. "Have a nice stay, Mister Clark."

Tentatively, he took the card and stooped to pick up his overnight case. Turning toward the front entrance, he paused to take a long look around. Following his gaze, I saw what he saw – overturned furniture, sloppy wet floors, and bits of broken glass everywhere.

And then, near the front entrance, there was Jake, standing in profile, with hard eyes and crossed arms. The way it looked, he was watching both the lobby and the street. We still hadn't had the chance to talk, but that time was obviously coming soon.

I gave Mister Clark a cheery wave as he hoisted his overnight case higher and turned toward the small bank of elevators. When the elevator door finally closed behind him, I breathed a giant sigh of relief and rushed out from behind the front desk.

"Come on," I told Jake as I scurried to the overturned sofa. "Help me lift this back up, will ya?"

He looked toward the sofa. "No."

I stopped to look at him. "Why not?"

"Because you're not lifting anything." Jake took a long look around. "Where the hell is the manager?"

"He's in the back office, and let's hope he stays there." I let out a long breath. "At least until I clean this up."

I circled to the other side of the fallen sofa and cringed as I felt glass crunching beneath my shoes. I looked down and saw what used to be the coffee table, lying in a million pieces. Who was I kidding? Cleaning up was one thing, but most of this stuff was beyond repair.

No matter what I did, I sure as hell couldn't put it back together again. Humpty Dumpty didn't just fall off the wall. He fell off the wall and was hit by an asteroid.

Eyeing the destruction, I felt my brow wrinkle. Should I call the police?

Jake moved toward me. "And the security guy?" he asked. "Where the hell is he?"

I shrugged. "I don't know. I don't think we have one."

"Yeah. You do," he said. "I saw the guy last night."

"Well, he's not here *now*."

"Yeah," Jake said. "I got that."

I stopped to look at him. "You know, if all you're going to do is stand there, looking mad at me, you might as well go up to your room." I froze as something else occurred to me. "In fact, what *were* you doing down here?"

His jaw tightened. "Is that a complaint?"

"No," I sighed. "It's not a complaint." My clothes were still damp, and so was my hair. I stifled a chill. If Jake hadn't shown up, I'd probably still be outside, standing in the rain. Vaguely, I wondered if Mister Clark had a spare umbrella.

Jake's voice softened. "You okay?"

"Yeah, I'm fine." I shook off the cold. "I'm sorry I didn't say it earlier, but uh, thanks. Really. Those guys were totally out of control."

"You think?" He shoved a hand through his hair. "Tell me

something."

"What?"

"Why the hell were you out here alone?"

"Technically, I'm not alone." I looked toward the closed office door. "The night manager's here." My voice faltered. "Supposedly."

Jake pointed to something behind me. "See that chair?"

I turned to look. He was pointing at an easy chair, situated right next to the front desk.

"Yeah," I said. "What about it?"

"That's where I should've been, reading a damn newspaper, no matter what you said."

"You read the paper?"

"What? You think I can't read?"

"Oh stop it," I said. "You just don't strike me as the newspaper type, that's all."

"Screw the paper," he said. "What I'd be looking at is *you*. Making sure you're okay."

At this, I felt that familiar mix of joy and frustration. I felt myself smile, and then frown. Why did it always come down to that?

"What is it?" Jake asked.

I bit my lip. "It's just that I don't like this."

"You don't like what?"

"I don't like that the only reason you're down here is to look out for me, like I'm still a kid or something."

Funny to think that's how Jake and I met, all those years ago. Back then, what I wanted more than anything was to be his girlfriend. If I were being completely honest, I still wanted to be his girlfriend.

Maybe someday, I'd want to be more than his girlfriend. I heard myself sigh. And people in hell wanted ice cream sandwiches.

Circling the fallen sofa, Jake moved toward me until we were close enough to touch. His gaze dipped to my lips. "You're no kid," he said. "You wanna know why I came down?"

"Why?" I asked.

"To talk."

"About what?"

His voice was softer now. "Us."

CHAPTER 26

Remnants of our last conversation drifted back to me, and I decided that my days of jumping to happy conclusions were long over. I kept my tone neutral. "What about us?"

"Come back," he said.

At those all-too-familiar words, I tried to laugh. "Oh no. Not this again."

"Not what again?"

"I'm *not* coming to work for you."

He shook his head. "That's not what I meant." Looking away, he blew out a long, unsteady breath before returning his gaze to mine. "You know what I am?"

I looked up at him. He was tall and dark, with chiseled features and tousled hair. He was sweet and dangerous. He was solid as stone, and unpredictable as hell. Just thinking of him, my stomach fluttered, and my knees grew weak.

I knew exactly what Jake was. He was a dream come true. And he was my worst nightmare. Because no matter what happened between us, I couldn't seem to get him out of my head.

"I don't know," I said. "What are you?"

He gave something like a laugh. "I'm a selfish prick."

"Oh, stop it."

"I am," he said. "And you wanna know why?"

"Why?"

"Because I'm finding it hard as hell to give you up."

Slowly, he moved closer. I heard the crunching of glass and my own intake of breath. He was so near, I could touch him if I wanted to. Desperately, I did want to. But more than that, I wanted to know what exactly he was telling me.

"What are you saying?" I asked.

In front of me, his eyes smoldered in that familiar way, and the destruction around us faded to nothing. There was just Jake, and there was just me. In a surreal way, it felt like there was nothing else in this whole world. Watching him, my palms tingled, and my breath caught. And yet, he still didn't answer.

Finally, just when his silence threatened to break my resolve, he spoke. "You were always my girl. You know that, right?"

"Actually," I said, "I'm pretty sure I was mostly a pain in your butt."

He smiled. It was a far-off smile, like he was seeing something in the far-distant past. "Yeah. You were."

"Hey!" I said.

"But then you weren't." His gaze softened. "And you weren't a kid anymore either."

I couldn't help but smile. "Oh, so you actually noticed?"

"I noticed a lot of things," he said, "but Luna, you meant something to me."

I swallowed. "I did?"

"Yeah. And you *still* mean something to me. And if I weren't such a selfish bastard, I'd do the same thing I did back then."

My heart clenched at the memory. I knew exactly what he had done. He had banished me – from him, from his friends, from anything to do with that group. There I was, seventeen years old, and I'd lost the thing I wanted most – him.

He was supposed to be my first. Instead, he turned out to be the guy who broke my heart. Until last weekend, I hadn't even gotten a kiss out of the deal.

"I'm not a teenager anymore," I reminded him.

"No. You're not. But you'd still be smart to run."

"Is that what you're trying to say?" I asked. "That we can't be—
" I hesitated, not knowing what word to use. "—friends?"

His lips formed the barest hint of a smile. "No. We can't be friends."

"Oh."

"Because the way I feel about you, there's nothing friendly about it." He visibly swallowed. "I love you." He reached for my hand. "I loved you long before this weekend, but—"

"No buts," I said. "Jake?"

"What?"

"I love you too." I felt a jolt of surprise that I'd actually come out and said it – not because I wanted to be coy, but because his earlier words were still haunting my thoughts.

I pray to God you never love me back.

Screw that. I threw back my shoulders and said it again, louder this time. "I love you. And if you've got a problem with that, well, I don't know what. But you'll be sorry."

"You don't know what you're saying."

"I know exactly what I'm saying. Listen, if you think you're doing me a big favor by sparing my feelings or whatever, you're not. I already love you. The damage is done." With my free hand, I gave him a soft poke to the chest. "So you might as well give it up, mister."

Slowly, he lowered his head to mine. His lips brushed my ear, and his voice was a caress. "Mister?"

I turned and silenced him with a kiss, just a small one, or at least, that was my original plan. But the moment our lips met, and his strong arms gathered me close, I couldn't help it. I clung to him like my sanity depended on it.

Maybe my sanity did depend on it. Because one thing was certain – I'd go crazy if I couldn't call him my own.

When we finally pulled away, I swear, I could feel my heart pulsing. It was pure bliss until I heard another sound – the sound of Rupert, croaking out, "You've *got* to be kidding me."

CHAPTER 27

Pushing away from Jake, I whirled to face my boss. Rupert was standing just outside the doorway to his office. Behind him, the door was open, and I heard the faint sounds of a television, or maybe a radio, coming from within.

Rupert's gaze darted around the lobby – from the toppled sofa to the fallen Ficus tree. Like the lone survivor of a zombie apocalypse, he wandered, dumbstruck, from around the front desk and into the main lobby area.

Standing near the lobby's center, he turned slowly around, not stopping until he had completed a full circle. When he finished, he turned toward me. His eyes were wide, and his face was flushed. "What the hell happened here?"

Desperately, I wanted to say something intelligent. I just didn't know what. I mean, forget the destruction. What *did* someone say when they were caught making out on the job?

Next to me, Jake turned to give Rupert a cold stare. "Yeah, what happened? That's a good question, isn't it?"

I gave Jake a pleading look. "I can handle this, okay?"

"No." Jake looked past me and said to Rupert, "Where's the security guy?"

Rupert's gaze narrowed. "Hey, *I'm* asking the questions around here."

"Your ass," Jake said. "Why the hell was she left alone?"

Rupert drew back. "Excuse me?"

"Last I checked," Jake said, "that wasn't supposed to happen."

"Last *you* checked?" Rupert said. "Are *you* the assistant deputy night manager?"

"No." Jake took a step toward him. "But I'm the guy who's gonna beat his ass if he keeps giving me the runaround."

I heard myself gasp. "Jake, seriously—"

In front of us, Rupert blurted out, "The security guy didn't show tonight. There, you happy?"

"No," Jake said, "Where the fuck were you?"

I grabbed Jake's elbow. "Just stop it, okay? You're not helping here. Can you *please* step away and let me deal with this?"

He turned to face me. His jaw clenched. He said nothing.

"Please?" I said.

Jake's gaze drifted to Rupert and then back to me. "If that's what you want," he said, not looking too happy about it. "I'll wait outside."

I glanced toward the windows. "But it's still raining."

"Not a big deal," he said.

"Can't you go upstairs or something?" I asked. "You know? Maybe hang out in your room?"

"Sorry, not gonna happen." He flicked his head toward the front entrance. "If you need me, that's where I'll be." With that, he turned and strode out the double doors.

Once outside, he turned around and stood, watching us, with arms crossed, oblivious to the falling rain. My skin felt icy just looking at him. Vowing to make this quick, I turned my attention back to Rupert.

"Is that your boyfriend?" he asked.

Was he? I wanted to say yes, if only to hear myself say it. But honestly, I didn't know.

"Well?" Rupert said.

I stuck with what I did know. "Actually, he's a guest." I looked around. "Here. At the hotel."

Rupert eyed me with disgust.

My face grew warm. Because nothing screams classy like making out with one of the customers.

"I *know* he's a guest," Rupert said. "You think I wouldn't recognize the guy? He's been a thorn in my side since he checked in."

That made me pause. "He has? How?"

"For one thing, the girls."

My gaze narrowed. "What girls?"

"Every time he walks in, they fawn all over him. It's disgusting."

I wasn't liking the sounds of this. "Which girls are you talking about?"

Rupert gave me the flinty-eye. "You, for one."

Oh. Well, that was different. I glanced away and heard myself say, "I wasn't exactly fawning."

"No, not you," Rupert said. "*You* were tongue-wrestling the guy." His voice rose. "On the clock."

"Technically," I mumbled, "there wasn't *that* much tongue."

Rupert looked around. "So, did *he* do this?"

"You mean did *Jake* trash the place? No. Of course not."

Rupert gave me a dubious look. "So that's your story? He had nothing to do with this?"

"Nothing except kicking out some trouble-makers."

Rupert's gaze darted outside. I turned to look. Jake still hadn't moved. His hair was wet, and his gray T-shirt clung to him like a second skin. Guilt washed over me. In this weather, he had to be freezing.

I wanted him inside, now.

I fought the urge to run out there and drag him upstairs for a hot shower. I wondered, and not for the first time, whether anyone had ever looked out for him.

And yet, there he stood, watching out for me yet again.

Rupert's voice broke into my thoughts. "You *do* know who the guy is. Don't you?"

"What do you think?" I said. "That I go around making out with random strangers?"

Rupert smirked. "So you admit you were making out?"

"It'd be pretty hard not to admit it, since you saw me and all." I mean, seriously, what did he expect me to say? That Jake was giving me mouth-to-mouth?

"Yeah, I *did* see you," Rupert said. "And him. That maniac."

"He's not a maniac," I said, "and it wasn't his fault."

Rupert crossed his arms. "How about *you*? Was it *your* fault?"

I hesitated. This was where things got complicated. Rango was my ex-boyfriend. He'd come in to give me a hard time. Did that make it my fault?

No, I decided. It didn't. It was Rango's fault. And Bianca's – because I just knew she was the one who told Rango where to find me.

"Look," I said, "I was just trying to do my job when some people came in and started giving me a hard time. They were drunk. They were rowdy. They weren't even guests." I pointed to the front entrance. "And get this, they locked me out."

Rupert's draw dropped. "Let me get this straight. You *left* your station?"

"Aren't you listening?" I said. "I was trying to make them leave. There were five of them. And just one of me." I glanced toward the office area. "I knocked on your door, but you didn't answer. Why is that?"

"If I were you, I'd watch your tone," he warned.

I didn't feel like watching my tone. I felt like screaming – at Rupert, who couldn't seem to understand what I'd been up against, at Jake, who was still standing outside getting soaked, and most of all, at me, for being so stupid in the first place.

Rango was my ex-boyfriend, after all. Why had I ever dated the guy?

With an effort, I took a deep, calming breath. "The person who started the trouble, I know him. I know his name. I know where he lives. You've got a security tape, right?"

"That's confidential." Rupert puffed out his chest. "Management only."

"Fine," I said. "Let's call the police. Let them sort it out."

Rupert looked at me like I was an idiot. "We're not turning the lobby into a crime scene."

"What's the difference?" I made a point of glancing around. "It already looks like one."

"Do you *see* a dead body?" he asked.

I shifted my gaze to Jake, who was eyeing Rupert through the front windows. There was something about his look that made me just a little bit nervous. "Not yet," I said.

Rupert held out his hand. "I'll be needing your name tag."

I glanced at the hand and then down at my torso. I wasn't a wearing a name tag. I was too new for a name tag. They were custom-made at corporate headquarters. Supposedly, mine would be here in a week.

Somehow, I had the distinct feeling I wouldn't be needing it. □

CHAPTER 28

"Five hours," I said. "Even for me, that's a new record."

Jake and I were walking side-by-side down the long, quiet corridor of the hotel's top floor, where his room was located. He was still soaking wet, and I felt another surge of guilt. If it weren't for me, he'd be warm and dry right now.

"A record for what?" he asked.

"Getting fired," I said. "I mean seriously, I didn't even make it one full night."

At the door to his hotel room, Jake turned to lounge sideways against the wall. "That job sucked. Getting fired? Best thing that ever happened to you."

"Oh sure, that's what you say *now*. Just wait 'til you get the bill."

"The way I see it?" His dark gaze met mine, and I saw the hint of amusement dancing at the corners. "Money well spent."

I still couldn't believe he'd told Rupert to put the damages on his bill – well, right before he told him to piss off, that is. The way it sounded, the damages would be at least a couple thousand dollars, maybe more. True, Jake had plenty of money, but I hated the idea of him spending a single dime on something that wasn't his fault.

I bit my lip. "You're not really going to pay for all that stuff, are you?"

"Well, I'm sure as hell not letting *you* get charged for them," he said, referencing Rupert's threat to hold *me* responsible.

The idea seemed pretty unrealistic, but it had made me nervous just the same. The only real money I had was Jake's, and I was planning to give that back.

I studied Jake's face. "But why would you do that?"

"You were worried," he said. "I didn't want you to be."

He was right. I *was* worried – that I'd get stuck with the bill, that somehow Jake would end up in trouble, and most of all, that Rupert would be pounded to a bloody pulp.

In the end, none of that had happened.

I pressed the issue. "Yeah, I *was* worried, but you were so mad, why'd you give in like that?"

"Because you wanted it to go away, so I made it. Erased. Forgotten." He reached for my hand. "You don't need to think about it anymore. Okay?"

"But what about Rango?" I asked. "I mean, it was *his* fault. Shouldn't he be the one paying?"

Jake released my hand, and his gaze lost any trace of humor. "Don't worry. He'll pay."

Something about the way he said it sent a chill up my spine. "What do you mean by that?" I asked.

"Forget Rango," Jake said, turning to insert his key card into the slot. "Come on. Let me grab my keys, and we'll head out."

I felt a twinge of surprise. It was the middle of the night. He had a room. We were right here. It was raining. Why go anywhere? "We're leaving?" I said. "To go where?"

"You pick," he said. "My place?"

"Or," I said with a half-hearted laugh, "there's always the job-trailer."

I had been staying in that trailer for only a couple nights, but already, it was a couple nights too long. Even with a curtained-off sleeping area, the arrangement was practically barbaric. It was messy, noisy, and way too small for one person, much less three.

And that didn't even take into account the porta-potties. I gave a little shudder. Seriously, what the hell had I been thinking? But I knew exactly what I'd been thinking. Better to tough it out in a trailer than have my heart broken someplace a whole lot nicer.

In front of me, Jake pulled the key card from its electronic slot, and I heard the telltale click of the lock releasing. He pushed open the door and flicked his head toward the open doorway. "After you," he said.

I gazed over at him. His hair was still dripping rainwater, and his soaked T-shirt shirt clung to his skin, accenting the outlines of his muscles under the thin cotton fabric.

I felt my tongue brush the inside of my lips. Even his jeans were soaked. Before going anywhere, didn't he want to change clothes? Tentatively, I reached out and touched his arm. His skin was ice cold.

I drew back my hand. "Oh my God. You're like a human icicle."

"Not a big deal," he said. "I've got a jacket inside."

He didn't need a jacket. He needed a hot shower. At the mental image of Jake naked, I felt my own temperature rise. I started to squirm. Here, the guy was soaked, and all I could think of was how amazing he'd look even wetter.

I should be ashamed of myself.

Pushing away the distraction, I strode into his hotel room, only to stop short at what I saw. The room looked absolutely pristine, vacant actually. My gaze drifted to the bed. The way it looked, no one had even sat on the thing, much less slept on it.

It seemed odd, considering that it was nearly morning.

Silently, I wandered to the window and looked out. What I saw was a perfect view of the construction site, mostly dark, but visible enough from the twelve-story vantage point. My gaze zoomed in on the job-trailer where I'd been staying with my brothers.

From ground-level, the trailer was hard to see, nestled among so many other temporary buildings. But from here, a hundred feet up, I had a dim view of the entire trailer, including its only door.

Inside the quiet room, I turned around. Jake was standing a few feet behind me, gazing at me with an expression that I couldn't make out.

"You were watching me?" I said.

I wasn't stupid. I had suspected as much. But to have it confirmed, I wasn't quite sure how I felt. Flattered? Or frightened? Maybe a little bit of both?

He gave a slow shake of his head. "No."

"Oh come on," I said. "You can't really expect me to believe that."

"Don't get me wrong," he said, moving closer. "I could watch you all day." His expression grew serious. "But that's not what this is about."

"Okay. Then what *is* it about?"

He glanced away, and I felt that familiar frustration. Countless times, I had asked him this question. Countless times, he had given me only vague answers. Why had I expected that this time would be any different?

"Let me guess," I said, "it's top-secret, right?"

"No. It's just ugly." He stepped forward and ran the back of his ice-cold index finger along my jawline. "And you're too damn sweet for any of this."

I didn't think of myself as sweet, but it made me smile just the same. "Oh please. I'm no saint, that's for sure."

"You think I want a saint?" His voice softened. "What would a sinner like me do with one of those?"

At something in his expression, my core ignited. Through lowered lashes, I gazed up at him. My voice grew breathless as I said, "I could think of some things."

On his lips, I saw the barest hint of a smile. "Yeah?"

Seeing that smile, my thoughts galloped in two opposite directions. On one hand, I wanted him so bad I could taste it. I wanted to warm his body with my own and melt myself against him. I wanted to drag my hands through his wet hair and feel his cool fingers harden my nipples.

I wanted a lot of things.

I felt myself frown. But what I really needed were answers.

The old Luna would take her pleasure now and let the future take care of itself. She'd forget that she had lost three jobs in one week and still had no place to call home. She wouldn't worry that she had no money, no references, and no real plan for tomorrow.

"Baby?" Jake said. "What is it?"

Breathlessly, I looked up at him. I felt myself swallow.

Screw tomorrow.

What I really needed was to get him out of those wet clothes.

For his sake.

Right?

CHAPTER 29

Breathlessly, I pressed forward until our bodies met. He was so cold and so hard that I shivered against him.

With a groan, he pulled back. Tucking his chin, he looked down at his soaked T-shirt. He frowned. "Baby, you're gonna get wet."

I couldn't help it. I laughed. After the last couple of days, the sensation felt almost new, and it made me feel just a little bit giddy.

"What?" he asked.

I edged closer. "I'm already wet."

His gaze dipped to my mostly dry clothes before it returned to my eyes. Whatever he saw in them made his lips curve into a slow smile. It was a nice smile filled with all kinds of implications that warmed me to the core.

Suddenly, I felt like crying – not sad tears, the other kind. "I missed you," I said.

Finally, his arms closed around me. He was cold and soaked, but I could hardly care. I lifted my face, and our lips met in a lingering kiss. His were cooler than I expected, making mine feel achingly hot and burning for more.

Breaking the kiss, he pulled back to look at me. His hair was still damp, and his skin looked paler than I recalled, even from just a few moments earlier. There was a new darkness in his eyes that took me by surprise.

"What's wrong?" I asked.

His voice was quiet. "Fuck hurting each other."

I shook my head. "What?"

His gaze was hungry, and his lips were parted. From somewhere between them, I heard the whisper of something that could only be my name.

I wanted to press tighter against him, to warm his skin and wash away the darkness, wherever it had come from. But somehow, I made myself stop. Because the way it looked, there was something he needed to say, something that for whatever reason, couldn't wait.

I tensed. Would it be something good? Or something bad?

Nervously, my hands toyed with the hem of his T-shirt. The cotton was cold and soaked against my warm fingers. I slipped my hands under the wet fabric until I felt his skin, cool and damp under my trembling touch.

As the silence grew, I studied his face. He might've been granite, except for his eyes, filled with such longing that I caught my breath.

"I won't," he said. "I swear to God, I won't."

"You won't what?"

"No matter what, I won't hurt you. And I won't make you hate me."

It was strange, really. Obviously, he was speaking to *me*, but somehow, I had the odd impression that the words were more for his own ears than for mine. Was it a threat to himself more than a promise to me?

"I never thought you would," I said.

He shook his head. "You don't know me."

"You're wrong," I said. "*You* don't know you." I tried to laugh. "Seriously, every girl we meet is half in love with you. They can't *all* be crazy."

"That?" he said. "It's all bullshit. I know it. You know it."

I gave him a look. "Well, I'm glad *you* think so."

"Why?"

"Because," I said, "less competition."

"Luna." His voice grew tender. "Don't you know? There *is* no competition."

My breath hitched. "Really."

He spoke into my hair. "And there hasn't been any for a long, long time."

I smiled against him and shivered as the dampness of his clothes burrowed its way into mine. "You know what I am?" I asked.

"What?"

"The most selfish person, ever."

"Why's that?" he asked.

"Because you're freezing. And you probably want a shower. But…"

"But what?"

Determined to lighten his mood, I gave a playful tug at his shirt. "I want you naked for other reasons."

For a long time, he said nothing. But then, when he finally spoke, the darkness had disappeared, leaving a smile in his voice that warmed my heart. "Oh yeah?"

Suddenly, almost before I could process what was happening, my feet left the ground as he swooped me up into his arms. "You want *me* naked?" he said, heading toward the bed. "What about what *I* want?"

Laughing, I pressed my cheek against his damp T-shirt and reached up to lace my fingers behind his neck. I heard a soft thud as one of my shoes hit the carpeted floor.

Jake stopped moving to look down. "Well, that's a start."

Deliberately, I flung off my other shoe, wincing as it almost crashed into the nearest nightstand.

"Nice," Jake said, cradling me closer as he moved toward the bed. Reaching it, he stopped. And then, counting as he went, he swung me forward once, twice, and three times, finally sending me tumbling amid laughter onto the mattress.

"Wait," I said through fits of giggles. "You're still not naked. This is so not fair."

With a crooked grin, he reached for the hem of his T-shirt. He lifted it a couple of inches, but then let go. He glanced down at his feet. A moment later, he kicked off his shoes.

I stifled another laugh. "Your shoes? Seriously? Is that really the best you can do?"

His gaze travelled the length of me. "How about you?" he said. "Is that the best *you* can do?"

Oh, he was so gonna pay for that.

On the bed, I sat up, tucking my legs underneath me. With a single hand, I reached up to toy with the neckline of my plain white blouse. It had lots of tiny buttons, straight down the middle. With a deliberate slowness, I started at the top, popping them open one-by-one as Jake watched with smoldering eyes.

When I finished with the last button, I stopped. Technically, the blouse was fully undone, but in truth, I had shown him nothing. I gave him a saucy smile. "You want more?"

Some of the color had returned to his face, making him look less like a pale statue and more like the guy I loved. His lips were parted, and his gaze was hungry. "You know I do."

I let my gaze zoom in on his T-shirt. "That's funny," I teased. "Me too."

His mouth twitched for the briefest instant before he reached for the hem of his still-damp shirt. Slowly, he lifted it upward, inch-by-inch, revealing those washboard abs, his broad chest, and those finely cut shoulders covered so perfectly in muscle and ink.

When his shirt finally hit the floor, my mouth was dry, and my core was on fire.

His body was glistening, and his hair was still damp. Suddenly, I longed for a camera, because I wanted to remember him just like this – wet, tattooed and half-naked. Or, better still, I decided, I could replay this scene over and over again in real life, as many times as he would have me.

I just hoped it was a lot.

For a long moment, our gazes remained locked. And then, his broke, drifting downward to caress my body in a way that felt nearly physical.

He flicked his head toward my blouse. "Your turn."

I ran a finger down the center of my unbuttoned blouse, nudging aside the fabric to expose the slimmest hint of bare skin, along with only the center portion of my lacy white bra. I stopped to give him a mischievous smile. "Does that count?"

"Not a chance."

"Hard-ass." Still smiling, I shrugged out of the blouse and let it fall onto the bedspread behind me. "How about now?" I asked.

His gaze drifted to my bra. "Only if you keep going."

Reaching behind my back, I unfastened my bra. Sitting up, I placed my hands over my breasts and dropped one shoulder, and then the other. The shoulder-straps fell aside, leaving only the cups in place, still covered by my hands. "How about now?"

His gaze was on fire. "Not by a longshot."

I looked down at his jeans. Damp and dark, they clung to him, showing off his long legs, his trim waist, and yes, because I was looking for it, the bulge that had grown noticeably bigger since I had started undressing. "What about *you*?" I asked.

"What about *me*?"

Keeping my hands in place, I gave a little shrug. "It seems to me, I'm doing a lot more undressing than you are."

He gave a slow nod. "You know what?" He smiled. "You're right."

And then, almost before I knew it, he lunged forward, tackling me onto the bed in a gentle tumble that somehow ended up with me cradled in his arms, with his hard chest pressed against my bare back.

I laughed as my hands fell free, and the bra slipped from my breasts. "That's not what I meant," I protested.

His voice was all innocence. "No?"

Before I could respond, I felt a cool finger at my left nipple. Whether from the temperature difference, or just the fact it was him, it practically jumped in response, hardening into a tight, hungry knob that made me whimper, longing for more.

"So," Jake continued, cupping both of his cool hands over my warm breasts. "You really expect me to fight fair?" Slowly, he spread his fingers and then, just as slowly, tightened them back up, capturing the tips of each nipple between his expert fingers.

I heard myself moan as I ground my hips backward, feeling his hardness surge against the back of my skirt. If only I *had* taken off more clothes. What the hell had I been thinking?

He gave my breasts a tender squeeze. "So here's the question," he said. "Do I finish undressing you? Or..." I felt a hand leave my breast and drift lower to hike up my skirt.

My answer was a half-moan, half-sigh. "Or what?"

"Or." He yanked my panties down my thighs. "Do I take you right here, like this?"

Oh my God. How did someone answer that?

I felt a hand drift up my leg. On instinct, my thighs parted as far as the panties would allow. Soon, I felt his cool touch exactly where I wanted it – on that hot knob of pleasure that was practically begging for attention.

"Well," he said, giving me a gentle stroke.

I ground forward into his touch. And then, I ground backward into his erection. I wanted both. I was almost too breathless to answer. "Well what?"

"Should I undress you?" His hips surged forward in a playful threat. "Or just take you?"

I was practically panting now. "Take me."

I made a motion to turn around, feeling like I should do something to move things forward. But he held me tight and gave me the best reason to stay still – another stroke against that special spot, and another, until I was slick and quivering with need and excitement.

I felt his body shift, and his hand briefly abandoned me to

unbutton his pants and shove down his jeans. Soon, I heard them hit the carpet. Desperate to have him, I shoved down my panties and kicked them off to who-knows-where.

A moment later, his hand was back, teasing and toying as he wrapped his body tight against my back. When his erection found my opening, I pressed my hips backward, moaning as his hardness found my softness and filled me nearly to bursting even as his hand continued to coax double the sensations out of my warm and willing body.

As we continued to move, I heard his voice in my ear, whispering, coaxing, claiming until I was utterly lost to everything but him. When at last, we shuddered together into that special place between heaven and Earth, I wanted to laugh with joy.

With no one else had it ever been like this — tender and fevered, rough and gentle. He was my own crazy set of contradictions. He was everything that he seemed, and yet, nothing that he seemed. In a hundred years, I'd never figure him out.

But in that moment, I just prayed I'd have the chance to try. □

CHAPTER 30

Later, after round-two — or maybe round two-and-a-half, depending on how I looked at it — we were tangled together under the covers. Blissful in his arms, I couldn't help but laugh, at least a little.

He was stroking my hair. "What is it?" he asked.

I burrowed deeper into his arms. "So much for being reformed."

"Reformed?" In his voice, I heard the hint of a smile. "How?"

With him so near, it was hard to think, much less put those thoughts into words. But I gave it a shot. "Growing up, my sister was always the responsible one." I sighed. "But me? I was always like, 'What sounds fun *now*,' you know?"

"Nothing wrong with that," he said.

"Well sure, nothing's wrong at the time. But what happens when the fun's over, and you're right back where you're started?"

"Who says the fun has to be over?"

I tried to smile. I didn't *want* the fun to be over, especially where Jake was concerned.

Images from the last couple hours danced across my mind. No matter what happened next, I'd have those memories forever. Maybe it hadn't been the smartest thing, but it was the only thing. That had to count for something, right?

Still, I felt myself frown against his skin.

"Baby, what is it?" he asked.

With a sigh, I sat up to look at him. "It's just that I still have no idea what's going on. Earlier, I started to ask, but, well, I guess you could say I got distracted."

In fact, looking at him lying there, bare-chested and tousled-looking, I was getting a little distracted now. It wasn't helping.

Grabbing a nearby blanket, I sat up and wrapped it around me. Determined to keep a clear head, I pushed off from the bed and wandered, barefoot, to the hotel window. I looked out. Once again, I zoomed in on the construction site, dimly lit, but clear enough.

"If you weren't watching me," I said, "what *were* you doing here?"

From behind me, I heard him move. Soon, I felt his arms close around me as I continued to gaze away.

"The truth?" he said. "I was watching for a friend."

"Who?"

"The guy who sent that text."

I turned around to give Jake a perplexed look. "What text?"

"Remember that morning I picked you up? At Maddie's place?"

I couldn't help but tease him. "Picked me up? Or dragged me out of there?"

In his gaze, I saw no hint of humor. "I had my reasons."

"Which were?"

"That text I showed you," he said, "you remember what it said?"

Actually, he had shown me a series of texts. As I nodded, bits and pieces of those messages came rushing back to me.

Looking for a girl from your old neighborhood.

To settle a score.

She stole something. I need to get it back. ASAP.

By now, I knew which "something" they meant – Rango's little black book, except, according to Jake, it didn't actually belong to Rango, but rather to Rango's boss. Who he was, I had no idea.

Supposedly, the book had account numbers, passwords, financial notes, that sort of thing. In truth, I hardly looked at it. All I had really wanted were two things – the passwords to Rango's social media accounts and to make Rango squirm.

"The guy who sent that text?" Jake said. "He's not someone I'd like you to meet."

I shook my head. "But you said he's a friend?"

"He was," Jake said. "These days, I wouldn't count on it."

"Why not?"

"Because I sent him packing."

"What do you mean? Like you told him to get lost?"

"No," he said. "Like I told him you were shacked up in Barbados with some banker."

I couldn't help but laugh. "A banker. Really?"

"Hey, it happens," Jake said.

"But why would you do that?"

"Because I wanted him away from you." His voice hardened. "And lying to the guy? Believe me, that wasn't my first choice."

I felt my brow wrinkle. "Then what was?"

He gave a laugh devoid of any real humor. "To kick his ass. Or worse." He shook his head. "But it wouldn't have been smart."

"And sending him to Barbados was?"

"It's a twelve-hour flight," he said. "Hard for him to find you when he's a mile high."

"But I'm still not following."

"Alright, let me back up," Jake said. "My friend – let's call him Bob – he hears about a bounty on a missing book. He starts digging and learns that Rango has access to the owner's house, where the book is kept."

"So he knows that Rango took it?"

"He suspects," Jake said. "Big difference. But anyway, he digs some more and learns that Rango has this ex-girlfriend who's been giving Rango a hard time on the internet, posting things under Rango's accounts. So Bob gets to thinking, 'Maybe Rango took the book, and the ex took it from Rango.'"

"Me?" I gave Jake a dubious look. "That seems like a pretty big leap, don't you think?"

"For most people? Maybe. But not Bob. He has an instinct for these things. He *knows* that Rango's a douchebag ..." Jake hesitated.

"Are you expecting me to disagree?" I asked.

"Just checking," Jake said. "Anyway, the way Bob sees it, it would be just like Rango to write his *own* passwords in the boss's book."

"Like peeing on another dog's hydrant?" I asked.

"More or less."

"So about your friend, you think he came back here? To Detroit?"

"Maybe," Jake said. "Maybe not. But I'm sure as hell not gonna take any chances."

"Because you think he's still looking for me?"

"I don't know," Jake said. "But he's good at finding things, people too."

"And you don't want him to find me?"

"No," Jake said. "Not alone, anyway."

Well, I guess that explained why he had dragged me to his penthouse and tried to keep me there. But it didn't explain everything. "Why not just give him the book?" I asked.

"Because," Jake said, "there's no guarantee he'll give it back to the owner."

I shook my head. "Why wouldn't he?"

"He might get more money from someone else."

"Like who?"

"People you don't want to know."

"Where's the book now?" I asked.

Jake glanced toward the far end of the room, where I spotted a dark jacket draped over an easy chair. "It's over there."

"So what are you gonna do with it?" I asked.

"The plan is to get it back to the owner, and you off the hook. But it's complicated."

"Why?" I asked.

His voice grew deadly serious. "Giving it back, that's not the complicated part."

I felt the color drain from my face. "But getting me off the hook is? Why would it be? I wasn't the one who took it."

Jake gave me a look.

I cleared my throat. "Well, not from the owner, anyway."

"Don't worry," he said. "I've got this. I've got some friends, they know the guy. It'll be fine."

Looking at him, that wasn't the only thing worrying me. "Can I ask you something?"

"What?"

I crossed my arms tight around myself. How to put this? "If it hadn't been for that book, or your friend, or whatever, would you have even looked me up?"

"The truth? No."

My heart sank. "But why not?"

"You know why."

I considered all he had told me, not just here, but at his penthouse. "Because you were afraid of hurting me?"

"Hurting you, dragging you into my shit." He gave a hollow laugh. "Ruining your life."

"And now?" I said. "Do you regret it? Finding me, I mean?"

"No." He moved closer to wrap his arms tight around me. "Yeah, the stuff with my friend, the book, all of it, it explains why I showed up. But do you know what it doesn't explain?"

"What?"

"Why I can't let you go."

CHAPTER 31

When I woke, he was standing by the bed, dressed in the same clothes that he'd been wearing the previous night. As for me, I was wearing what I had fallen asleep in, absolutely nothing. I felt myself smile. The last time I'd looked, he'd been wearing nothing too.

How long ago was that?

Sunlight filtered in through the hotel windows, making me squint as I gazed up at him. "What time is it?" I mumbled.

He smiled down at me. "Still early. Not yet eight."

I turned and groaned into my pillow. Technically, it wasn't *that* early, but considering that I'd been asleep for only a couple of hours, it felt like the middle of the night, sunlight or not.

When I felt the mattress shift, I turned to look. Jake was sitting on the edge of the bed, gazing down at me with an expression that made me want drag him back under the covers.

With a sleepy hand, I reached out and touched his shirt. It was still damp. Perplexed, I moved my hand to his thigh. So were his jeans.

I shivered under the warm covers. "You put on your wet clothes? Why?"

"They were the only ones I had."

"You didn't bring any luggage?"

"Nah," he said. "I wasn't sleeping here. Remember?"

"Oh. I guess." My brain wasn't quite awake yet. "But, aren't you freezing?"

"Nah, not a big deal. I've got some stuff in the car, so..." He let the sentence trail off as he tucked the covers tighter around me.

"So, where are you going?" I asked. "Should I get dressed?"

He shook his head. "You stay. I've got to run out for something." His voice softened. "You go back to sleep. I'll be back in a few hours. Then we'll figure things out." He glanced toward the door. "Want me to bring you back anything?"

"Just you," I said.

"I'll give you a call if I'm running late." He leaned over and brushed his lips against mine. "Don't go anyplace, alright?"

I had to smile. Where would I go? I made a show of closing my eyes. "Not unless I sleepwalk."

His hand brushed my cheek, and a moment later, I heard the door open and shut behind him. Snuggling deeper under the covers, I felt myself smile. For someone who'd just lost her third job in one week, I felt surprisingly content.

I drifted off, thinking of Jake, and didn't wake until the shrill sound of a telephone ringing jolted me out of my dream state. Confused, I sat up and looked around, half-forgetting where I was.

My gaze landed on the room's ugly beige telephone, sitting on the nearby nightstand. Should I answer it?

Before I could decide, it stopped ringing. I was glad, actually. It saved me the trouble of a decision, especially when I wasn't quite awake.

Next to the phone was a digital clock that read 9:02. So Jake had been gone how long now? An hour? Had *he* been the one who called? Resisting the urge to go back to sleep, I stumbled out of bed and dug through my purse in search of my cell phone.

I pulled it out and felt myself frown. It was dead, of course. What if he had tried to call my cell first, and then called the room as a last resort?

Embarrassingly, I couldn't even call him back, because I didn't know his number by heart. Mostly, I just pressed the Jake button from my contact-list. Stupid cell phone. I didn't even have a charger on me.

Too wired to sleep, I went to the bathroom to freshen up and get dressed. I was nearly done when the hotel phone rang again. This time, I dove for it and picked it up with a breathless, "Hello?"

On the other end, I heard a woman's voice that sounded vaguely familiar. "Laura? Is that you?"

"Uh, sorry," I said. "I think you have the wrong room."

She hesitated. "So this *isn't* Laura Moon?"

Oh crap. Laura. That *was* me. Damn it. Maybe Jake was right. Maybe I *should* go by my birth name, as weird as it was. If nothing else, it might reduce my odds of looking like an idiot. "Oh. Sorry," I said. "I must've misheard you."

"It's Suzanne." She cleared her throat. "From the front desk?"

Of course. Suzanne. I'd been her co-worker for less than a day. I could only imagine what she thought of me. I tried to keep my tone friendly. "Oh, right," I said. "Hi."

Her voice was deadpan. "Hi. You've got a visitor."

"A visitor? What do you mean?"

"Someone at the front desk."

"Who?"

"A gentleman. He says his name is Vince."

"Vince Hammond?" I asked. Vince was a hotshot sports agent – and more to the point, Jake's mortal enemy. Or at least, that was my impression.

"That's the one," she said.

I recalled the incident with Bianca just yesterday. She had tried like crazy to reach Jake in this same hotel room, with absolutely zero luck. How had Vince pulled it off?

More to the point, what on Earth was he doing here? We were on friendly enough terms, but I still didn't want to see him. The last time I'd seen him, he'd offered me a job. Jake had been livid, even more so after someone had claimed that Vince and I were playing swallow-the-salami in the elevator to Jake's building.

"So, are you coming down?" Suzanne asked.

What if I didn't? Would Vince stick around? Would Jake see him when he returned? And if he did, what would happen? The last thing I needed was another ugly scene in the hotel lobby.

"Yeah, sure," I said. I'll be down in a minute."

While I was at it, I decided, I'd need to get rid of him in half that time. ☐

CHAPTER 32

When the elevator doors opened into the crowded lobby, I spotted him instantly, a good-looking blond guy in a stylish business suit. He was leaning against the front desk, chatting with Suzanne, who the way it looked, was utterly charmed.

The place was busier than I'd ever seen it, with two other hotel-employees, not including Suzanne, manning the front desk. I guess that made sense. It *was* nearly check-out time, after all.

I took a deep breath and moved toward the lobby's center. I'd thrown on my clothes from the previous night – the standard black skirt and white blouse. I guess they looked reasonably okay, which had to be some kind of miracle, all things considered.

Catching my eye, Vince motioned me to the lobby's main seating area. I glanced toward it and tried not to show my surprise.

It didn't look nearly as bad as I'd anticipated.

Sure, it was minus one coffee table, but all in all, the area looked nothing like the war zone I'd been expecting. I saw no broken glass, no shattered ceramic, no scattered flower arrangements, and no other sign whatsoever of last night's altercation.

Obviously, someone had been very busy during the five hours I'd been upstairs.

After we said a brief hello, Vince motioned to the nearby sofa – the same one that Chet had toppled over the previous night. "Want to have a seat?" he asked.

"Sorry," I said. "I've only got a minute, so I'd better not get too comfortable."

"What you mean to say is you don't want *me* to get too comfortable." Vince gave me an easy smile. "Am I right?"

I felt my cheeks grow warm. I had only met him a few times, but he had this maddening way of cutting straight to the point with an easy charm that made me feel like an oaf in comparison.

"You want the truth?" I asked.

"Sure," he said. "Hit me."

"Honestly," I said, "I really didn't want to talk to you at all, no offense." I glanced around. "But Jake will be here soon, and I figured it would be best for everyone if you guys didn't run into each other." I glanced toward the entrance. *Hint, hint.*

"So what you're telling me is to get to the point and get out?" Vince gave a slow nod. "I can respect that."

What did someone say to such a thing? I studied his face. He actually looked sincere.

"Alright," he continued, "I'm here to offer you a job."

I felt my brow wrinkle. "You already did that. Remember?"

He'd done this at the door to Jake's penthouse of all places. At the time, Jake hadn't been home. Jake wasn't around now either. Obviously, that was no accident. Vince either had terrific timing or inside information.

"By the way," I said, "how'd you know I was here?"

Of course, I already knew the answer to that. Bianca was working for him now. The way it looked, she was quite the blabbermouth. I was dying to see if he'd admit it.

"I have my sources," he said.

I crossed my arms. "Bianca?"

He shrugged. "She might've mentioned it."

"Right," I said. "And about the job, thanks, but the answer is still no."

"Can I ask why?"

"You already know why," I said. "One, you're not hiring me for my qualifications. And two, Jake wouldn't like it."

"Do I have time for a rebuttal?" he asked

"Not really."

"Come on," he said with a smile, "just hear me out, alright? Aren't you curious?"

In truth, I *was* curious. Vince was a top sports agent. His company represented some of the biggest names in sports entertainment. It did billions in revenue and had offices all over the place, including one right here in Detroit.

Into my silence, Vince said, "About your qualifications, you're selling yourself short."

I gave him a skeptical look. "Am I?'

"You are," he said. "You've got the right degree and just enough experience. Plus, I like the way you handle yourself. This business? It can get a little rough sometimes. I need someone who's not afraid to go toe-to-toe with personalities that others might find intimidating."

At this, I actually laughed. "I think you've got the wrong girl. I don't go toe-to-toe with anyone."

"Not true," he said. "I've seen the way you handle Jake."

"I don't 'handle' Jake," I said. "We've been friends a long time."

"Okay. Sorry." Vince held up his hands, palms out. "Bad choice of words. The point is, you're not afraid of him."

"Why should I be?"

"See, that's what I'm talking about," he said. "It's that kind of attitude that wins in this business. Now, as to your other objection–"

"That Jake wouldn't like it?" I said. "Yeah, that's a pretty big one, isn't it?"

"Not as big as you'd think." Vince looked around the hotel lobby. "You think he'd like *this*?"

"What do you mean?" I asked.

"You," Vince said, "working nights?"

Oh God, he thought I still worked here? When I'd been fired?

Well, this wasn't awkward or anything. "Actually," I said, "that's not a problem anymore."

"I *know* Jake, remember?"

What did he mean by that? "I guess I'm not following," I admitted.

"Knowing him, he's worried about your safety. You take the job with me, and he won't need to worry anymore."

I almost laughed. "So take the job for him? That's what you're saying? Well, I've got to give you points for creativity."

"Be honest," Vince said. "It drives him crazy, doesn't it?"

Funny, it had driven Jake crazy. But I knew what would make him a whole lot crazier – me, working for Vince. But that wasn't the topic at-hand, was it? "Actually," I said, "I think your information is a little outdated. I don't work here anymore."

"You don't?"

"No. Didn't Suzanne tell you?"

"Tell me what?" he asked.

I didn't bother to sugar-coat it. "I was fired."

"No kidding?"

"No kidding. My first night, by the way." If that didn't discourage him, nothing would.

"For what?" he asked.

"There was sort of a mini-riot in the lobby, and uh, well, the management wasn't pleased."

At this, Vince laughed. "A mini-riot, huh?" He was nodding now. "See, that's exactly the kind of experience I'm looking for."

Didn't this guy ever take no for an answer? "Well, you're going to have to look somewhere else, because as I told you, Jake wouldn't like it."

"So," Vince said, "you're going to let *him* dictate your career path?"

"He's not dictating anything," I said.

"But?"

"But you guys don't get along. And out of loyalty, well, let's just say I'm not going to change my mind, okay?" I glanced toward the entrance. "Now, I don't want to be rude, but you should probably get going."

"Hang on. One last thing." He reached into the inside front pocket of his sports jacket. He pulled out a folded sheet of paper and held it out toward me.

Reluctantly, I took it and opened it up. I scanned several paragraphs of typewritten text and felt my eyebrows furrow. I looked up. "You can't be serious?"

"I'm dead serious," he said. "And I've got the check to back it up."

I scanned the letter again. "A signing bonus? Of five-thousand dollars?"

"The way I see it," Vince said, "it's a good investment."

I handed the letter back. "Not for me, it isn't."

"Why not?"

"Because I'm not gonna sell my relationship to Jake for any amount of money."

"Who says you have to sell anything?" he asked. "Keep seeing him. In fact, it's better for me, if you do."

"And why's that?" I asked.

"Because," he said, "it'll cut the odds of him harassing my clients."

I made a scoffing sound. "So you think you're buying influence?" I almost laughed in his face. "More likely, he'd never speak to me again. And then you'd be out five thousand for nothing."

"Not the way I see it," Vince said.

I gave him a look. I knew exactly what he meant. If Jake were hurt by this, it wouldn't bother Vince in the least. In fact, that was probably the whole point, wasn't it?

The logical part of me actually understood. The way it sounded, Jake had cost Vince a lot of money. But the emotional part of me? My heart? That belonged to Jake, and only Jake.

I glanced toward the doors. "I think you'd better leave," I told him.

"Can't blame a guy for trying," he said.

Actually, I could. And I did. Because nothing could entice me to stab Jake in the back like that – or so I thought, right up until my next nasty surprise.□

CHAPTER 33

At the door to Jake's hotel room, I pulled out the key card. I slid it into the slot, still thinking about Vince's ridiculous offer. Like my loyalty could be bought with a decent job and a signing bonus.

I hesitated. The job was more than decent actually. Just before leaving, Vince had thrown out a salary figure that almost made me regret I couldn't take it. Almost, but not quite. The way I saw it, some things were a whole lot more valuable than money.

Entering the hotel room, I paused at the sounds of running water coming from the bathroom. I felt myself smile. He was back. And earlier than expected too.

I was just about to call out to him when something saved me the trouble. That something was a voice – unfamiliar, and worse, female – coming from behind the closed bathroom door.

"Hey Jake," she called out in a flirty voice. "I'm running a bath. You wanna join me?"

I froze, feeling the color drain from my face as my mind started churning on overdrive. Everywhere Jake went, girls threw themselves at him. A lot of those girls, Jake didn't even know. Was that the case here?

It had to be.

A moment later, I heard the voice again. "Sorry I didn't call first, but my phone is totally on the fritz. Would you believe I dropped it *again*?" Her laughter rang through the door. "It reminds me of that time in Vegas. Remember how mad I made that dealer?"

I was still staring, dumbstruck, at the door, when it opened just a crack, and a female head peeked out. She was drop-dead gorgeous, with sun-kissed hair and big blue eyes. When she saw me, those eyes widened and she gave a little gasp. "Oh my God," she said. "Shoot. Wait. This isn't what it looks like."

I felt my eyebrows furrow. Stupid or not, I still wasn't quite sure what it *did* look like. I mean, I knew the obvious conclusion, but I refused to jump there.

"Um, hi," I said. "So you're, uh...?"

Her gaze darted around the room. "The cleaning person," she said. "Just let me finish with this, uh – I'm cleaning the shower, actually, and I should be done in five minutes..." She gave me a half-smile, half-wince. "..., if you'd like to come back?"

I didn't bother to hide my disbelief. "So you're saying you're from housekeeping."

"Yes. That's it. Housekeeping."

In my head, I compiled a short list of things this girl *could* be. And nowhere on list did the word housekeeper appear.

Whatever she saw on my face, it obviously wasn't good, because a moment later, the bathroom door slammed shut, and I heard rummaging coming from within.

Beyond confused, I stood there like an idiot, staring at the door while she did God-knows-what behind it. Maybe a minute later, the door flew open, and there she was, wearing a skimpy red dress with matching shoes. She scurried out of the bathroom, lugging a white overnight case with her.

Housekeeping, my ass.

She'd gotten maybe two steps when I jumped to block her path. "Just who *are* you?" I said. "And don't say 'housekeeping' because I'm not stupid."

We were only inches apart. And in truth, she was a bit taller than I was. But there was no way in hell I was letting her waltz out the door without giving me some answers.

"I'm nobody," she said. "Wrong room, that's all." She gave a shaky laugh. "Happens to me all the time. I really need to get my eyes checked."

I gave her a look. "How do you know Jake?"

"Who's Jake?" She made a show of looking around. "Oh, is this *his* room? Is he your husband or something? I am *so* sorry." She gave an exaggerated eye-roll. "I am *so* embarrassed. Honestly. I don't know how this happened."

"Nice story," I said. "But tell me, how'd you get in here?"

She frowned. "It was, um, open?"

I'd met some pretty dishonest people in my life. Some were good at lying. Others, not so much. But this girl? She was the worst liar, ever.

"Look," I told her, "I can tell you're lying, so just tell me. What, exactly, are you doing here?"

"Listen, Luna—"

I froze. "How do you know my name?"

Her face blanched. "Oh shit. I mean, it was, uh." She glanced around. "I've gotta go." And with that, she pushed around me and made a mad dash for the door. I dove after her, lunging for her arm. I held it in a death grip as she whirled to face me.

"Who *are* you?" I demanded.

Her gaze darted from the door to me. Her shoulders slumped. "Look, don't be mad at him, okay?"

I swallowed. "Him? You mean Jake?"

"We're just friends," she said. "Honest."

"Friends?" My gaze narrowed. "Or friends with benefits?"

She glanced away. "Just friends."

"You are so full of it." I gave her a no-nonsense look. "I *heard* you."

She blinked. "Heard me what?"

Through gritted teeth, I said, "I heard you inviting him into your bath."

She gave me a pleading look. "Listen, I'm no threat to you, if that's what you're worried about. I mean, I'm a flight attendant, so I'm not home a lot, you know."

"No," I ground out. "I don't know."

She gave me a sympathetic look. "He's crazy about you. You know that, right?"

I thought I did. Now, I wasn't so sure.

"It's just that sometimes," she continued, "a guy likes a variety, you know? You can't really blame him. I mean, seriously, look at the guy."

At something in my expression, she drew back. "But you're his number-one. I mean, that is *so* obvious."

I didn't want to be his number-one. I wanted to be his only. Words utterly failed me.

She glanced at the door. "Look, I'll get out of your hair. Sorry for getting my wires crossed, alright?" She gave me a shaky smile. "Are we good?"

I wasn't good, that was for sure. When I didn't answer, she hurried out the door, taking her overnight case with her.

As for me, I sat back on the bed to wait.□

CHAPTER 34

When Jake walked into the room maybe an hour later, I was still sitting there, dumbstruck, on the edge of the bed.

At the sight of me, he stopped short. "What's wrong?"

"I don't know." And it was the truth. I *didn't* know. Or maybe I did know, and I didn't want to accept it.

He approached the bed. "Baby, you okay?"

I glanced up at him. Sometime while he'd been out, he had changed into fresh clothes similar to the ones he'd been wearing earlier. Where had he gone, anyway? Back to his place? And if so, why hadn't he invited me to join him? Was he planning to meet that girl *there* instead? Was *that* what she meant by getting her wires crossed?

He sat next to me on the bed and took me into his arms. For the briefest moment, I soaked up the feel of him, everything from the muscles of his chest to the tenderness of his embrace. I wanted to forget – not just the girl, but everything that was wrong in my life. I had no job, no place to live, and no real sense of where I was going next.

But over and over again, it came back to one thing – the girl.

I wrenched myself free and turned to stare at him. I searched for clues in his face while I tried to find the words that were eluding me.

He gave me a perplexed look. "What is it?"

"Where'd you go?" I asked.

"When?"

"Just now," I said. "Where *were* you?"

"What's wrong?" His gaze darkened. "Did something happen while I was gone?"

"You could say that."

"What?" His voice was calm, with the slightest edge. "Tell me."

"No," I said. "You tell me. Where'd you go?"

"Back to my place," he said. "And ran a couple of errands. Why?"

"Why didn't you take me with you?" I asked.

"You've gotta ask?"

"Yeah," I said. "I do. And I am. So just answer the question, alright?"

"I didn't take you because you were sleeping."

"I was not," I said. "I was awake when you left."

"Bull," he said. "You were *half* awake and tired as hell. I don't remember you arguing about staying in bed."

The words felt like salt on my raw nerves. "What are you implying?" I asked. "That I'm lazy?"

He gave me an odd look. "What's up with you, anyway?"

"When you were gone," I said, "were you alone?"

"Yeah. Why?"

I studied his face and couldn't see any sign he was lying. But what did that prove? Maybe the person he was *supposed* to meet ended up in the wrong place. "I've got to ask you something."

His voice was wary. "Alright."

"Were you supposed to meet anyone?"

"Like who?"

"Just answer, okay?"

"Alright. The answer is no. I wasn't 'meeting' anyone. Why?"

"Because you had a visitor." I swallowed. "Here. In the room."

His muscles tensed. "What happened? Someone try to hurt you?"

"Yeah," I said, "actually they did."

His voice became fierce. "Who?"

"You. And some girl."

He gave his head a slight shake. "What?"

"Some girl," I said. "She was *here*. In the shower." I hesitated. "Or maybe the bath. I don't know."

He glanced toward the bathroom before turning his gaze back on me. "When you were sleeping?"

"No," I said. "When I went down to see Vince."

He froze. "What?"

"Yeah. Vince Hammond," I said. "You know."

"Damn straight I know. What the hell did you see *him* for?"

I drew back. "Because he stopped by, and I figured I'd give him the brush-off before you got back."

His jaw clenched. "So I wouldn't find out?"

"No, so there wouldn't be a scene."

"You stay away from him."

"Why?" My tone grew snotty. "Because you guys are arch-enemies?"

"No," he said, "because that guy's an asshole. I don't want you around him."

"Well maybe *I* don't want you around Bath Girl."

"Who the hell is bath girl?"

I crossed my arms. "You tell me."

"I can't," he said, "because I don't know who the hell you're talking about."

Desperately, I wanted to believe him. I tried to rein in my frustration as I searched for some clues that might help me sort this out. "She's a flight attendant. She said you two were in Vegas together? There was something about a dealer..." I pushed my hand through my hair. "You two are supposedly friends?" I cleared my throat. "And um, more than that?"

Jake pushed himself off the bed. "It's a load of crap."

"What is?"

"There *is* no other girl."

"Or maybe," I said, "there are so many girls, you can't keep track."

"Yeah," he said. "In my past."

Sitting on the bed, I gazed up to study his face, watching as it grew stonier with every second that passed in silence. I knew what he wanted to hear. He wanted to hear that I believed him, that I trusted him over all evidence to the contrary.

I wanted to trust him.

But what did that mean?

During my freshman year of college, I had this roommate who literally caught her boyfriend in the act of screwing his lab partner. The guy swore up and down that the girl was just there by mistake. It was all just a big misunderstanding, not what it looked like at all.

As far as my roommate, she actually believed him. At the time, I thought she was a flaming idiot. And a few months later, so did she, when she caught the guy again, this time with her best friend.

But if my old roommate was an idiot, what did that make me? Was I an idiot too?

It was Jake who broke the silence. "I'm not doing this."

"Doing what?"

"This."

"What's this?" I asked.

"I'm not watching you look at me like that."

"Like what?"

"Like I hurt you." He glanced away. "For no good reason."

"So you admit you hurt me?" My heart sank. "So you *did* know her?"

"Shit, I don't know. Probably."

I squinted up at him. "What?"

"Look Luna, there's a lot of girls in my past." He shoved a hand through his hair. "*A lot* of girls. Stuff like this, it's gonna happen. And you're gonna get hurt."

"I wouldn't be 'hurt' if I knew you weren't planning to hook up with her."

"So that's what you think?" He made a scoffing sound. "That I've got you – the girl I love – and I'm gonna risk it all by having a cheap fuck stop by in the same hotel room you're at?"

"I don't know," I admitted. "She said something about getting your wires crossed, so it could've been a mix-up?"

His voice was flat. "A mix-up."

"Like maybe you were supposed to meet her someplace else?"

On his face, I saw rage simmering just beneath the surface. But when he spoke, his voice was eerily calm. "I'm not doing this."

It was the second time he'd said that, and for some reason, that made me nervous. "What do you mean by that?" I asked.

He turned toward the door and began walking.

"You're not leaving?" I said.

But obviously, that's exactly what he was doing. With his hand poised on the door handle, he stopped and turned around. "I've got the room for a week. Paid. So stay. Or go. Your choice."

"What about you?" I asked. "Are you coming back?"

As an answer, the only thing he did was walk out the door.

Sitting there like an idiot on the edge of the bed, I stared after him, doing a slow burn. It was the second time he'd walked out on me like that.

The first time, we'd been at his penthouse. Later that night, when he had finally returned, I'd practically thrown myself at him. And yet here I was. Waiting. Again.

Pathetic. That's what I was.

Before I knew it, I was pushing myself off the bed and grabbing for my things – my purse, my phone, and yes, the toiletries from the bathroom, out of spite, mostly.

At the hotel room door, I stopped and turned around, much like Jake had. But where he'd been looking at me, I saw nothing – just a temporary place for temporary bliss.

My gaze landed on Jake's jacket, lying across the chair. Last night, he'd mentioned that Rango's black book was in there. Was it still? A few seconds later, I had the answer.

Yes. It was.

But not anymore.

I shoved the book into my purse and strode out the door.

Two could play at that game.

Right?☐

CHAPTER 35

Anger carried me down the long hall and through the short elevator ride. But by the time the elevator doors opened into the crowded hotel lobby, the anger had mostly subsided, replaced by a dull ache in the center of my chest.

Either Jake had been lying about that girl. Or he hadn't.

Either way, I was an idiot.

If he *had* been lying, I'd been incredibly stupid to fall for someone who, let's face it, wasn't a one-girl kind of guy.

And if he *had* been telling the truth? In that case, I was dumbest person on Earth, because I'd just walked out on the most amazing guy I'd ever met even though he had done nothing wrong.

Striding past the front desk, my steps faltered as reality knocked me sideways. Jake had walked out on me, not the other way around. It wasn't exactly a comforting thought.

I was so lost in my own troubles that I didn't realize someone was calling out to me until I was nearly at the exit. Of course, it didn't help that the name they were calling wasn't technically my own.

It was a guy's voice. "Laura!" he called. "Where do you think *you're* going?"

I turned toward the voice and stifled a groan. It was Rupert of all people. Why now? For that matter, why ever?

As he hustled toward me, I stopped to give him an annoyed look. "What?"

He was carrying a clipboard, clutched close to his chest. "You're still working tonight, right?"

"You've got to be kidding," I told him.

"No. Why?"

"Because you fired me, that's why."

"No, I *suspended* you," he said. "For one night. Remember?"

"I hate to break it to you," I said, "but when you fire someone, it makes an impression. So no, I don't remember any 'suspension.' What I remember were two little words. 'You're fired.'"

"Alright, fine. You got me. Guilty as charged." He gave a nervous chuckle. "Throw the book at me, your honor."

Funny, I had a book. And I *was* tempted to throw it at him. I only wished it were bigger and made of brick.

Rupert cleared his throat. "Okay, here's the truth. I need a favor."

"Yeah, good luck with that."

"Aw come on," he said, "I'll make it worth your while, okay?"

I gave him a dubious look. "Is that so?"

"Yeah. And I'm not just talking about getting your job back." He glanced around. "I'm talking cash." He lowered his voice. "Fifty bucks."

If I weren't so distraught, I might have laughed. "Wow, fifty whole dollars, huh?"

He gave a frantic nod. "Yeah. Cash-money."

This, I had to hear. "For doing what?"

He handed me the clipboard. "Get these signed for me, will ya?"

Holding the clipboard, I glanced down. On it, I saw a printed black and white image, obviously from the hotel's security camera. It was of Jake, last night, as he plowed through Rango's friends to let me back inside the hotel. Looking at the picture, my heart ached. Had that really been only a few hours ago?

"Here's the thing," Rupert said, "I saw on the internet that Jake never signs anything."

Was that true? I had no idea. "So?" I said.

Rupert pointed to the clipboard. "So, you get these signed, and they'll be collector's items."

Oh for crying out loud. "Except, as you just said, he doesn't sign stuff." I tried to shove the clipboard back at him.

He pushed it back toward me. "He'll sign them for you. I can tell. The way he came to your rescue? I thought he was gonna kill those guys."

As the wheels in my head turned, I couldn't help but stare at him. "Wait a minute. How would *you* know?" I mean, the guy had been hiding out in his office the whole time.

Rupert glanced away. "Um, well, there was the security camera—"

"Did you watch that after-the-fact?" I heard my voice grow harder. "Or in real-time?"

"Well, I didn't watch *all* of it in real-time," he said. "I had some popcorn in the microwave, so…"

I glared at him. "You've got to be kidding me. I was *dying* out there."

"Hey, you don't think I've dealt with my share of drunks? Trust me. I've seen a lot worse than that. I warned you. Remember?"

"What I remember," I said, "was you hiding out in your office and letting me deal with those idiots alone."

"Aw come on," he said. "You did fine."

"Until I got locked out," I said.

"Eh, rookie mistake. Happens to the best of us."

Again, I shoved the clipboard back toward him. "Take it. I'm not your signer girl." My heart clenched. I wasn't Jake's girl either. Was I? Somehow, I doubted he'd be coming to my rescue if such a thing ever happened again.

Again, Rupert nudged the clipboard back toward me. "But there's not just the one," he said. "There's like ten. How about this? Fifty bucks a photo. Just look at them before you say no, okay? Some of them could be worth some serious money."

For too many reasons to count, the answer would definitely be no. But in spite of myself, I was curious. Or maybe I was just desperate to see Jake's face. Slowly, I went through the photos, feeling a fresh pang of longing each time I saw him. But it was the last photo that knifed me straight in the heart.

It was a photo of Jake. With Bath Girl.

Silently, I stared at the thing. I couldn't tell exactly when the image had been taken, but the location was obvious enough. It was in the hotel elevator. She had her hand on his arm, and was giving him the flirty eye while he smiled down at her.

My hands were shaking.

That asshole.

I shoved the clipboard back at Rupert. Again, he didn't take it. This time, I let go anyway. It clattered to the floor, sending images scattering. Ignoring whatever Rupert was saying, I turned and rushed toward the main entrance, trampling a couple of printouts in my wake.

Thirty seconds later, I was standing on the sidewalk just outside the hotel. I was having a hard time catching my breath. I glanced across the street at the construction area, buzzing with activity.

Home sweet home, huh?

No.

I was done with that.

I reached into my purse and yanked out my cell phone. Studying the display – or lack thereof – I heard myself curse, not lady-like and not quietly either.

Near me on the sidewalk, an older man in business attire stopped to give me a startled look.

"What's the matter?" I said. "You've never heard the word 'fuck' before?"

He drew back, and I felt my righteous indignation crumble. Oh God, I was turning into Maddie. And Bianca. Cripes, I was a walking parody of every girl that Jake had ever been with. In the end, they were all the same – crazy, loud – my shoulders sagged

— heartbroken.

I turned to the guy and choked out, "I'm really sorry about that. Honest."

Before he could answer, I was already halfway across the street. I heard tires screech and a horn honk. Something whizzed by my back – a pickup truck. Damn it. Blindly, I kept on going until I reached the opposite sidewalk.

Once there, I stopped, dumbstruck, to stare at the fence that surrounded the construction zone. I laughed – not a good laugh, the other kind, the kind you hear in horror movies just before some co-ed gets it with a chainsaw.

From gaps in the chain link, bits of colorful silk and satin were flapping in the wind. Yup, my undergarments.

Some pervert had dug them out of the trash and strung them around the metal like some sort of ode to undies. *My* undies, in fact.

I lowered my head and plowed forward, pushing through the gate and making a beeline for the job-trailer.

Blindly, I threw open the door and stumbled inside. It was empty. Thank God.

I threw what little stuff I had into my crappy suitcases and glanced around. I spotted Steve's cell phone atop a random pizza box and dove for it. Clutching the phone, I dug through my purse until I found the business card I was looking for.

I dialed. And waited.

I didn't have to wait long. He answered on the second ring.

My voice was shaky, but my resolve was firm. "Hello Vince?" I said. "About that job offer…"

CHAPTER 36

That day, I changed everything – my job, my home, and even my name. For once, I decided, I'd go by the one I was born with.

Luna Moon.

Heaven help me.

Why use the name after all this time? I still wasn't sure. Maybe I just didn't care enough to pick a new one. Or maybe it was sentimental, some pathetic tribute the name that Jake liked best – assuming I could believe anything he had told me during those few days of bliss.

As for the money Jake had given me, I'd returned it by mail through a certified check. I had been planning to return it anyway, but somehow, it seemed important to just get it over with already.

I'd been at my new job for exactly one week, and so far, it was everything Vince had claimed and then some. I had a private office, a company car, a great salary, and the work was surprisingly interesting.

During my first week, I'd spent most of my time helping to organize events and publicity appearances for the sports stars that Vince represented. Just like Vince had predicted, my degree and experience were actually coming in handy.

So why, I wondered for the millionth time, wasn't I happy? But I shouldn't have wondered, because the answer was all too obvious.

It was because of Jake.

Our story wasn't supposed to end this way.

But it had, just like it had for all the other girls in Jake's life. But unlike them, I vowed, I'd move on. I'd just forget him. Not a big deal. In a month, he'd feel like ancient history.

"Yeah, right," I muttered.

From my open office door, I heard a male voice say, "What?"

I looked up to see Vince, standing in my doorway, frowning.

No wonder, with his employees talking to themselves and all.

"Sorry," I said. "Just thinking out loud."

He strode into my office and shut the door behind him. "We need to talk."

Great. Just what every new employee wanted to hear. Still, I looked up and gave him a smile. "Sure. Is there a problem?"

"You might say that." He glanced to my right, where my computer was located on a side-desk, with the screen facing me. "He's done it again."

I turned to look at my computer screen. On it, all I saw was a spreadsheet detailing expenses for an upcoming publicity event.

"I guess I'm not following," I admitted. "Who is 'him'?"

"Your boyfriend."

"Jake?" I hesitated. "Actually, we're not together. I did tell you that, right?"

Of course, I knew the answer to my own question. I *had* told him. Repeatedly. But somehow, this approach seemed more polite than telling him he was full of crap.

Vince's face tightened. "Your 'friend' then."

"I don't mean to quibble," I said, "but actually, we're not quite friends anymore either."

In fact, I hadn't even talked to Jake since that awful day at the hotel. I hadn't called him, and he sure as heck hadn't called me. Then again, calling me wasn't exactly easy these days, since I had a new phone number, courtesy of my new employer.

"You were supposed to solve this," Vince said.

I shook my head. "Solve what?"

With a sound of irritation, he reached over to my computer and brought up an internet browser. After a few keystrokes, I saw a still video image that made my heart clench. It was Jake in a blood-spattered white shirt.

"Oh my God," I said. "Is that *his* blood?"

When Vince said nothing, I turned to look at him. He was staring at me like I'd just gone off the deep end.

"No," he said through clenched teeth, "that would be the blood of our newest client, Doc Rochester."

I shook my head. "The boxer?"

"No," Vince said, "the heart surgeon."

"Huh?"

"Of course it's the boxer." He pointed toward the screen. "Do you know how much that stunt is gonna cost me?"

I winced. "How much?"

"Let's put it this way," Vince said. "More than the guy's worth."

"Who?" I asked. "Doc?"

"No." Vince glowered at me. "Jake. Remember him? The guy who thinks it's hilarious to start fights with my clients?"

"I'm not sure he thinks it's hilarious," I said. "Funny maybe. But not hilarious funny. I mean, I've never seen him laugh about it or anything."

"Yeah, whatever." Vince glanced again toward the computer screen. "You wanna watch it? Go ahead. Hit play."

Actually, I didn't want to watch it. I felt myself swallow. "Sure. If you think I should?"

"What I think," Vince said, "is that you need to figure out where your loyalties lie."

Boss or not, something about this little visit was setting my teeth on edge. "Wait a minute." I flicked my head toward my computer screen, where the image of Jake remained. "Do you think *I* had something to do with that?"

"Yes," he said. "I do."

I studied Vince's face. Was he serious? I couldn't tell. "I guess

I'm not following," I said.

"Alright. You want the truth? Ever since I hired you, he's been coming at us harder and faster. I didn't want to say anything before, but this is the third hit this week. It's like the guy has lost his damn mind."

I didn't know all the details about how Jake operated, but I did know one thing. He never hit first.   Probably, it was the only reason he wasn't rotting in jail somewhere. Or maybe, knowing Jake, he wasn't the sucker-punch type. Either way, it was pretty obvious that there was a lot more to this story.

"What do you mean?" I asked. "He's not attacking those guys, is he?"

"Does it matter?" Vince said. "In the end, they get asses handed to them just the same."

"But Jake isn't sucker-punching them or anything." I hesitated. "Is he?"

Vince gave me an annoyed look. "Sucker punching?"

"You know, hitting them first, like when they're not looking?"

"No," Vince said. "He's not 'sucker punching' them. But he *is* pushing their buttons."

"Yeah," I admitted, "he's kind of good at that."

Vince crossed his arms. "You wanna know why Doc made me his new agent?"

"Why?" I asked.

"Because I *said* I could rebuild his image, get him better endorsement deals, a bigger slice of the pie." Vince glared at the computer screen. "Not so easy *now*, isn't it?"

"Because he's fighting in public?"

"No," Vince said. "Because he just got his clock cleaned by some douche bag."

Without thinking, I slid my gaze to my computer screen, where the frozen video image of Jake remained. His hair was damp, and his shirt was bloody. But his face — that face I loved so well in spite of everything — it was the same as always, all angles and shadows of masculine perfection. And his body? Well, it was the same work of art that I recalled in my dreams.

Douche bag? Hardly.

He looked so good that I wanted to die.□

CHAPTER 37

That night, Steve and Anthony showed up at my new apartment with pizza. It wasn't exactly a surprise. They'd been showing up nearly every night – sometimes with pizza, sometimes to ask me what was for dinner.

The sad thing was, I never felt like cooking, whether for me, or for my brothers. So, in the short week that I had been living in my new place, I'd become an expert on ordering takeout. But it wasn't the food or my lackluster company that kept my brothers coming back. It was the other thing.

Steve elbowed his way through my apartment door and tossed the pizza boxes onto my kitchen counter. "I've gotta shower," he said, turning to Anthony. "You'd better save me some pepperoni. Or else."

As Steve, with his duffle bag slung over his shoulder, headed down the short hall that led to my bathroom, Anthony called after him. "Yeah? Well, you'd better save me some hot water." His tone grew mocking. "Or else."

Standing at my kitchen counter, Anthony opened the top pizza box and pulled out a slice. He shoved half of it into his mouth and asked, "How's it going?"

"Good," I said.

He motioned to the pizza. "Then why aren't you eating?"

"I will," I said. "Probably."

"Yeah, sure you will. You see the latest video?"

Like I wanted to be reminded. "Of Jake and Doc Rochester?" I shook my head. "Nah, I mean, I heard about it and all, but I didn't actually watch it."

Part of me wanted to watch it. But the other part of me wanted to ignore the whole thing entirely. With Jake, all of these contradictions were making me crazy. I hated to watch him fight. And I loved to watch him fight. I heard myself sigh. Just like I loved and hated the guy himself.

I was like Gollum, sitting on a barren rock, calling Jake my Precious.

"Nah, not that fight," Anthony said. "I'm talking about the one at the hotel. Where you worked." Anthony gave a small chuckle. "Well, for like half a night anyway."

At the mere mention of that hotel, I was glad I hadn't eaten anything. Still, I couldn't help but ask, "Which video do you mean?"

"The one with you," he said. "In the lobby with all those drunks. The thing was a riot."

"What are you saying?" I asked. "That Jake posted a video of what happened with Rango?"

"Nah. I mean, yeah, that was the video, alright. But Jake wasn't the one who posted it. It was some new guy. Get this." Anthony grinned. "He goes by the name of Raging Rupert."

"Rupert?" I said. "My old boss?"

"I dunno," Anthony said. "Never met the guy. But the way it looks, the video was pulled from hotel security footage. The thing's making the rounds. You seriously haven't seen it?"

"No," I said. "Why?"

"Because you're like the star," Anthony said. "It's got everyone talking."

"Who's everyone?" I asked.

"You know, like people on-line. They're all like 'Who's that chick he's so into?'"

I shook my head. "What?"

"Yeah," Anthony said. "It was like the second video that you've been in, so people are thinking you two are an item."

"Except," I pointed out, "it wasn't Jake's video. And technically, there wasn't really much of a fight."

"Like *that* matters. Besides, there's that big makeout scene." Anthony made a face. "Like I wanted to see *that*."

I gave him a look. "Then maybe you shouldn't have watched."

"Yeah. Whatever," he said. "But now, people are like, 'Who's that girl?'"

"Oh right," I said, "I've seen his videos, remember? There's always a ton of girls around."

"Yeah, but the thing with you," Anthony said, "is people are saying there's more to it." His voice grew higher, as if imitating a female fan. "See the way he looks at her? You can tell he's *totally* in love."

My heart clenched. "Except it wasn't like that. Was it?"

Anthony shrugged. "Hell if I know, since you never told us what happened."

It was true. I hadn't. Somehow, I just couldn't bring myself to admit that I'd been such a fool, or that Jake had been the man-slut that everyone expected him to be. Some things were just too sordid to share, especially with my younger brothers. I would never hear the end of it.

I swallowed the heartache and said, "Nothing happened. Not really."

"Like I believe that," Anthony said. "Anyway, Jake stopped by again."

"Huh?" My breath caught. "Where?"

"The job-trailer. Where else?"

I shook my head as the other half of his statement caught up with me. "And what do you mean 'again'?"

"Well, there was that first time, the day you took off—"

"Wait a minute," I said. "You never told me that."

"I know," he said. "I figured Steve did."

"Why would you figure that?"

"Because he came to see you that night."

I was having a hard time following. "The night I moved?"

That whole day had been absolutely crazy. I mentally checked off everything I had done within that short timeframe. I had met with Vince, signed the employment paperwork, cashed my signing bonus, and took a week-to-week lease on my new place, which happily came furnished. And then, I'd spent the rest of that night crying myself to sleep.

All in all, it had been a pretty full day.

Pushing those painful memories out of my mind, I gave Anthony a perplexed look. "Steve never came over. Or at least, not while I was home."

"Well, there you go," Anthony said.

There I go? That hardly seemed a sufficient explanation. "When Jake stopped by," I said, "what did he want?"

"The first time or the second time?" Anthony asked.

"Both."

"Well, the first time, I thought he was gonna tear the place apart looking for you. He was all like 'Where the hell is she?'"

"What'd you tell him?" I asked.

"Told him you got a new job, working for that Vince guy."

"Oh crap," I breathed. "How'd *that* go over?"

Anthony reached for another slice of pizza. "Well, there was a lot of swearing."

"At you guys?" I asked.

"Eh, hard to tell, "Anthony said. "But he looked really ticked off. And then he was all like, 'Where's she staying?' And we're all like, 'None of your business, dude.'"

Through the heartache, I almost laughed. "You really said that?"

"Hell yeah, we said that. You said you didn't want to be found."

It was true. I'd been adamant about that. But somehow, it almost surprised me that my brothers had actually listened for once.

"So anyway," Anthony continued, "he rips through the place, which takes like five seconds as small as it is, and he leaves all pissed off."

"And what about today?" I asked. "You said he stopped by again?"

"Yeah, it was just more of the same." Anthony glanced toward the fridge. "Got any beer?"

"No," I said. "Sorry."

"Bummer." Anthony reached into his pocket. "Anyway, he asked us to give you something."

"What?" I asked.

From his pocket, he pulled out a cell phone. "This."

"A phone?" I took it from Anthony's outstretched hand. "Why?"

"That's what *I* asked him."

"What'd he say?"

"He said, 'Just give it to her.' And Steve's like, 'Fine, but it'll cost ya.'"

"Cost him what?" I asked.

Anthony pointed to the pizza boxes. "Dinner."

"Oh my God. Seriously? You made him buy you pizza?"

"Not just for us," Anthony said. "For you too. And besides, he just gave us the cash. It's not we dragged him to the pizza joint or anything."

Again, I glanced down at the phone. It was similar to my last model, and the way it looked, it already had service. I checked the contacts. I saw only one name – Jake, listed as my top favorite, my only favorite in fact.

Anthony stood to peer over my shoulder. "You gonna call him?"

Was I? Honestly, I didn't know.

I was still debating it when my other cell phone rang. Since the phone number was practically brand new, my list of potential callers was embarrassingly short. I pulled out the phone and glanced at the display. It was my sister. Clutching the phone, I ducked into the apartment's only bedroom and answered with a rushed, "Hello."

"Oh my God," she said, "You actually answered."

She had a point. It wasn't that I'd been avoiding her, exactly, but she *was* engaged to Jake's brother, and I was drowning in too many complications already.

"Sorry," I told her, "it's just been really crazy lately."

"Yeah. I heard. But you're away from Jake, right?"

Like she didn't know. My brothers could be surprisingly blabby when it came to such things.

"I guess," I muttered.

"Good. Because you saw what he did, right?"

I hesitated. Jake did so many crazy things that I practically needed a catalog to keep up. "You're gonna have to be more specific than that," I told her.

"It's this huge fight," she said. "I think it's at a biker bar. I'm watching the video right now. You want the link?"

"No," I blurted out. "Definitely not."

"Why not?" she asked.

The answer was too complicated for words. Seeing Jake in any form was a temptation nearly impossible to resist. But now, after everything that had happened, it was like grinding salt into a giant, festering wound, especially if Jake was doing something dangerous.

And one thing about Jake, he was *always* doing some dangerous.

I dodged Selena's question with some lame excuse about running low on data.

"Oh," she said. "So you want me to tell you about it? Because seriously, that guy's nuts. You're so lucky you're away from him."

Before I could stop myself, I said, "I don't feel lucky."

She quiet a long moment and then said, "Oh crap."

"What?"

"You're in love with him."

"I am not." I hesitated. "Okay, well maybe I am, but –"

"Oh no," she groaned.

"Hey," I said, suddenly feeling the urge to defend him. "He's not so bad as everyone thinks. Steve and Anthony like him."

"Yeah," she said. "They also like the Three Stooges and Kung fu."

Well, there was that. But that was beside the point.

"You're one to talk," I told her. "You're marrying his brother."

"Yeah, but they're nothing alike."

"Oh come on," I said, "they're practically twins."

"I'm not talking about how they *look*. I'm talking about how they *act*."

"Either way," I said, "I've got to ask you something."

"What?"

"What if I ended up with him?"

"Jake? You wouldn't."

"But what if I did?" I persisted.

She was quiet a long moment. "Under this scenario, is he good to you? Or bad to you?"

That was the million-dollar question, wasn't it? When Jake was good to me, life was like a big happy dream. When he was bad to me, it like was walking nightmare. The only thing was, I still wasn't totally sure he'd been bad to me at all.

For simplicity's sake, I said, "Good to me. Definitely."

"If that were really true," she said, "I'd be happy for you. A little scared. But happy."

I didn't bother to point out the obvious. Her fiancé was pretty scary himself. Funny, she never saw it that way. Maybe my sister and I were more alike than I realized.

Or maybe I was grasping at straws. Because I couldn't deny it. I missed Jake like crazy. And against all my better judgment, I wanted like hell to make that call.□

CHAPTER 38

"I heard you're in trouble," Bianca said.

Sitting at my desk, I looked up and spotted her, standing in the doorway to my office. I gave her an irritated look. "What are you talking about?"

It was the morning after I'd gotten the mysterious cell phone from Jake, and I still hadn't used it. Honestly, I was afraid to. Jake had always been my dream guy, and in spite of everything with Bath Girl, I still loved him – too much for my own good, it seemed. So I had settled on a simple strategy – avoidance.

Cowardly, but effective.

Now, if only I could stop thinking about him.

Bianca walked into my office without an invitation and sank into my visitor's chair. She crossed her legs and leaned forward to say in a hushed voice, "Yeah, big trouble."

It wasn't even eight o'clock in the morning yet. What was she doing here, anyway? As for me, I'd come in early for two reasons – to get caught up on work, and more to the point, because I hadn't slept a wink last night.

Even if she didn't know it, Bianca was playing with fire.

"Funny," I said, "you're in big trouble, too."

Her brow wrinkled. "Why?"

I motioned her closer and said in the same hushed tone that she'd used on me, "Because I haven't had coffee yet."

She drew back. "Are you threatening me?"

Was I? Probably not. But in this case, I figured silence was golden.

"Fine," she said, "I *thought* I was doing you a favor, but oh well, I guess you can find out on your own."

"Good," I said. "It'll give me something to look forward to."

I wasn't even worried, not about that, anyway. Bianca had this nasty talent for implying things that weren't quite true. I wasn't going to let her get under my skin, especially since we were supposedly on the same team now.

She gave me a smirk. "Want to know what *I'm* looking forward to?"

"Not particularly."

"What I'm looking forward to," she said as if I hadn't spoken," is my lunch date on Friday." She ran a hand through her long, dark hair. "I don't want to give too much away, but let's just say his initials are J.B."

I caught my breath. J.B.? As in Jake Bishop? In spite of my best intentions, my insides turned to ice. Still, somehow, I made myself smile and say, "Goodie for you."

"And just so we're clear," she said, "his last name's Bishop."

Right. As if I were too stupid to figure that out on my own.

She spent the next ten minutes, going on and on about the restaurant they were going to, and how much she was looking forward to it. The way she made it sound, food wasn't the only thing on the menu.

When she finally left, my face literally hurt from concealing my true feelings. Did I believe her? I didn't want to believe her. But it bothered me just the same.

Trying for a distraction, I threw myself into work and didn't look up until later that afternoon when my door was darkened yet again — this time by Vince, who looked more unhappy than he had the last time he stopped by.

"We need to talk," he said.

I wanted to groan. Again?

Before I could respond, he strode into my office, shut the door behind him, and claimed the exact same spot where Bianca had sat earlier that morning. He leaned forward and frowned. "You *do* know our phone policy, don't you?"

What was this? A pop-quiz? In school, I hated those things. I still hated those things. I never did well, especially when the teacher was staring at me like he knew I hadn't studied.

"Actually," I said, "I'm not sure which part of it you're referring to."

In truth, I didn't even know there *was* a phone policy.

Stupid quizzes.

He crossed his arms. "Personal calls."

I glanced toward the edge of my desk, where my company cell phone sat. I didn't have a land-line in my office, so the cell phone served as my office phone too. It was true I had made a few personal calls on the thing, but those were mostly after hours. And really, no one had told me that I couldn't.

"Oh," I said, feeling my face grow warm under his cold scrutiny. "I'm sorry, Vince. I didn't realize we weren't supposed to make any personal calls on them." I glanced toward the cell phone. "But I'll stop using it right away, okay?"

"I'm not talking about your cell phone," he said.

"You're not?"

"No. I'm talking about the main office line."

I shook my head. "But who's calling me?"

"Guess."

I bit my lip. I didn't want to guess.

When I said nothing, Vince said, "Jake."

"He's calling here?" I said. "Why?"

"Other than to threaten me, you mean?"

Oh jeez. This just got better and better. "He's threatening you?"

"You might say that."

"I'm really sorry," I said, "but you know, I don't have any

control over what he does."

"Don't you?"

"No. I don't."

"He's been asking for you," Vince said. "And the way it sounds, he's having a hard time taking no for an answer."

"The way it sounds?" I said. "So you've actually talked to him?"

"No," Vince said. "Bianca has. She's been running interference."

Well, this was just great. "How nice of her," I said.

"What?" he snapped. "You've got something to say?"

"Yeah. I do, actually." I crossed my arms. "I don't believe it."

"You don't believe what?"

"I don't believe he's threatening you, and I don't believe he's calling for me."

"So Bianca's making it up? That's your theory?"

"Well, she and I aren't exactly the best of friends," I said. "I mean, you knew that going in, right?"

"What I know," he said, "is that Jake has cost me a lot of money. And a lot of grief." He stood. "So you'll have to excuse me if I'm not eager to think the best of him."

"Vince, come on," I said. "Bianca doesn't even answer that phone."

"She does now," Vince said. "We're routing the main number to her cell."

"But why?" I asked.

"Because Lisa's out with the flu," he said, "and Bianca volunteered to help out."

I gave him a look. "Well, isn't that convenient."

Five minutes later, Vince was gone, and I was wondering what on Earth I'd gotten myself into. The way I saw it, things were bad either way. If Bianca was telling the truth, Jake was seriously losing it. And if she wasn't, I'd be the one losing it sooner or later – meaning of course, my job.

But then again, I was used to that.

Or at least, that's what I kept telling myself.☐

CHAPTER 39

"My boss was a jerk today," I said.

I was inside the job-trailer of all places, sprawled out with Steve and Anthony while they inhaled yet another pizza. It was nearly ten o'clock at night, and somehow, I just couldn't bring myself to face my apartment alone.

"But you said he was a nice guy," Steve said.

"Yeah," I said. "He was. For a whole week. But get this. I was written up this morning." I made air quotes as I used the official term. "Reprimanded."

"For what?" Steve asked.

"Mostly," I said, "I'm pretty sure it was for being a smart-ass."

"Nice," Steve said.

"No," I said. "Not really." The truth was, I should have kept my big mouth shut. Mental note – calling your co-worker a liar isn't the best way to win points, especially if the co-worker may, or may not, be sleeping with the boss. I let out a long sigh. "You know what the real problem is?"

"What?" Steve asked.

"Jake. My boss hates him. My co-worker is obsessed with him. And then there's me, stuck in the middle."

Anthony spoke up. "Speaking of Jake, did you end up calling him? You know, with that new phone?"

I shook my head. "No. I powered the thing down. Remember?"

"Yeah," Anthony said. "But I figured you'd power it back up after we left."

Sure, like I needed *that* temptation. There was something about the guy that made me absolutely stupid. Was I so stupid that I'd return to him, even after what had happened? I didn't like to think so, but I couldn't afford to take any chances.

My jangled thoughts were interrupted by a knock on the flimsy trailer door.

I felt myself tense. "Are you guys expecting someone?"

What if it was Jake? Was I really prepared to see him? Should I hide? I glanced around the job-trailer. There weren't many hiding places. Come to think of it, there were no hiding places, unless I wanted to dive under a blanket, or maybe pile of pizza boxes. There were a lot, after all.

Steve pushed away from the table and peered out the window. "It's that guy again," he said.

I sagged in relief, even as part of me battled the teeniest bit of disappointment. "What guy?" I asked.

From outside the trailer, I heard a vaguely familiar voice call out, "Hey, I know you're in there. Open up, alright?"

"Or what?" Steve asked through the door.

"Or my boss will kick your ass."

Suddenly, I realized why the voice sounded familiar. I'd met the guy, a few times in fact. It was Trey, Jake's assistant.

What on Earth was *he* doing here?

I found out a minute later, when Steve opened the trailer door to let him in.

Trey was lugging a giant expensive-looking suitcase. "I brought Luna's…" He froze in apparent shock at the sight of me sitting on a bottom bunk, trying to pretend I was invisible. He dropped the suitcase onto the trailer floor and stared at me. "You're here," he said, reaching toward his back pocket.

I spoke up. "Touch that phone, and you're a dead man."

He froze in mid-motion. "For real?"

I hesitated. How did one answer that? It wasn't like I'd really murder the guy for calling Jake. But I wouldn't be happy either.

Steve spoke up. "I wouldn't risk it, man. She's pretty nuts."

"Hey!" I said.

Trey glanced around the trailer as if weighing his options.

"Look," I said, "you could call Jake, but what good would it do? I'd just leave, and you'd be bothering him for nothing." Trying to shift the focus away from Trey's cell phone, I glanced at the suitcase. "What's that?"

"It's your stuff," Trey said. "I was supposed to give it to your brothers to give to you, but since you're here, I guess I'll just give it to you directly, huh?"

I looked at the suitcase. Even from here, it looked was way nicer than anything of mine. "But I already have my stuff," I said.

Trey shook his head. "That's not what Jake said." Trey glanced down at the suitcase. "Do you know he had someone come in and professionally pack this thing?"

I squinted at him. "What do you mean?"

"It was crazy," Trey said. "It was this professional shopper lady or something. She came in and packed the stuff all special like, so it wouldn't wrinkle."

I stared at the suitcase for a long moment until it dawned on me. Unless I was mistaken, I knew exactly which stuff was in there. During my weekend with Jake, he had insisted on taking me shopping. In spite of all my protests, the clothes he bought were nicer than anything I had ever owned.

When I'd left his penthouse, I hadn't taken any of it, well, except for the undergarments, and look how well *that* had turned out. I stifled a shudder. Parts of them were still stuck in the fence.

I stared at the suitcase, trying to decide what to do. "What if I don't want it?" I asked.

Trey gave me an odd look. "Why wouldn't you?"

The answer was complicated. I didn't want to be just another girl, taking whatever Jake offered, no questions asked. But I also knew that when we were shopping, Jake's heart had been in the right place. It seemed almost cruel to send the stuff back, like a picky dinner guest whose steak was overcooked.

Jake and I had been friends once, after all.

Stalling for time, I said, "I don't have my suitcases here, so…" I shrugged and let the statement speak for itself.

"So what?" Trey said.

"So I don't know how I'd get the stuff back to my place."

"Do you *not* see the suitcase?" Trey asked.

"But that's Jake's," I said. "I'm sure he'll want it back."

"No, he won't," Trey said. "Jake has his own luggage. He bought this for you. Personally."

Somehow, I couldn't envision it. "He did? Really?"

"Well he sure as hell didn't buy it for me," Trey said.

Desperately, I wanted to ask how Jake was doing. But for all kinds of reasons, I didn't want to do it in front of an audience. I glanced toward my brothers. "Could you give us a moment alone, maybe?"

Anthony turned to Trey. "Got any beer money?" he asked.

Trey gave him a puzzled look. "No. Why?"

Anthony showed no sign of moving. "No shit?" he said. "You work for some rich dude, and you've got no cash?"

"I'm not broke," Trey said. "I use a credit card."

Anthony held out his hand, palm up. "Eh, that'll work."

"Oh for God's sake," I said, reaching for my purse. Looking down, I rummaged through it while Steve and Anthony watched. Finally, I pulled out a twenty and handed it over. "Get me some juice or something, will you?"

Anthony took the twenty and shoved it into his pocket. A moment later, both of my brothers headed out the trailer-door.

I turned to Trey. "I know I probably shouldn't ask," I said, "but how is he?"▢

CHAPTER 40

"You want the truth?" Trey said. "He's an asshole."

I stared at him. "What?"

"Yeah. He's ticked off all the time. Taking dumb-ass chances." Trey gave me a sour look. "He's no fun anymore." His shoulders slumped. "My job sucks."

Dumbstruck, I stared at him for a long moment. Somehow, this was the last thing I'd expected from Trey, someone whose favorite responsibility, it seemed, was kissing Jake's butt. "Did you just call him an asshole?"

"What? You want me to candy-coat it?" Trey said. "You screwed him over bigtime. You expect *anyone* to be happy about it?"

Well that was rich. "I screwed *him* over?"

"Yeah. The guy goes out to kick the ass of the douchebag who's giving you a hard time, and you take off on him."

My jaw dropped "What?"

"Aw shit," Trey said. "Nothing."

My gaze narrowed. "You said *something.*"

"No, I didn't."

"Get real. I heard you." If there was an ass-kicking, I was determined to find out what happened. I crossed my arms. "Who's 'ass' are you talking about?"

"Mine, if you go blabbing."

I gave him a pleading look. "I'll make you a deal. Tell me, and I won't blab."

"No way," Trey said.

"Why not?"

"Because you're the enemy. I'm not telling you squat."

"Oh for God's sake," I said. "We're not enemies."

He stuck out his chin. "You hurt Jake, you hurt me."

My heart twisted. "I hurt him?"

"Damn straight you hurt him. I mean, it's not like he says so, but I can tell. Since you took off, it's like the guy's got a death wish or something."

I frowned. I *so* didn't like the sounds of this. "What are you talking about?"

Trey clamped his lips shut and glanced toward the door. I held my breath, fearful he would try to bolt. When he didn't, I sidled toward the door and claimed a spot beside it. I wasn't exactly blocking his escape, but I was definitely within tackling range.

"Trey," I said. "Tell me. Please?"

"I dunno," he mumbled.

"You might not know this," I said, "but I've known Jake since I was like twelve. So we have a history together. You know?"

"I know," he said.

"You do?"

"Yeah," Trey said. "He's got a picture of you in his wallet."

"He does? You mean like a recent picture?"

"No," Trey said. "Like a picture from way back in your hometown or something." With a clinical detachment, he studied my face. "You look the same. But different. You know?"

"Actually," I said, feeling a little overwhelmed, "I don't know what I know anymore."

"Well here's something you didn't know," Trey said. "He thought you were a stripper."

"What!"

"Yeah," Trey said. "A couple weeks ago. He was looking for you. Remember? Well anyway, his only lead was that call you made to your sister."

"You mean the one I made from Maddie's strip club?"

"Yeah," Trey said. "You should've seen him. I thought he was gonna kill someone. He was *so* ticked off."

"At me?"

"Hard to tell," Trey said. "But that first night he went in there, to the club, you know, looking for you, I just knew he was gonna drag your ass out of there."

I almost laughed. "And what? Give me a firm talking to?"

"Well, he sure as hell didn't like the idea of you stripping, that's for sure."

"That makes two of us." It suddenly occurred to me that for all of Trey's earlier hostility, he was being surprisingly open. At the risk of ruining our shaky truce, I said, "Seriously, tell me. Was it Rango's ass that Jake was going to kick?"

"Maybe," Trey said.

"I'll take that as a yes." I tried to keep my tone casual. "So was he planning to film it or something?"

"Hell no," Trey said. "He wasn't gonna film that."

"Why not?"

"Because," Trey said, "he was gonna kick his ass but good." He began scowling again. "You don't even know what he was risking."

I rolled my eyes. "I think he could take Rango."

"Screw Rango," Trey said. "I'm talking about his dad."

I gave my head a little shake. "Rango's dad?"

"You ever meet him?" Trey asked.

"No," I said. "I mean, it's not like Rango was a big family person."

"The guy's seriously connected."

"What do you mean connected?"

"Put it this way," Trey said. "He's not the kind of guy you mess with. Jake's still looking for him, you know. I mean Rango, not his dad."

I swallowed. "He is?"

"Yeah," Trey said. "And the guy's proving hard to find, which is okay by me. It's not like *I* wanna see Jake dead or anything."

I gulped. "Dead? You're talking figuratively, right?"

Trey shrugged. "I dunno. Maybe I've seen too many gangster movies. But I'm telling you, I don't like it."

A slow queasiness settled over my stomach. "I don't like it either."

Next to me, the door flew open. I jumped, and that's when I saw him – Jake, looking mad as hell.

CHAPTER 41

For the longest moment, nothing happened. In the narrow doorway of the job-trailer, Jake looked larger than life, half-demon, half-angel, with his dark eyes and hypnotic face.

Staring at him, I caught my breath and somehow managed to choke out, "What are you doing here?"

His gaze shifted to Trey. "You can head out," Jake said. "I've got this."

I whirled toward Trey. "Oh, so that's why you were so chatty all of a sudden? You were stalling?" I shook my head. "I should've known."

"Yeah. You should've," Trey said. "Because I work for Jake, not you."

"Butt-kisser," I muttered.

"Ingrate," he shot back.

"Trey," Jake said in a warning tone. "I *said* I've got this."

I turned to Jake. "So what *was* this?" I asked. "Some sort of setup?"

It was Trey who answered. "Hardly. When you were oh so busy looking for beer money, I texted him and told him you were here." Looking beyond smug, he added, "You didn't even notice. Did you?" He gave a slow, self-satisfied nod. "Yeah, I'm a pretty fast texter. Comes in handy, you know?"

"Trey," Jake said. "See you tomorrow, alright?"

Still looking way too pleased with himself, Trey sauntered out, squeezing past Jake and leaving the suitcase behind. I stared down at the thing, wondering just how much of that conversation was actually real. Had Trey been only spinning stories to keep me occupied? Was there truth any of it?

Feeling suddenly deflated, I sank down onto the nearest bunk and sat there, gazing up at Jake. I wanted to say something meaningful, or at the very least, something that wouldn't make me look like an idiot. "So," I said, "you sure got here fast. You didn't fly here by chance, did you?"

As soon as the words left my mouth, I regretted saying them – not because they were offensive or anything, but because they weren't remotely meaningful. And I *still* sounded like an idiot. Fly here? Was that *really* the best I could do?

"Your job?" Jake said. "You need to quit."

Of all the things I had expected him to say, that was *so* not on the list. Here he was, the guy I'd been thinking about non-stop, and what were we discussing? My job.

How depressing.

"Is that so?" I said. "And why is that?"

"Because it's not safe."

I was so tired of this routine. "Because of your friend? The one who may – or may not – be after for me, looking for Rango's book?"

"No," Jake said, "because Vince is an asshole."

"Funny," I said. "From what I hear, Trey's employer is an asshole too. You think *he* should quit?"

"We're not talking about Trey," Jake said.

"So you're not denying it?"

"That I'm an asshole? No. Why would I?"

I glanced toward the trailer door, still open just behind him. "Can you please shut the door?" I asked. "It's freezing in here."

In truth, it wasn't just me I was worried about. Earlier today, a cold front had swept in. And Jake was decidedly underdressed in faded jeans and a thin gray T-shirt. It occurred to me that his clothes were almost identical to what he'd worn on the night he had rescued me from Rango and his drunken friends.

At the memory of that night, I felt a pang of something that could only be regret. Was it regret that I had loved him? Or regret that we weren't together anymore? As usual, it was probably a bit of both.

Hardening my heart, I recalled the scene with Bath Girl. Whether I felt regret or not, three was definitely a crowd. Throw us together in a tub, we were one rubber ducky shy of a freak show.

Jake kicked back his foot, slamming the flimsy door with more force than required. He crossed his arms and leaned back against it. The muscles in his arms and neck were bulging as if the act of standing motionless was taking all of his strength, which let's face it, was considerable.

He gave me a hard look, and the silence between us loomed large, filling the tiny space to near suffocating levels.

"I'm not quitting my job," I said.

"That's what you think."

"What are you gonna do?" I asked. "Quit on my behalf again? Well don't. Because it won't work. You *do* know that, right?"

"Yeah. I know," he said. "Or I wouldn't be asking."

"You're not asking," I said. "You're demanding."

His gaze darkened. "You want me to ask nice?"

"I don't want you to ask at all," I said. "The job is fine, and so is Vince."

Through clenched teeth, Jake said, "He's fine?"

"Yeah, in fact he is," I said. "And just so you know, I'm not talking romantically. He's been the epitome of professionalism."

The guy had even written me up. If that didn't make him a regular boss, what did?

"So far," Jake said. "But give it time."

I gave Jake a stiff smile. "Thanks. I will."

"That's not what I meant, and you damn well know it."

"Maybe," I said. "But it's what *I* mean. So far the job's good. I don't want to leave it. And I'm not going to."

Sure, it wasn't all sunshine and roses. And sure, I'd been in trouble more than I would like. But it was a terrific opportunity for someone like me. Even if the job didn't last forever, I needed it on my resume.

"If something goes wrong," Jake said, "he won't have your back."

"Nothing's going to go wrong."

Jake made a low scoffing sound. "You know what kind of animals he represents?"

Actually, I still didn't know nearly enough about Vince's clients. The company's main office was in New York. The Detroit office was just a satellite operation, with only a handful of people. Even Vince, from what I'd heard, wasn't local.

Why he was spending so much time here lately was anyone's guess. I mean, Detroit wasn't exactly the mecca of the sports-entertainment world, was it?

Jake's voice broke into my thoughts. "You ever meet Doc Rochester?"

"No," I said. "Not in person anyway."

"Good," Jake said. "Keep it that way. The guy's trouble."

I gave Jake a good, long look. If anyone looked like trouble, it was him.

"Oh, get real," I said.

"You think I'm kidding?"

I gave a half-hearted shrug.

"A few months ago," Jake said, "the guy was caught up in a sex scandal." His gaze darkened. "Of the unwilling kind."

"What do you mean?"

"You *know* what I mean."

"But I never heard about it," I said.

"Yeah. And you can credit Vince for that."

"For what?" I asked.

"For the fact it's not news."

"I'm still not following," I said.

"Thanks to Vince, it all went away. Charges dropped, girls won't testify, the usual bull."

"And you know this, how?"

"I just do," Jake said. "And I'm telling you, Vince represents the worst of the worst, which means that's the last place you should be."

"Oh come on," I said.

"You think I'm lying?"

"What I think is that you'd say just about anything to make me quit."

"You're right," he said. "I would. But that doesn't make it a lie."

I heard myself sigh as I shoved a tired hand through my hair. "It's been fine. Honest."

"Right. It's been 'fine' for a week." Jake's voice ground to a low menace. "You think that just because he wears a suit and acts like a nice guy that you can trust him? Well, he's not nice, any more than I am."

I'd heard this before. The last time Jake told me this, I had claimed that he and Vince were both nice. Now, I wasn't so sure about either one of them. It was making my head hurt. "I don't want to talk about it," I said.

"And," Jake said, "you wanna know *why* he hasn't hit on you?"

"Actually, I don't care, because he's not my type. He's my boss, not my boyfriend."

"He's not hitting on you, because Bianca's keeping him distracted."

I narrowed my gaze. "What do you mean by that?"

"I mean she's been keeping him too busy to think about anyone else."

At the implication, I felt myself grow just a little bit queasy. "What are you saying? That you've got Bianca banging Vince to keep him away from me?"

"Does it matter?" Jake said.

"Yeah. It does, in fact."

"She was gonna 'bang him' anyway," Jake said. "Let's just say I didn't discourage her."

"How nice," I said. "So you and Bianca are on speaking terms again?"

An edge crept into his voice. "Do you care?"

I did, probably too much for my own good. But I'd die before admitting it. Still, anger made me reckless. "I don't know," I said. "Does Bath Girl care?"

His jaw clenched. "There is no 'Bath Girl.'"

"Yeah, right," I said. "I saw the picture."

"What picture?"

"Of you two together."

"If you saw a picture," he said, "it sure as hell wasn't recent."

"It was too," I insisted. "It was taken just last week." At the mental image, I wanted to throw up. "At the hotel."

He gave me a hard look. "Who showed it to you?" He almost spat the word. "Vince?"

"No," I said. "Someone else. Practically a stranger, actually."

"Right." His eyes were blazing now. "Let me tell you something. My whole life? I've loved exactly one girl. Just one. And maybe that's where you and I are different, because it would take a shitload more than some photo from a stranger to make me walk out on her." He made a sound of disgust. "But hey, you think what you want."

I stared at him, stunned by the veiled accusation. "Oh, so I'm supposed to ignore a naked chick in our hotel room? And I'm supposed to ignore a photo of you two in the elevator?" My voice rose. "What next? I'm supposed to ignore you screwing her right there in front of me? I mean, come on, Jake. How naïve do you think I am?"

"Forget it," he said. "Think what you want."

"I don't *want* to think it," I said. "But I'd be stupid not to."

He moved toward me, almost like he couldn't help himself. "Do you want to know what *I'd* be stupid to do?"

My voice was clipped. "What?"

"I'd be stupid to risk losing some important to me, someone I love, for a cheap thrill. But you know what? Maybe I am stupid, because for fuck knows why, I still care what you think of me."

My voice broke. "If you care so much, why'd you walk out on me?"

His accusing eyes met mine. "I came back. You were gone."

"But why'd you leave at all?" I asked.

"I left to cool off." He paused to give me a long, serious look. "You? You left forever."

Like a dark cloud, the words hung there, casting an eerie shadow over the small space. Forever? I had always liked that word. Now, not so much. At least, not in this context. I didn't want to be gone forever. But I didn't want to share him with anyone either, at least not in that way.

Desperately, I wanted to believe him. I gave him a pleading look. I had known Jake a long, long time. In that time, I'd seen him with tons of girls. He was a bastard. And he was cold as hell when he wanted to be. But the whole time I'd known him, he had never been a liar.

And if he was telling me the truth, he had every right to hate me.

I opened my mouth. "Jake—"

But before I could say a say anything else, someone pounded on the door so loud that I practically jumped out of my skin. Jake turned toward the sound, shielding me from whoever was out there.

"What?" Jake said.

A deep male voice called back, "Security. Open up."

Oh crap. □

CHAPTER 42

It was the night after Jake's visit to the job-trailer, and I was sacked out in my apartment with my two new roommates – Steve and Anthony.

I looked around, taking in the pizza boxes, dirty laundry, and duffle bags filled with who-knows-what. It's not like my place was super-nice before or anything, but now, it was a cramped, cluttered pigsty.

"You guys really are slobs," I said.

"Hey," Anthony said, "did *we* complain when you messed up our place?"

I gave him a look. "It was messy before I got there."

"Well there you go," he said.

I rolled my eyes. "Yeah. There I go."

Steve was sprawled out across the apartment's only sofa. "Quit your griping," he said. "You were the one who got us kicked out of the trailer."

It was true. I *had* gotten them kicked out, at least as far as staying there overnight. Apparently, having a raging argument in a place that was supposed unoccupied tended to draw attention. Who knew?

"Stupid security guy," I muttered.

"No kidding," Anthony said. "You know, that was the first time I saw him?"

I let out a long sigh. "Lucky me."

"Yeah," Anthony said. "I know, right? I mean, we'd heard about the guy, but I thought he was like Bigfoot, something you don't actually see in person." He frowned. "Unless you're wasted."

Recalling the scene in the job-trailer, I wanted to get wasted *now*. And if I became so wasted that I saw Bigfoot, that was fine by me. The whole thing with the security guy had been a total nightmare.

Steve and Anthony had returned just as the guy had decided to make a stink about it. Worse, when confronted, my brothers were total smart-asses, not only to the security guy, but to Jake too, who looked like he wanted to kill all three of them with his bare hands.

The whole thing had been a giant powder keg, just waiting for a match.

In the end, I had claimed I was crashing there alone and bought off the guy with the rest of the pizza, along with Steve and Anthony's beer.

And then there had been the worst part. I never had the chance to tell Jake…well, I didn't know what, exactly. But it was pretty obvious that I needed to say something, because things between us were far from settled.

Maybe I was stupid, or maybe I was blind, because Heaven help me, I was almost starting to believe the unbelievable – that the thing with Bath Girl had been a big, stupid misunderstanding. The only question now was, what was I going to do about it?

Sometime after midnight, when my brothers were zoned out in the living room with some Kung fu movie on cable, I snuck into the bedroom and pulled out the cell phone that Jake had given me. I stared at the thing for a long time.

If I called him, I couldn't hold back. I'd have to trust him in spite of all evidence to the contrary. I'd have to be willing to fall hard and not care where I landed.

Was I ready for that?

Images of Jake flooded my brain. For as long as I could

remember, he had been everything I had ever wanted. He made my pulse race, and my heart melt. He was sweeter than chocolate, and harder than granite. He made me laugh, and he made me cry. He had rescued more times than I could count, and those were only the times I knew of.

With trembling hands, I powered up the phone and hit the call button.

He didn't answer.

But I did get his voicemail, so in a hushed tone, I left my message after the beep. "Jake, I've been thinking. You were right. I should've at least tried to believe you. And I'm sorry." I wanted to say more, but not like this, so I added, "Maybe you could call me? And we can talk?"

I sat by the phone for at least a half-hour, willing him to call me back. When he didn't, I wandered, still clutching the phone, out into the main living area, to hang out with Steve and Anthony. I didn't really want to talk or anything, but I sure didn't feel like being alone.

Ignoring their grumbling, I squeezed in between them on the sofa and watched the television screen in a mindless stupor. He *would* call back, right?

"Hey, be quiet, will ya?" Steve said. "We're almost to the best part."

I gave him an annoyed look. "But I didn't say anything."

"Yeah, but you're breathing heavy," he said. "It's distracting as hell."

"Oh shut up," I said. "I am not."

"What he means," Anthony said, "is that you keep looking at that phone and sighing. And yeah, it *is* distracting. Sorry."

Steve reached for the remote and turned up the volume. Trying to be inconspicuous, I snuck another quick glance at the phone. He still hadn't called.

And for all I knew, maybe he never would.

Wondering if by some miracle, he might have tried me on my

other cell phone, I stood and retrieved it from the bedroom. Scrolling through it, I found zero phone calls and one text – from Rango.

Just great.

Without much enthusiasm, I pulled it up. The way it looked, he had texted me a photo. I opened the image and felt my eye grow wide.

The photo was of a personal check, made out from Rango to me. I sucked in a breath. The amount was for twenty thousand dollars. With the photo, was a short message. *For you. Once you give me the book.*

In a fit of irritation, I tossed the phone aside. Obviously, he thought I was an idiot. Even if the check were real, he'd probably refuse to turn it over. Or he'd void it. Or he'd simply call the bank to put a stop-payment on the thing.

By now, I knew how Rango worked. Given half a chance, he'd cheat me, and then, afterwards, he'd make it look like my fault.

Screw that.

Besides, he wasn't the guy I wanted to hear from. And he wasn't even supposed to have that number. Probably, I could thank Bianca for that too.

In a fit of irritation, I blocked Rango from calling again, at least from that number, and tossed the phone aside. I decided to forget Rango. And his stupid book.

Now, if I could only forget another guy.

There was only one problem.

I didn't want to.☐

CHAPTER 43

"Good news," Vince said.

Sitting at my desk, I looked up. I'd been so lost in my own thoughts that I hadn't realized he was standing in my doorway until he'd actually spoken.

I summoned up a smile. "What kind of good news?"

"Training period's over," he said. "Time for you to hit the field."

I froze, trying hard to keep my smile in place. Field? What field?

He leaned sideways against the door jamb and continued. "I'm thinking Saturday night. One of our clients is hitting some clubs. You'll be on deck with Bianca." He gave me an easy smile. "Sound good?"

With Bianca? Good wasn't exactly the word *I'd* use. My smile *was* still there, right? I nodded and managed to say, "Sure. Sounds great."

With something like a laugh, he ducked into my office and shut the door behind him. "I know what you're thinking."

"Really?" I said. "What?"

"You're thinking she won't do a good job and that you'll end up in hot water. Am I right?"

Hot? More like boiling. "Maybe a little," I admitted.

"Don't worry," he said. "She knows what she's doing. And

she'll make sure that you do, too."

Well, it was good to hear that *somebody* knew what they were doing, because honestly, I had no clue what Vince was talking about.

At something in my expression, he paused. "You do know what I'm referring to, right?

Oh screw it. "Actually," I said, "I have no idea."

At this, Vince laughed. In the quiet office, the sound was surprisingly pleasant, and missing the contempt I might have expected. "I like your honesty," he said. "In this business, it's something you don't see often."

What did someone say to that? "Oh?"

He sank down into my visitor's chair. "Trust me, if you do this long enough, you'll see all kinds." He gave me a smile that somehow managed to look boyish. "Listen, I know I've been riding you hard lately..."

Technically, Bianca was the one he'd been riding, at least in the naked sense – assuming Jake had been telling the truth. But that kind of honesty was definitely off limits. "It's been fine," I told Vince, "really."

"The thing is," he said, "your boyfriend—"

"He's not my boyfriend." Even as I said it, something inside me twisted. Jake never did call me back, and now, in the light of day, I tried to tell myself it was for the best. After all, his claims about Bath Girl still defied any reasonable explanation.

Was it the light of day that had me seeing things differently? Or the fact that Jake was giving me the silent treatment? Still, I *so* wanted to believe him.

"Well, your 'friend' then," Vince continued, "he's got me chasing my tail." His tone grew serious. "You know we've had to hire extra staff, right?"

I winced. "Actually, I didn't know that. I mean, I haven't seen them around or anything."

"Yeah. You haven't," Vince said. "Because I've got half of them out on damage-control, and the other half providing extra security. You add that to the money that Jake's already cost me, and you can see where I'd be on edge."

In truth, I could see. Whatever had happened between Vince and Jake, it was pretty obvious that Jake's activities were wreaking havoc on Vince and his clients. Loyalty to Jake aside, it was hard not to feel at least a little sympathy.

After a minute of idle chit-chat, Vince left my office with the promise that Bianca would stop by to tell me everything I needed to know.

Like *that* was any comfort.

By the time she darkened my office door an hour later, I was feeling surprisingly edgy about the whole thing. She didn't make me feel any better when she gave me a long, predatory look and said, "Well, somebody didn't get any sleep last night."

She was right, of course.

My brothers' Kung fu marathon had extended until two o'clock in the morning, and I'd hung with them the whole time, praying that Jake would return my call. And then, when he didn't, I'd slept like crap and woken up to the realization that I was probably an idiot for making that call in the first place.

But I'd die before telling Bianca any of this.

She sank into my visitor's chair and said, "Well?"

"Well what?"

"Well, aren't you going to respond to that?"

I blinked over at her. "You didn't get any sleep? Gee, sorry to hear that."

"I wasn't talking about *me*," she said. "I was talking about *you*."

"Oh. Then I'm even sorrier."

She gave her head a little shake. "What?"

Okay, even to me, that didn't make much sense. It was definitely time to change the subject. "Vince said you and I are going out in the field Saturday?"

"Right." Bianca made a face. "Baby-sitting duty."

"What do you mean?" I asked.

"I mean we've got to tag along with one of his high-maintenance clients and make sure he doesn't get into serious trouble." She frowned. "Or more likely, once he *has* gotten into trouble, we'll be the ones left smoothing it over."

"Smoothing it over how?" I asked.

"Any way we can," she said, giving me a meaningful look.

Something about that look was making me nervous. But then again, this was Bianca. She had a way of implying the worst possible things, only to make me look like a moron afterwards. I wasn't falling for it. Not this time.

"Sounds great," I said.

Her gaze narrowed. "Doesn't that bother you?"

"Doesn't what bother me?"

She lowered her voice. "*You* know."

"Actually," I said, "I don't know. So if you want to spell it out, I'm all ears."

She pursed her lips. "If I have to spell it out, you're a lot greener than I thought."

"Or maybe I'm getting wise to your tricks."

"Oh, get over yourself." She gave me a thin smile. "I don't have any reason to 'trick' you."

I did a mental eye-roll. This whole thing was *so* grade school.

"Good," I said, "then *I* won't have any reason to hide a clown in your closet."

Her brow furrowed. "What was that? Another threat?"

Actually, I didn't even know what that was. I was losing it, definitely.

Still, I made myself say, "Oh please. The threat of what? Clownage?"

Her gaze narrowed. "You *do* know why you were hired, right?"

At this, I felt a twinge of discomfort. I wasn't totally clueless. I knew that I wouldn't have been hired in the first place if it weren't for whatever was going on between Vince and Jake. But I also knew that I was willing to work hard and prove myself in this business. If I had my way, I'd be earning my keep and then some.

I felt my own brow furrow. Or maybe I'd just done it because I'd been so angry with Jake. Maybe *I* was the grade-schooler here.

"You were hired," Bianca continued, "because you were supposed to handle Jake." She made a show of looking around my office. "I mean, let's be honest here. You — someone with nearly no experience and zero connections — managed to get a private office, a company car, and a salary that's well beyond your qualifications." She gave me a smirk. "Did you really think it had anything to do with *you?*"

Ouch. Score for one for Bianca. Trying hard not to show it, I stood. "Are we done here?"

"For now." With a long, languid motion, she rose to her feet. "Want some friendly advice?"

"From you?" I made a scoffing sound. "No thanks."

"Quit, before you get fired." She smiled. "Again."

Heat flooded my face. Desperately, I searched for a snappy comeback. "Do *you* want some friendly advice?" I asked.

She crossed her arms. "What?"

"Tonight, don't open your closet," I said, "because I'm pretty sure you'll find a clown in there."

After she left, I sank back into my seat and pondered my own stupidity. My comeback was more pathetic than snappy, and my chances of success here were looking slimmer all the time.

Somehow, it reminded me of all the other mistakes I'd made in my life. And then, there was my number-one mistake — Jake. Somehow, with him, I'd managed to do everything wrong.

Sitting at my desk, I closed my eyes, trying to envision his face. A wave of melancholy washed over me so hard that I swear I could hear his voice.

But then I realized something. I *was* hearing his voice, literally. And if I wasn't mistaken, he was just down the hall.

CHAPTER 44

Surprised, I pushed up from my desk and rushed to the doorway of my office. I poked my head out and glanced around. I didn't see him. Was I hearing things?

But then I heard Jake's voice again, saying something about an ass-kicking. I felt my brow furrow. Who was he talking to?

I hurried toward the sound, which led me to the suite's only conference room. I stopped just outside the doorway. The room was dark, and the door was mostly shut. But I *was* hearing his voice from somewhere within. I was sure of it.

I froze, wondering if I should knock or maybe poke my head in for a quick look.

But before I could do anything, the room fell silent, and the door flew open, revealing Vince, looking like he wanted to kill someone. "What?" he barked.

I shrank back. "Sorry," I stammered. "I just thought I heard a voice."

"Whose voice?" His tone grew sarcastic. "Your boyfriend's?"

"He's not my—"

"Cut the crap," Vince said. "You were supposed to solve this shit."

Startled, I tried to peer around him. "I don't know what you mean."

"Is that so? Then who are you looking for?" He made a grand

sweeping gesture toward the inside of the conference room. "You wanna see him? Is that it?" He gave a bitter-sounding laugh. "Go ahead. Be my guest."

I took a small step backward. The guy looked nearly unhinged. Trying hard to keep my voice level, I said, "Vince, what's going on?"

As an answer, he grabbed my elbow and practically dragged me into the darkened space. He spun me toward the far end of the room, where a still-motion image was frozen onto a big white video screen. It was Jake. His shirt was torn and splattered with red. He was standing in front of a rumpled bed in what looked like a low-budget hotel room.

Next to him, seated haphazardly across a faded blue chair was a petite, college-aged blonde in a cheerleader's uniform. Her hair was a mess, and her face was bloody. Her eyes were red-rimmed and bloodshot, like she'd been crying for hours. Her mouth was open, as if she were in the middle of saying something to whoever held the camera.

"Oh my God," I breathed. Suddenly, I felt like throwing up. I couldn't be seeing what I thought I was I was seeing. But there it all was, in full, ugly color.

I could hardly bring myself to look. I had known Jake for years. Never, not even once, had I thought him capable of this. That poor girl. I whirled toward Vince. "Who is she?" I asked. "A client?"

He looked at me like I was too stupid for words. "Who is who?" he asked.

"The girl."

"Screw the girl," he said. "You see the guy behind her?"

As if I could miss him. My voice was barely a squeak. "Jake?"

"No," Vince said through clenched teeth. "The other guy."

Was he being sarcastic? From the tone of his voice, I couldn't be sure.

With a growing queasiness, I turned back to the screen. That's when I noticed something lying across the floor — cowboy boots, pointed toes-up. The boots were attached to long denim-clad legs, which the way it looked, were attached to a prone body, lying on the floor somewhere just behind the bed.

Trying to make sense of everything, I stared at the image. "You mean the guy in the boots?"

"Yeah," Vince ground out. "The guy in the boots." He made a sound of disgust. "That, Luna, is Doc Rochester. Remember him?"

The more he talked, the more confused I grew. "The boxer?"

"Not just the boxer," Vince said. "*My* client. Or should I say *our* client, since you supposedly work here."

I drew back. Supposedly? What was that supposed to mean?

Stepping forward, Vince continued. "You know how much this is gonna cost?"

"Who?"

"Doc. And, more importantly, me."

My head was swimming. How could he think of money at a time like this? I sure as hell couldn't. Still, I made myself stammer out, "You mean in endorsement deals?"

"You really don't get it, do you?"

The whole ugly scene aside, I was getting a little tired of him talking to me like I was a piece of garbage. "No. I guess I don't get it, because none of this makes any sense." I glanced toward the still image. "That girl? What happened to her?"

Vince shoved a hand through his hair. "Shit," he said. "Fuckin' Jake."

My gaze narrowed. "But Jake didn't do that. Did he?" I leaned toward him and spoke very slowly. "Who is the girl?"

"She's nobody," Vince said. "Get over it."

I stared at him. "Get over it? Is she gonna be okay?"

Vince gave a choked laugh. "Oh, she'll be okay. But it won't be cheap."

I shook my head. "What?"

"Everyone has their price," he said.

"What do you mean?" I felt my lips curl in disgust. "Hush money?"

"What are you a Girl Scout?" he said. "That girl? She's a pro. She gets it, even if you don't."

"What do you mean pro?" I asked. "You mean like a pro cheerleader?"

"If you think that," he said, "I've got a bridge to sell you somewhere." He lowered his voice to say, "You fix this. Or I will."

"What's that supposed to mean?"

"I mean, it's time for you to start earning your keep around here."

As I stared at Vince, all of Jake's warnings skittered across my brain. Why hadn't I listened? But I knew why. It was because I had only seen what I wanted to see – a chance to break out of my employment rut and actually make something of my life.

Forget that.

I'd rather be unemployed than sell my soul for a nice office and a paycheck. I crossed my arms. "No."

"No what?"

"No. I'm not having any part of this."

"That's what you think."

"What are you gonna do? Fire me? Well, you don't need to." I straightened my spine and met his gaze head-on. "Because I quit."

At this, Vince laughed. It sounded nothing like any laughter I had heard from him before. "Is that so? Fine. Your call. I'll just be needing that signing bonus back." He smiled. "Unless you've already spent it."

My mouth fell open. The signing bonus? Oh crap. I *had* spent most of it, and none of it on luxuries either. I did a quick mental tally. Between the rent and security deposit on the apartment, not to mention living expenses, I didn't have a whole lot left.

It didn't help that I still hadn't received a paycheck. But maybe if I played it right, that could be a good thing. Somehow, I made myself speak. "Fine. Just take it out of my check."

"Sorry, not good enough. You quit."

"So?"

"So and you forfeit your first month's pay. Or didn't you read your contract?"

I did read it, in fact. The thing had been pages and pages long with all sorts of clauses and details that ran together into one big blob of confusion. But it was a little late to complain about it now, wasn't it?

I glared at him. "Don't worry. I'll have your money."

"I don't want the money." He pointed toward the screen, where the still image of that ugly hotel scene remained. "I want your help in making this go away."

I gave him a look. "Dream on," I said. "Even if I wanted to, I couldn't make that go away. The thing's gotta be all over the internet by now."

"Not the way it looks," Vince said. "It was delivered on a disk."

"I don't care if it was delivered by unicorn," I said, turning to leave. "I'm not fixing this for you, and you wanna know why? Because Jake was right. You *are* an asshole." □

CHAPTER 45

When I walked into my apartment an hour later, the Kung fu marathon was still going strong. I stopped to stare at my brothers. The way it looked, they hadn't moved all day. Steve, as usual, was hogging the whole sofa, while Anthony was sacked out on the easy chair next to him.

"Why aren't you guys working?" I asked.

"Because it's raining," Steve said. "You didn't notice?"

Like I wouldn't notice the raging downpour that had just soaked me to the skin. After forfeiting my company car, I had taken the bus home. The bus stop was a half-mile away, and I had no umbrella.

"Oh, I noticed," I said. "But seriously, raining or not, don't you have to work anyway?"

"Not the way I see it," Steve said.

I glanced around, taking in the snack wrappers, pizza boxes, and empty soda cans. "Must be nice," I muttered.

"Like you should talk," Steve said. "It's like one o'clock in the afternoon. Why aren't *you* working?"

I gave a long sigh. "You don't wanna know."

"Wait," Steve said, holding up a hand. "Fired or quit?"

I gave him a dirty look. "Oh shut up."

"Seriously," he said, "what was it?"

"Does it matter?" I asked.

From the easy chair, Anthony spoke up. "It does, actually.

Steve and I got a bet."

Well, that was special. I kicked aside a pizza box and claimed a spot on the floor, where I sat cross-legged facing them. "For your information, I quit. There. Are you happy?"

Steve frowned. "Well I'm sure as hell not happy."

"Why not?" I asked.

"Because," Steve said, "that means I owe Anthony twenty bucks." He gave me a sour look. "Thanks a lot."

Anthony was grinning. "Yeah," he told me, "Thanks."

"And," I said, "I've got to come up with five thousand bucks by Monday."

"Why?" Anthony asked.

I pushed a hand through my soaked hair. "Because I've got to pay back my signing bonus."

"You know what you should do?" Steve asked.

I glanced at him. "What?"

"Get Jake to pay it. I mean, he's rich, right?"

"Just stop it," I said. "I don't like him because he's rich. And besides, this isn't his problem."

Thinking of Jake, my heart sank even lower. He still hadn't called me back, and I was getting a sick feeling that he never would. But even if he did, I wouldn't be asking him for money. Dignity aside, the last time I'd borrowed money from a guy, it had cost me my car.

On a cheerier note, I didn't have a car anymore, so that wasn't exactly a problem these days, was it? Nothing like looking on the bright side.

Desperate for a distraction, I turned my attention to the television screen, where a monk was cooking with one hand and fighting off assassins with the other. Somehow, I could almost relate.

When the show went to a commercial break, I stood and headed toward the kitchen, praying there was a bottle of wine in there somewhere. I hesitated. Two bottles might be better.

I'd gotten maybe three steps when a vaguely familiar female voice made me stop in my tracks. I couldn't quite place it, but I was sure I'd heard that voice before.

I turned to look and heard myself gasp.

"What?" Steve asked.

With a shaky hand, I pointed toward the television. "That girl. In the commercial. I've met her."

In unison, my brothers turned to look. It was a local advertisement for a low-budget used car lot. Wearing nothing but high heels and a skimpy red-white-and-blue bikini, the girl was perched on the hood of a classic Chevy muscle car.

She was talking about free floor mats and air fresheners with every purchase. Smiling into the camera, she ended her pitch by hollering out, "So come on down to Morrey's Used Car Emporium, and tell 'em Candy sent you." The commercial ended with Candy giving a big sideways wink toward the camera just before it faded out to poorly rendered graphics of fireworks exploding.

When the next commercial began, I was still standing there, dumbstruck. She might call herself Candy, but I knew her by another name. Bath Girl.

An hour later, I was down at the used car lot, braving the rain in search of answers. In spite of my brothers' best efforts to convince me otherwise, I'd come alone, having wheedled the keys out of Steve, who hadn't looked too happy about it.

I was standing in the rain for maybe ten minutes when a hard-looking woman with dripping wet, over-processed hair cornered me in the truck section. "You looking for a good deal?" she asked.

"Actually," I said, "I'm looking for Candy."

The woman's eyebrows furrowed. "We don't sell no candy. You lookin' for a truck?"

I cleared my throat. "Sorry, what I mean to say is that I'm looking for the actress in your commercials. I think her name is Candy? By any chance, do you know her?"

"Know her?" the woman said. "I had her."

"Excuse me?"

"She's my daughter." The woman gave me a toothy grin. "And you know what?"

"What?"

"She's gonna be famous."

Fifteen minutes later, I knew more than I ever dreamed of – of the woman, of pickup trucks, and of Candy, an aspiring actress, who surprise, surprise, had just signed with a hot new talent agency, courtesy of some sports agent with New York connections.

Gee, I wonder who that could be?

My head was spinning. An actress? Inside the hotel room, the girl had claimed to be a flight attendant. I wanted to cry.

Had the girl realized that she was ruining my life? Or did she think it was some prank for fun? Did it matter? Either way, the result was the same. I had bought her act, hook, line and sinker. Worse, I'd thrown away something good because I'd fallen for a lie.

Later that night, sprawled across the bed in my darkened bedroom, I called Jake, using the cell phone that he had given me. I held my breath as it rang once, twice, three times – and went to voicemail.

Damn it.

I disconnected the call and wrapped myself around my oversized pillow, squeezing it hard against my chest. Probably, it was time to face facts. He was done with me. And I couldn't say that I blamed him.

Everything he had told me – about Vince, about Bath Girl, correction – Candy, about everything, it had all turned out to be true. And yet, in none of those cases, had I given him the benefit of the doubt. Was I just like everyone else? All too willing to think the worst of him?

I squeezed my eyes shut as images of him flashed across my mind. He was the cocky teenager who'd rescued me from bullies.

He was the twenty-something bad-ass, who'd banished me from his life to protect me from his friends. He was the guy who had loved *me* of all people, in spite of the fact he could have any girl he wanted.

He deserved better.

But there was something else he deserved. A heartfelt apology. A *real* apology. If I couldn't at least give him that, I wasn't worthy to even call him my friend.

Screwing up my courage, I clutched the phone and called again. This time when it went to voicemail, I took a deep breath and said, "Listen, I don't blame you if you don't want to talk to me. But there's something I need to tell you."

My voice cracked. "I'm sorry. I wish you were here. I'd tell you in person. If you wanted, you could even laugh at me. I'd totally have it coming. Get this. The thing with Bath Girl? I'm pretty sure it was all just a setup."

I tried to laugh. "She was an actress, if you can believe it. You see, I saw this hotel picture of you. With her. In the elevator. Not naked or anything, but it looked bad, even though it probably wasn't. Stupid I fell for it, huh? Anyway, I just thought you should know, I mean, in case it happens again with someone else."

At the thought of Jake with someone else, I couldn't bring myself to say another word. With a heavy heart, I disconnected the call. After a long, depressing moment, I wriggled out of my jeans, and crawled under the covers, wearing only my T-shirt and panties. In my makeshift cocoon, I curled into a ball, listening to the muted sounds of Kung fu coming from the living room.

When at last, I fell into a fitful sleep, I dreamed of him. And I heard his voice, low and tender, close against my ear. "Luna?"

Unwilling to wake up, I yanked at the covers, pulling them upward until I met resistance – warm and hard resistance that jolted me wide awake.

He was here, a shadowed figure kneeling beside the bed. His voice was quiet. "Don't worry. It's just me."

I bolted upright. "Jake? What the hell?"

CHAPTER 46

In spite of my outburst, his voice remained steady. "You want me to go? Just say the word."

Confused, I glanced around the darkened room. "How'd you get in here?"

He pointed toward the far wall. "The balcony door."

My mind was whirling. "But I'm three stories up."

"You're telling me."

I rubbed at my eyes. "Huh?"

"And why wasn't it locked?" he asked.

I gave my head a little shake. "What?"

"In this neighborhood?" He leaned closer. "You've got to be more careful."

I almost laughed. "*I've* got to be more careful?"

"I'm not kidding."

"Hey, I locked my *bedroom* door," I pointed out.

Through the shadows, he frowned. "So you locked your *inside* door, but kept your outside door wide open?"

"It wasn't wide open," I said. "It was unlocked. And besides, only a maniac would climb up this high."

"Exactly," he said. "You lock it from now on. Alright?"

Jake might not know it, but the whole debate was pointless. My lease was week-to-week. Since I was officially dead-broke again, I'd be moving in just a few days. Where to, I wasn't quite sure. But the way I saw it, the whole balcony door thing was hardly a long-term problem.

"Well, I will *now*." I told him. "Now that I know there's a maniac on the loose."

When he said nothing, I reached out a hand, suddenly fearful of shattering what might yet be a dream. "You're really here?" I asked. My fingers brushed the side of his face, and I wanted to sigh with contentment. "Why didn't you call?"

In his voice, I heard the hint of a smile. "I did. You didn't answer."

"When?" I asked.

"Maybe an hour ago."

"So you came over?" I said. "Why?"

"Because you asked me to."

At this, I did laugh. "Since when do you do anything I ask?"

He was quiet a long moment before saying, "You want the truth?"

"Definitely."

"When I called and you didn't answer—" He hesitated. "I had to see you."

I felt myself smile. "Yeah?"

"And," he continued, "I figured that if I got here, and you told me to take off, well, at least I'd know you're okay."

"Jake?" I said.

"What?"

"I really am sorry."

"Yeah, I heard the message. But don't be."

"But I am," I insisted. "And I'm not ashamed to say so. I should've believed you."

"Why?" he asked. "It made sense not to."

I felt myself tense. "What are you saying? That there *is* another girl?"

"There's only one girl I want," he said, "and she's way too good for the likes of me."

"How can you say that?" I said. "If anything, just the opposite is true."

He shook his head. "No."

"Yes," I insisted.

"Luna." He leaned his head closer. "I'm no saint."

"I don't care." I recalled something he had once told me. "Besides, what would a sinner like me do with one of those?"

"You're no sinner." His finger brushed the side of my face. "You're the sweetest thing I've ever known."

From somewhere out in the living room, I heard the echo of battle cries, followed by the lingering clang of what could only be a giant gong.

Jake glanced toward the noise.

"Kung fu," I said.

He nodded like he totally got it. Why should I be surprised? He was a guy after all.

"It's just my brothers," I added.

"Yeah? Good to know."

"Oh, like it would be anyone else." My voice grew coaxing. "But just to be safe, you might want to hide out with me under the covers. You know, in case of ninjas or something."

He gave a slow nod. "Subtle."

Although he was obviously joking, I couldn't help but say, "Tell me something."

"Hmm?"

"Am I chasing you? You know? Like all those other girls?"

Clothes and all, he crawled under the covers. "Other girls?" he said. "No such thing."

"It's a serious question."

"Alright." He turned sideways to face me. "Here's my serious answer. No."

Somehow, in the darkness, it was easy to be honest. "Oh come on," I said. "I mean, you've got to know that I've been in love with you since I was like twelve. I've never even been a challenge." I felt myself frown. "But I guess you don't get many of those, huh?"

At this, he gave a low laugh.

"What?" I asked.

"A challenge?" he said. "That's your issue?"

"It's not an issue," I said. "It's just that you've always had it easy with me."

"Have I?"

"Sure," I said. "Even way back before, one snap of your fingers, and I'd have come running."

"Right," he said.

"It's true. Seriously, where's the challenge in that?"

He slid a hand up the back of my T-shirt. His hand felt big and warm, and something in my shoulders eased.

"Want to know what's a *real* challenge?" he asked.

I felt myself nod.

"A real challenge," he said, "is seeing a girl who's something special, a forever kind of girl." He leaned his forehead against mine. "...and knowing you can't have her, *shouldn't* have her, because your life is too messed up, and she deserves better."

At his words, my heart melted into a gooey glow. Still, it seemed almost too far-fetched to be real. "That can't be true," I whispered.

"Why not?" he asked. "You think it's easy to stay away from what you want? To keep quiet when you want to say something? To stand still when you want to move forward?" He pulled me close. "Luna, if you think it's been easy for me, you've got the wrong idea."

I felt myself smile. "Be honest. It couldn't have been *that* hard to keep quiet."

At this, his tone grew teasing. "Is that so?"

"Definitely."

"So," he said, running his hand lower until it caressed my hips. "You wanna test that theory?"

Something in his voice sent my pulse jumping. "How?"

"Give me fifteen minutes," he said. "*You* stay quiet, and later, you can say, 'I told you so.'"

My breath caught. "What if I don't stay quiet?"

I felt his hand slip under the backside of my panties. When he cupped my ass, I felt ready to squeal already.

His voice was low. "Not gonna happen."

I had to laugh. "Cocky, are you?"

He pressed his hardness against me. "What do you think?"

I heard myself giggle. "No fair. You've got a secret weapon."

"Not gonna need it," he said, tugging down my panties.

I stifled a groan as the lacy fabric disappeared somewhere under the covers. My hips, seeking his hardness, surged forward like they had a life of their own.

"You're not gonna win that way," he warned.

I was just about to argue when I felt a long finger brush the inside of my thigh. My breath hitched. Again, my hips pressed forward. He was wearing jeans of all things. Desperately, I reached for the button at his waist.

He reached for my hand, stopping me in mid-motion. "The game isn't 'Make *Jake* Squeal,'" he teased.

My voice was breathless. "So it's a game?"

"No." He planted a soft kiss just between my neck and shoulder. "But you'll like playing anyway."

Again, I felt his hand move between us. By the time he touched me again, I was already slick with yearning. If this was a game, I was the biggest loser ever, because I wasn't even willing to fight it.

With one expert finger, he stroked that special spot again and again, around one way and then another. When he slipped a finger inside me, I bit my lip to keep from begging for more.

At that moment, I swear, I could almost read his thoughts. He had done something very similar with his fingers the very last time we were together. And I had liked it. I had liked it a lot.

I hadn't exactly been shy about it either.

He pressed his lips close to my ear and said, "You're my

forever girl. You know that, right?"

Did I know? I wanted to. On impulse, I said, "Can I confess something silly?"

He moved his head lower and nuzzled at my earlobe. "Anything."

I smiled at the memory. "The first day we met, I told myself that I'd marry you someday."

I waited for him to laugh.

He didn't.

He stiffened.

I felt myself cringe. "Well, but you know, I *was* twelve, so…" I gave a stupid little laugh.

"Why is it silly?" he asked.

I wasn't sure what to say to that. "I don't know. It just is. Right?"

His fingers began moving again. "What's the matter?" He tone grew almost playful, but not quite. "You think I wouldn't make a good husband?"

Oh wow, how did one answer something like that? Jake was untamable, irresistible, and impossible to predict. And right now, he was driving me to distraction. Breathlessly, I said, "Actually, I can't quite picture you married."

"Is that so?"

His fingers were moving achingly slow now. Desperate for more, I ground against him. In truth, I wanted more than his fingers, and more than his lips. I wanted all of him. Half forgetting his question, I nodded as my hips surged forward like they had a mind of their own.

His fingers picked up the tempo, and I felt his lips teasing my earlobe again. His voice was a whisper. "How about you?"

With everything he was doing, I could hardly speak. "Me?"

"Yeah." His tone, along with his fingers, grew teasing again. "Can you picture yourself married?"

I could, in fact. But for some reason, I didn't like the thought of saying so. When his fingers grew coaxing, I whispered, "Sometimes."

"Well," he said, "the next you picture it, and the guy's not me, you're gonna have some explaining to do." With that, he did this wonderful thing against that special spot, and a small moan escaped my lips.

As he did it again, he said, "Got it?"

Breathlessly, I nodded.

"Good," he said, doing it again.

This time, my moan was just a little louder. Heat flooded my face. Too loud? Did I care?

"You like that?" he asked, doing it yet again.

Conscious of the Kung fu marathon just down the short hallway, I clamped my mouth shut and nodded against him.

The tempo of his fingers increased, and soon, all I could do was pray for some sort of noisy, ninja attack, because I couldn't stop myself from giving in completely to everything he was doing. Soon, I gave up and turned my face into the pillow and just prayed I didn't wake the neighbors.

When something like sanity returned, a different kind of craziness took its place. Desperate to have him inside me, I yanked feverishly at the waistband of his jeans. Why on Earth had I let him crawl into bed with those things on in the first place?

When the button finally popped free, maybe even literally, I joined Jake in tugging them downward, along with his briefs – assuming he'd been wearing briefs. In that moment, I wasn't quite sure of anything.

But the next second, I was flipped on my back, and he was inside me. I felt his hands on my ass, and his lips near my ear. "I love you," he said, "and don't you forget that. No matter what."

Breathless and crazy for him, I somehow managed to gasp out, "I love you too. And don't *you* forget." Reaching up, I tore at his shirt, yanking it over his head and throwing it somewhere across the room.

It was too dim to see, but not too dim to feel, so I let my hands roam wildly over his body, soaking up the feel of him. His body felt so damn good, and the things he was doing with it were driving me utterly insane.

At the end, I think I must've screamed, because a moment later, I heard the television go suddenly quiet. Soon, one of my brothers — I couldn't even tell which one — was pounding on the bedroom door and calling out, "Hey, you okay in there?"

CHAPTER 47

My brothers were still knocking. Against my shoulder, Jake was shaking – maybe with laughter, or maybe with the throes of spent passion.

Somehow, I managed to call out, "It's okay. I'm good."

Through the door, I heard the voice again, Anthony's. "What happened?"

"Um, nothing. Leg cramp."

"You need help?"

"No," I blurted out. "I mean, I'm fine. I'm just going back to sleep."

Into my hair, Jake said, "That's what *you* think."

"Shhhh!" I said, waiting for them to go away.

When a minute later, I heard the television return to normal, I turned toward Jake and whispered, "Do you think they bought it?"

"Depends on the quality of the Kung fu," he said.

I stifled a laugh. "Seriously?"

His tone grew solemn. "You doubt me?"

"I don't know. Should I?"

As an answer, he gathered me close to him and said, "You're dangerous. You know that?"

This time, I did laugh. "I am? To who?"

When he spoke, his voice held no hint of humor. "Me."

I didn't know what to say to that, so I pressed my cheek against his bare chest and listened to the steady rhythm of his heart. The sound – not to mention the mind-blowing sex – had nearly lulled me into a dream-state when I remembered something.

I sat up. "I forgot to tell you. I quit my job."

In his voice, I heard a smile. "Yeah?"

"Oh yeah," I said. "You were right. Vince was a total asshole."

"Got that right." His hand brushed my face. "And, if you were willing to work for one of those, you should've taken *my* job offer."

"I couldn't."

"Why not?"

"Because," I said, "what if I turned out to be the next Bianca?"

"How?"

"Well," I said, struggling to put it into words, "you know how she worked for you?"

"Yeah?"

"She wanted more. And then, when she couldn't get it, she turned into a total basket case. And I saw the contempt you had for her." I let out a long breath. "I didn't want that to be me."

"It wouldn't have been."

"Why not?" I asked.

"Because you're not Bianca." Reaching for me, he pulled me back into his arms. "You're the girl I love. Big difference."

I smiled against his chest, and for a fleeting moment, I wondered if this was, in fact, all just a dream. If it was, I decided, I didn't want to wake up, ever.

Later on, when I did wake, he was gone. I sat up in bed and looked around, half-afraid the previous night had all been a dream after all. Bleary eyed, I stumbled, naked, out of bed, threw on a silky bathrobe, and wandered into the main living area.

It was just after dawn, and my place was empty. Outside the window, it was clear and sunny, which explained why the only signs of my brothers were empty pizza boxes and damp towels, draped over the furniture.

They really were slobs. Still, I knew I'd be missing them soon. Based on what they told me the previous night, they would only be in town for a couple more days. Apparently, their small part in the giant construction project was nearly over, which meant they'd be soon returning to our hometown, two hours north.

I glanced around. In spite of the mess, the place suddenly felt way too empty. Or maybe I was just missing Jake. Desperate to confirm that I hadn't merely imagined last night's visit, I dashed to my bedroom and retrieved the cell phone that he'd given me. I pulled up his name and hit the call button, waiting for the dreaded voicemail to kick in.

But this time, he answered with a warm, "Hey, so you're up?"

I let out a long, relieved breath. "Yeah. When did you leave?"

"A couple hours ago."

I just had to ask. "By balcony?"

"Well I sure as hell wasn't going through the Kung fu zone."

"Why didn't you wake me?" I asked. "I could've made us waffles or something."

His voice was low and seductive. "Because, you looked way too sweet to wake. And it wouldn't have been waffles on my mind."

Heat shot straight to my core. I clutched the phone with both hands and said, "You could come back and not have waffles now. I mean, it's not like I've got to work or anything."

He gave a dramatic groan. "You're killing me."

"Why?" I asked.

"Because *I've* gotta work, and it can't wait."

"Why not?"

"Because it involves you," he said.

"Me? How?"

"You wanna come to my office?" he asked. "I'll show you what I've got."

"I would, but I don't have a car. I mean, I could take the bus, but—"

"Screw the bus," he said. "I've got a car waiting for you."

"You do?"

"Yeah. Right outside your building. Whenever you're ready."

I felt myself smile. "I'll be ready in a half-hour."

Sitting in the back seat of a luxurious sedan, I pulled up to Jake's building an hour later, feeling surprisingly nervous. I hadn't been inside since that awful day that I'd left with my brothers. How long ago *was* that? A couple of weeks? Strange. It felt like longer.

But when the doorman greeted me like an old friend, it gave me the boost I needed to smile as I made my way inside the building and into the nearest elevator. Recalling where Jake's office was located, I pressed the button for the floor just below the penthouse, where he lived.

When the elevator doors opened, Trey was standing there as if waiting for me.

He gave me a glum look. "I told you."

"You told me what?" I asked.

"That you were screwing him over." He crossed his arms. "Remember?"

Actually, I did remember, and I wasn't afraid to admit it. "Look, I was wrong. Okay? And I'm sorry."

"You don't have to be sorry to me," he said. "You have to be sorry to Jake."

Behind him, I heard Jake's voice. "Trey, you were supposed to watch for her, not give her a hard time when she showed up. Alright?"

"I guess so," Trey muttered, turning away.

I glanced in the direction of Jake's voice and felt myself smile. He looked amazing, larger than life and hot as hell in dark slacks and a stylish grey, button-down shirt that looked way too civilized for the likes of him.

I wanted to pounce on him and rip that thing off. But first things first. I reached for Trey's elbow. "Trey," I said. "Wait up, okay?"

He turned around to give me a sullen look. "What?"

"I mean it," I said. "I'm sorry." I felt a smile tug at my lips. "You want to know something?"

He gave a half shrug. "I guess."

"I like how you stick up for Jake. He's lucky to have you, and I'm sorry that I didn't give him the benefit of the doubt."

Trey's posture relaxed. "Yeah?"

I nodded. "Totally."

He was grinning now. "Well, okay then, because you're gonna love what I've got to show you." □

CHAPTER 48

I leaned forward. "Oh my God. That's her."

We were clustered around a computer screen, watching hotel security footage from earlier in the month. Along with Jake and Trey, I studied the moving images of Jake and Candy inside the elevator.

Both of them were staring straight ahead, not talking, not interacting – seemingly strangers.

As I watched, Candy gave Jake a sideways glance. A moment later, her purse slipped from her hands and tumbled onto the elevator floor. She stood utterly still, as if momentarily confused.

Glancing downward, Jake bent down to retrieve the fallen purse. When he handed it back to her, she slung it over her shoulder and placed a hand on his elbow while she smiled up at him. For the briefest instant, Jake returned the smile, looking more polite than actually interested.

A split-second later, he broke eye contact, reaching into his pocket to pull out his phone. As I watched, he studied the screen, seemingly oblivious to the girl standing next to him.

"Stop," I said.

Trey hit a button, and the image froze.

"Now back it up a few frames," I said.

Trey did as I asked and stopped when I indicated.

I pointed. "That's it. The picture that Rupert showed me."

"Who's Rupert?" Trey asked.

"My boss," I said. "At the hotel."

Jake and Trey exchanged a look.

"What?" I asked.

"Show her," Jake said.

I looked over at him. "Show me what?"

"Hang on," Trey said. "I've got it saved off in a separate file." He worked the computer keyboard, and a moment later, a new image appeared on the screen. It was a shot of Vince Hammond in the hotel lobby, slipping some cash to who else, but my old boss.

"That jerk," I said.

"Which one?" Trey asked.

"Both of them," I said. "Definitely."

Trey was nodding now. "Yeah, I thought you'd like that."

Technically, I didn't like it, but that wasn't the point was it? I stared at Trey. "How'd you get this?"

"I have my ways," Trey said.

Somehow, I didn't doubt it. This was, after all, the guy who had hacked into my email account. Unprompted, another video image flashed across my brain – the one of the battered cheerleader in the cheap hotel room.

"Hey," I said, "I've gotta ask you guys something."

"What?" Jake said.

How to put this? "I saw some footage of a cheerleader..." I began.

"That was for Vince," Jake said, "not you."

I gave him a confused look. "So you know what I'm talking about? The cheerleader?"

His jaw tightened. "You weren't supposed to see that."

"Why not?" I asked.

"Because it's ugly." He reached over and pulled me close to his side. "And you shouldn't have to see stuff like that."

"And besides," Trey said, "she wasn't really a cheerleader."

That was *so* not the point. Still, I couldn't help but ask, "So then who was she?"

"A call girl," Trey said. "You didn't know that?"

"No," I said. "Why *would* I know that?"

"Because," he said, "you don't see a lot cheerleaders dressed that way off the field. I mean, you don't see football players running around in uniform, do you?"

"Forget that," I said. "What happened? Is she okay?"

Jake's arms tightened around me. "She's okay."

"But how'd *you* end up there?" I asked.

"We had a tip," Jake said, "showed up, caught him in act."

I swallowed. "Of what?"

Trey spoke up. "Beating the crap out of her. You saw that, right?"

"I saw enough." I pushed away from Jake as a horrible thought occurred to me. "So you filmed it?"

"Well yeah," Trey said. "How else are we gonna stop it? Besides, Jake totally kicked his ass. You should've seen him. In the end, Doc was screaming like a girl."

"So afterwards," I said, "you sent the video to Vince? As what? Some sort of message?"

"Something like that," Jake said.

I turned to give Jake a good, long look. "Tell me something. How'd you end up doing what you do?"

"I already told you," he said. "I'm good at two things – fighting and pissing people off. Seemed a natural fit."

"Oh stop it," I said. "There's more to this story, isn't there?" As I studied his face, pieces started to click and I worked them out aloud. "What you do is find guys who treat people like crap—"

"Not just people," Trey said. "Girls mostly. Kids too. Remember the Chainsaw? Whacked that kid in the face with a football? He totally had an ass-kicking coming."

I glanced at Jake. He didn't deny it. But he didn't look eager to discuss it either. I might have found this strange, except it was vintage Jake. There was always a lot more to him than anyone ever saw.

"So now what?" I asked.

Jake grinned over at me. "Now, we hit back."

Trey didn't look nearly so confident. "Too bad Bianca's not in on it," he said. "We'd be golden then."

"Why?" I asked.

"Because she's sneaky," Trey said. "That's why."

Well, there *was* that. It also reminded me of something. It was Friday. I turned to Jake. "Aren't you meeting her for lunch today?"

He shook his head. "No. Why?"

"Because," I said, "earlier this week, she told me she had a lunch meeting with you on Friday."

Jake's eyebrows furrowed. "Were those her exact words? With Bianca, that's important."

He was right. I had to remember who I was dealing with. "Well," I said, "she told me their initials were J.B., so I just assumed…"

Jake finished the sentence for me. "Exactly what she wanted you to assume."

"Yeah, I get that," I said. "But she told me flat-out that his last name was Bishop."

Next to me, Jake froze.

"What's wrong?" I asked.

"It's Joel," he said.

I stared up at him. "Your brother? But why would Bianca be meeting with *him*?"

"Not just Bianca," Jake said. "Vince. That weasel's gonna try to sign him." ☐

CHAPTER 49

Jake and I arrived at the restaurant just after noon. We found Vince and Bianca in a private dining area, sitting with a guy I barely recognized as Joel, Jake's youngest brother.

The last time I'd seen him, he'd been how old? Sixteen? That would make him, what, twenty-one now? If it weren't for the family resemblance, I might have doubted it was the same person.

He had the same dark hair and dark eyes that I recalled, but sometime in the last five years, he'd grown up. Correction – he'd grown up and then some, acquiring the same muscular build as his brothers, along with an edge I wouldn't have expected from a kid who I always remembered as surprisingly nice, especially for a Bishop.

Now, as he looked at his older brother, all I saw was attitude of the worst kind. "What the hell are you doing here?" he asked.

Across from him, Vince leaned back in his chair as he studied us with obvious annoyance. "That's a good question." His gaze shifted to me. "I suppose I have *you* to thank for this?"

I snuck a quick glance at Bianca, sitting beside him. Technically, she could claim credit for this visit, even if she'd never admit it.

Jake strode forward to tower over the table. "This meeting's over."

Joel shot to his feet. "You're not the boss of me."

"I'm not talking to you," Jake said. He turned to give Vince a hard look. "I'm talking to *him*."

Vince gave Jake a stiff smile. "Except, you're not the boss of me either."

Jake turned to Joel. "If you're seeking representation, get it somewhere else. This guy? He's an asshole."

"So what?" Joel said. "I'm not looking for a mommy. I'm looking for an agent."

From what Jake had told me on the way over, Joel had been making a name for himself on the underground fighting circuit and was looking to go legit.

In a way, it made sense that he'd consider signing with Vince's agency. From my own short tenure there, I knew just how much money could be made going that route. But Vince was *so* not the best choice.

I spoke up. "If it's about the money, you can get that somewhere else."

Joel turned to me. "Yeah? Well, maybe I don't want to go somewhere else."

"Smart guy," Vince said, "because we're the best."

I whirled toward him. "No, you're not. You're the worst. And by the way, the next time you send a girl to Jake's hotel room? Well, don't, because I'm on to your tricks now."

Vince didn't even flinch. "I have no idea what you're talking about."

"Sure you don't," I said, turning back to Joel. "Seriously Joel, this guy reps the worst kind of people, and the things he does? It's bad. Seriously bad."

Joel gave me a good, long look. "So don't associate with 'bad' people." He gave a laugh. "Is that what you're saying?"

I squared my shoulders. "Yeah. It is."

With a scoffing sound, Joel made a show of looking at his older brother. "Then maybe you should take your own advice."

"You don't know what you're talking about," I said.

I gave Jake a sideways glance. If the taunt bothered him, he didn't show it. In fact, he was smiling now. It was cold smile that almost gave me a shiver. He stepped toward Vince and said, "So you wanna rep him, huh? Why?"

"Just look at the kid," Vince said, "he's got star written all over him. And I'm not talking just fights. I'm talking about endorsement deals, maybe some acting, modeling. The kid's got the looks, the body. With the right agent, he's golden."

The words sounded way too rehearsed, and it was pretty obvious that the audience for that little speech wasn't Jake so much as his younger brother. I looked over at Joel, expecting him to look flattered.

He didn't.

"I'm not a fuckin' model," he said.

"Eh, give it time," Vince said. "For the right amount of money? Trust me. You'll see it differently." He gave a half shrug. "I'm just saying, we'll keep our options open."

Bianca leaned forward to give Jake a pleading look. "Look," she said, "I know you guys have had your differences, but on this? Vince is right. We can do great things for your brother."

I looked down at her. "We?"

"Well, yes," she said. "I mean not just Vince, but the whole team." She turned to Joel. "It's a top-notch firm. The best."

I snorted. "You mean the best for covering up sexual assaults."

"It wasn't like that," Vince said. "The girl was willing. And she was paid plenty."

Incredulous, I stared down at him. "To get beat up?"

"Hey, stuff happens," Vince said. "So get off your high horse or ride it somewhere else."

Jake leaned over the table, pressing his palms flat against the surface. In a very low voice, he told Vince, "Yeah. Stuff happens. Sometimes, it happens to girls. And sometimes, it happens to pricks in thousand-dollar suits."

Vince stood. "Is that a threat?"

Jake pushed himself up. He was grinning again. "I don't know. Is it?"

"Hey," Vince said, "you've been making my life hell for months. If anything, I should be threatening you."

Jake spread his arms. "Go ahead."

"Go ahead and what?" Vince asked.

"Threaten me. Hit me. Whatever." Jake made a forwarding motion with his fingers. "Come on, Vince. Take your best shot. I'm waiting."

Suddenly, a crash sounded as the table was upended, sending dishes and glasses smashing to the floor. We all looked to see Joel standing there, white-faced and unmoving, his hands still poised in the upward motion that had sent the table tumbling.

"You guys want a fight?" he said. "Bring it on. Right here."

Before anyone could respond, a waiter rounded the corner and stopped short. Taking in the mess, he stammered out, "Um, is everything okay in here?"

Vince turned to glare at him. "If we want you, we'll call you. Until then, get the hell out." His voice rose. "I paid good money for this room, and I'd like some fucking privacy."

After the briefest of hesitations, the waiter backed slowly away, shutting the previously open door firmly behind him. I looked over at Vince. His pants were covered in some sort of curly pasta and globs of red sauce. It was oozing down his tailored slacks like some sort of alien life form.

I couldn't help it. I snickered.

Slowly, he turned toward me. "You see something funny here?"

"Actually," I said, "yeah. You look totally stupid."

As he stared at me, his shallow breathing seemed to fill the whole space. I glanced toward Jake. He was eyeing his brother with something that looked like admiration. Oh my God, like that temper tantrum, or whatever it was, was something to be proud of.

Bishops – I'd never figure them out.

Brushing the pasta off his pants, Vince turned to Bianca and said, "You. Fix this."

Her eyes widened. "Me?" She glanced down toward the destruction. "You mean the plates, or—"

"Screw the plates," Vince said through clenched teeth. "You get him out of here. Now."

Bianca's gaze shifted to Jake. "I don't suppose you'd consider leaving?"

Before he could answer, someone else turned to walk away. It was Joel, who called over his shoulder, "I need a ride. You guys coming or what?" □

CHAPTER 50

From somewhere in the back seat, Joel said, "A fuckin' model. Can you believe that shit?"

I turned around to look at him. "I dunno. You might look cute in a sundress."

He gazed at me with hooded eyes, looking anything but amused.

Next to him, Bianca turned sideways to give him a long, speculative look. "The money's no joke," she told him. "Swimsuits, underwear. I could see it."

Joel turned to look at her. He said nothing, but his expression said it all. He'd rather gnaw off his own ass than model underwear.

She drew back. "Hey, I'm just saying, you could make some serious cash."

I turned to glance over at Jake, sitting in the driver's seat. With his rugged face and finely cut body, he'd look good in just about anything. "How about you?" I teased. "Do *you* want to model underwear?"

He gave me a sideways glance. "For you? Any time."

From the backseat, I heard Bianca mutter something that sounded an awful lot like. "Where's a barf bag when I need it?"

I turned around to face her. "Did you say something?"

"No." She sank down in her seat. "And thanks, by the way, for getting me fired."

In truth, Vince had fired all of us – me, Bianca, Jake, and even Joel – even though none of us were technically his employees. Even as far as Bianca was concerned, Vince was her client, not her boss. Still, in the aftermath of that doomed lunch, none of that seemed to matter.

On his way out, Vince had fired a table of four, a random busboy, and the same waiter who'd popped in to check on us. But based on the tip that Jake handed the guy on the way out, he looked like he'd be happy to serve us all over again, with or without the collateral damage.

"Cheer up," I told Bianca. "Tomorrow's Saturday."

"So?" she said.

"So, just think," I told her, "we were supposed to be baby-sitting that client. Now, we don't have to. See? Things aren't all bad."

From the driver's seat, Jake said, "What client?"

At this, Bianca launched into a long, detailed explanation – giving Jake way more information than she had ever given me.

This was why, on the following night, I found myself lost in the commotion of a packed nightclub, accompanied by Jake and Bianca of all people.

Supposedly, she was working – for Jake this time, not Vince. What her responsibilities were, I still wasn't sure. And actually, I hadn't asked – probably because I'd been a little preoccupied with Jake, who had distracting me in all my favorite ways.

One of those ways, it seemed, was dragging me out to a club that I'd been dying to visit ever since it opened a few months earlier. The place, named Stage Left, used to be an old theater forever ago. But tonight, it was jam-packed, with a huge dance floor, crazy lighting, and techno music blaring out across the crowd.

Around the club's perimeter, high balconies jutted out from the second and third levels, giving its occupants a bird's-eye view of the action below.

Still, based on what Bianca had told us in the car, I knew there was a lot more to this whole club scene than a simple night out. Standing just inside the front entrance, I turned to Jake. "I still don't get it," I said. "Why exactly are we here? Because of Vince?"

"No," Jake said. "Because of you." He reached out for me, pulling me close to his side while the crowd surged around us. Over the pulsing dance music, he said, "But at midnight, you need to make yourself scarce. Alright?"

"Why?" I asked.

"Because I've got a fight."

I felt my body tense. "What?"

"Yeah," he said. "So you'll need to hang loose. Stay with Bianca. Okay?"

I pulled back, feeling myself frown. "Why didn't you say something?"

"I just did."

I gave him a look. "I meant before."

He reached out to tuck a stray lock of hair behind my ear. "Don't worry. I've got this."

"That's still no kind of answer."

He grinned down at me. "I didn't want you to worry. But trust me, when it's over? You'll be happy."

Around us, the music was pulsing harder now, making it almost hard to concentrate. Standing a few feet behind us, Bianca was squinting into the crowd as if searching for someone. After a long moment, she pointed. "There."

I turned to look. She was pointing at an upper balcony area – no doubt a throwback from the building's old theatre days. But what, exactly, was she pointing at?

"Go snag our table," Jake told her. "We'll be up in a few."

Bianca frowned. "You want me to go by myself? Why?"

"Because I'm paying you to," Jake said. "And I've got something important to do."

"Fine. Whatever," she said, stomping off toward the direction she had just pointed.

After I watched her disappear into the crowd, I turned to Jake. "What is it you have to do?"

He leaned close and said in a low, seductive voice, "Last night, someone filed a complaint. You remember what it was?"

I felt myself smile. I had made the briefest passing comment that he had never once danced with me. I hadn't even realized he'd been listening. But when he reached for my hand and tugged me toward the dance floor, I couldn't but laugh as we waded through the crowd, heading toward the center.

Over the noise, I called out to him, "Don't you want a drink first?"

He stopped and turned around. "Do you?"

"No." I smiled up at him. "But you're a guy."

"So?"

"So I've never known one who's willing to dance sober."

His gaze met mine, and he wrapped his arms tight around me. "With you? *You're* my drug. Anything else? Don't need it."

I pressed myself close to him. "You're my drug too," I said, although in all the noise and commotion, I had no idea whether he even heard me.

So I let my body do the talking, pressing myself against him, and feeling his hips grind against mine as one song led to another. As the beats changed, I lost track of time, along with the crowd surrounding us.

A few songs in, I felt a tap on my shoulder. When I turned to look, I spotted Julie of all people, the same girl who'd been with Rango that awful night at the hotel. She was flanked by who else, but the same blond as before.

The blond, who tonight, was dressed like a naughty schoolgirl, was doing this half-dance, half-stagger thing as she gazed at Jake, with her tongue hanging out of her mouth. She gave him a sloppy wave and called out, "I love you!"

When I glanced at Jake, I couldn't help but laugh. He wasn't even looking at the girl. He was still looking at me. So together, we ignored them, probably in hopes they'd go away.

"Oh come on!" Julie called. "The more the merrier, right?"

Laughing, Jake shook his head. "Sorry, I don't share."

Blondie edged closer to call out, "It's not *her* we want." She licked her lips. "I mean, unless you're into that sort of thing."

"I'm not," Jake said, wrapping his arms tighter around me to form a cocoon of protection against everything – the crowd, the noise, random ho-bags. Whether they wandered off or not, I had no idea, because I was soon utterly lost to everything but him.

When his lips found mine, I sagged against him, not caring who was around, or whether our tempo matched the music. We made our own rhythm, and it seemed to go on forever. Finally, when I was almost too breathless to move, I pulled back to look at him. His hair was damp, and his eyes were twin coals of desire. I felt myself swallow and suddenly wished we could get out of here, now.

When the music changed tempo yet again, to a slow, sultry love song with sexual undertones, he pulled me tight against him once more, and I gave up thoughts of anything but this. His chest felt hard against my cheek, and his arms felt strong around my back, shielding me, caressing me, claiming me – until his body suddenly stiffened.

I stopped moving to gaze up at him. "What?"

"Nothing," he said. "Go find Bianca, alright?"

"Why?" I asked.

He glanced at something behind me. "Because you're not gonna want to see this."

CHAPTER 51

I turned around and stifled a groan. Working his way through the crowd was Rango, my jerk of an ex-boyfriend. Elbowing his way forward, Rango gave Jake a murderous glare. "This is *my* house," Rango yelled over the noise. "You need to get the fuck out."

I glanced around. "Your house?" I called back. "What's that supposed to mean?"

Next to me, Jake spoke in a low, amused voice that even over the music, somehow managed to carry well beyond arm's reach. "It means he's a tough guy when he thinks he has backup." Jake looked toward Rango and said, "Am I right, Dingo?"

Oh brother. Not this again.

Standing only a few feet away now, Rango looked ready to explode. "It's Rango, asshole."

Jake's brow furrowed. "Rango Asshole?" He glanced toward me. "I thought his last name was Marzoni, but hey, whatever."

Still worried about Jake's "backup" comment, I looked past Rango to scan the crowd. I saw nothing, just bodies moving in time with the music. I gave Jake a concerned look. "What'd you mean by backup?"

Rango swaggered forward. "I don't need backup," he told Jake. "I need you to get the fuck out. Now."

"Luna." Jake said, "remember what I told you before?"

About finding Bianca? Sure, I remembered. But I wasn't going to back down and leave Jake to deal with *my* ex while I scurried off to hide in the shadows. I looked to Rango and said, "I'm not going anywhere."

Rango bared his teeth. "Been missing me, huh?"

I laughed. "In your dreams, dumb-ass."

Rango's face reddened, and he took another step forward. Jake stepped sideways to block his path. That's when I noticed something. I wouldn't need to find Bianca, because the way it looked, she was coming up behind Rango, fast.

Around us, the music was still blaring, but no one was dancing, not near us, anyway. As I watched, Bianca weaved her way through the crowd, getting closer with each passing second. I glanced back at Jake. For someone who'd just been told to leave, he looked pretty comfortable where he was.

He grinned at Rango and said, "Tell me something."

Rango glared at him. "What?"

"Do you work at being a douchebag, or does it come naturally?"

Rango made a low growling sound. His fist flew backward and plunged toward Jake. Jake caught the fist with one hand. He gave it a squeeze. Rango let out a squeak and fell to his knees.

Jake turned to me. "Told you he was a pussy."

It was true. He had. Repeatedly. But that didn't make the situation any less awkward. Plus, Trey's words from the job-trailer came back to haunt me. The way it sounded, Rango's family was connected. If that was true, Jake was risking life and limb out here. Rango was *so* not worth it.

"Jake," I said, "let's go, okay?"

"Not a chance." Jake flicked his head toward Rango. "You wanna hit him?"

"Me?" I drew back. "No."

He grinned over at me. "You sure?"

I looked down at Rango. His face was beet-red, and his eyes were blazing as he glared up at us.

The guy had squashed my car and tried to ruin my life. He had scared me more than I wanted to admit. Part of me did want to hit him, but that hardly seemed sporting.

"Yes, I'm sure." I told Jake. "Now, come on."

Jake gave a half shrug. "Not yet." Leaning over Rango, he said something low near Rango's ear. Rango glanced around, looking suddenly like a sky-diver without a parachute. A moment later, Jake shoved his hand forward, releasing Rango onto the floor. Rango slid backward a couple of feet before coming to a shaky stop near a familiar pair of high heels.

The heels belonged to Bianca, who plunged forward and reached out a hand – not to Rango, but toward my wrist. "Come on," she said.

With a confused shake of my head, I glanced toward Jake. He stepped toward Rango, who had jumped to his feet and stood glaring around the dance floor. "Get the fuck out of here," Rango bellowed. "All of you!"

Nobody moved. A guy near the front reached for his phone. He held it out and snapped a picture. The girl next to him laughed.

"I mean it!" Rango yelled.

Jake was grinning again. "You tell 'em, Dongo." And then, Jake's smile disappeared. He flicked his head toward the exit. "Five minutes," he told Rango. Without waiting for a response, Jake turned to me and said, "Go with Bianca. I'll see you later."

"Why?" I asked. "Where are you going?"

"Outside."

"For what?" I asked.

With a sound of impatience, Bianca reached out and grabbed my hand. She gave it a yank. I resisted.

"Come on," she hissed, "before we get kicked out."

My gaze narrowed. "I don't care if we get kicked out."

Jake turned toward me. "Trust me," he said. "Just go with her, alright?"

I hadn't always trusted him. And honestly, I didn't want to now

– for his sake, not mine. But I guess I owed him this. So with a small nod, I yanked my hand out of Bianca's grip and motioned for her to lead the way.

As I weaved my way through the crowd, I turned to glance over my shoulder. But Jake was already gone.

Reluctantly, I followed Bianca up a wide stairway to the third level. Soon, I was settled with her at a small private table in one of the club's many balconies.

From my new vantage point, I looked down on the crowd – dancing, gyrating, drinking. The energy was pulsing, but I couldn't bring myself to care, not when I didn't know what was going on with Jake.

I scanned the crowd, but saw nothing useful. Had they really gone outside? And if so, were they coming back? Or at least, was *Jake* coming back?

I dug out my cell phone and checked the time. It was half past eleven. I felt my eyebrows furrow. Jake had warned me about a fight at midnight. Had he meant with Rango? If so, things were running way ahead of schedule.

I scanned the dance floor, and then the neighboring balconies, seeking something – anything – to distract me from my own thoughts. I found the distraction in the next balcony over, where a private party was spiraling way out of control. □

CHAPTER 52

In the nearby balcony, a massive guy with a bullet-shaped head was the center of some sort of commotion. He was surrounded by two girls and a couple of guys – all dressed to kill, and louder than loud, even in the noisy club.

I watched from the corner of my eye as the guy, laughing like a maniac, slammed his drink onto the table, and said something that I couldn't make out. The rest of the table roared with laughter.

The two girls cozied up close to the big guy's side. The girl on his right, a buxom brunette who could've been a model, tipped her head upward and gave his neck a long sensual lick.

The guy threw back his head and laughed again. Instantly, everyone else joined in. They were still laughing when a petite, blonde cocktail waitress arrived with a tray of drinks. With a shaky smile, she began placing the drinks on the table, one in front of each person.

When she placed the drink in front of the big guy, he stopped laughing. He glared up at her. Around him, the table grew silent.

"What the fuck is this?" he yelled, glancing down at his drink. The girl to his left, a platinum blond in a tight purple dress, giggled and said something that I couldn't understand.

After a long, tense moment, the big guy laughed. Immediately, the rest of the table joined in. The waitress, with a smile still frozen in place, picked up the guy's drink and put it on her tray.

When she turned to leave, one of the guys — a player type with overly styled hair, tossed a wadded up cocktail napkin at her back.

When it bounced off her shoulder, her steps faltered before she kept on going.

"Hey!" the player type yelled to her receding back. "Aren't you gonna pick that up!"

Again, the table erupted in laughter. The guys at the table exchanged high-fives. The big guy planted a kiss on the brunette, and then the blonde.

"Jeez," Bianca said. "What's got *your* panties in a knot?"

I whirled to face her. "What?"

"You look like you want to kill someone." She gave me a smile that was all innocence. "It's not me, I hope?"

I motioned toward the table of rowdies. "Who *is* that guy?" I asked. "Do you know?"

She craned her neck and gave him a quick look. "Oh *him*? You seriously don't recognize him?"

"Should I?" I asked.

"Let's put it this way." She made a face. "You and me? That's the guy we were supposed to be baby-sitting tonight."

I felt my eyes widen. "Really? So that's Vince's client?"

"Not just any client," she said, "the guy's Tank Penetta, first round draft pick."

I looked around. "So if *we're* not watching out for him, who is? I mean, who's gonna smooth things over if they go to crap?"

At this Bianca gave a cat-like smile. "Funny you should ask. The way I hear it, his new baby-sitters ended up at the wrong place."

Against all my instincts, I felt myself smile back. "How'd *that* happen?"

"Cash," she said, "and plenty of it."

"Whose?" I asked.

"Jake's. Who else?" She glanced over at Tank's table. "Get this.

He was paid ten grand to be here tonight."

"You're kidding," I said. "Why?"

"Oh come on," she said. "You know why."

Okay, so I knew how these things worked. Celebrities were paid all the time to show up at certain clubs or restaurants. But why on Earth would anyone want Tank? From what Bianca had told us in the car, he was a lot more trouble than was worth.

"Well obviously," I said, "it's for publicity. I *do* know that. But why *him*?"

"Got me," she said. "I didn't make the deal, just like I didn't pay off your signing bonus."

I shook my head. "What?"

"Haven't you heard?" She gave me a sour look. "Jake repaid it. All five grand."

I drew back. "To Vince? Why would Jake do that?"

"Gee, I wonder," Bianca said.

"But he hates Vince."

"Yeah," she said. "But that wasn't really about Vince, now was it?"

I had no good answer to that, so I returned my gaze to Tank's balcony. The waitress was back with a new tray of drinks. One by one, she went through the same routine as before. Tank picked up his drink and gave it a look. He took a quick sip, frowned, and then slammed the glass back down.

The waitress flinched. He gave the glass a hard push, sending it toppling over the side of the table, where it splashed onto the floor, garnishments and all.

Silently, the waitress leaned down and picked up the glass, along with the little toothpick fruit-thingy. Tank laughed, and his companions followed suit.

Tray in hand, the waitress turned away, facing me as she navigated the narrow walkway. Her face was red, and her eyes were glassy. As she walked past, my heart went out to her. I'd never been a cocktail waitress, but I *had* been a bartender. I'd taken a lot of crap, and knew firsthand that the waitresses took even more. Under the table, my fists were balled into knots.

"Hey!" Bianca said, clapping her hands near my face. "Is anyone home in there?"

Startled, I turned to face her. "What?"

She scrunched up her face. "Are you hard of hearing or something?"

"No. Why?"

"Because," she said, "I've got to practically scream to get your attention. It's pretty annoying, actually."

"Annoying?" I said. "Really?" I raised my hands and gave them a good clap near her face.

She jerked her head backward and looked at me like I'd just lost my mind. "What'd you do that for?"

"Sorry," I said, giving her a look that was all innocence, "I thought's how we were communicating now."

"Oh forget it," she said, "I'm hitting the ladies room. You coming?"

"No."

She pursed her lips. "I'm not supposed to leave you alone."

"Oh c'mon," I said. "You can't be serious."

"Jake was very specific," she said.

"So what are you saying?" I asked. "That you're baby-sitting *me* now? Jeez. Just go. I'll be fine."

She bit her lip as she gazed around. "Alright," she finally said. "But remember, if he gets all mad about it, it was *your* move, not mine."

Watching her go, I actually felt relieved. If I was really lucky, there'd be a huge line in the ladies' room, and I wouldn't see her for hours.

I pulled out my phone and glanced at the time. It was fifteen minutes until midnight. Where *was* Jake, anyway?

I glanced again at the table of rowdies. Tank was raising his glass in salute to the guy sitting across from him. He took a long, deep drink and slammed the now-empty glass onto the table. That's when I noticed something. The guy across from Tank had no drink. Had he given his to Tank?

Utterly disgusted, I turned away, only to see a welcome sight appear at the entrance to our balcony – Jake, finally. □

CHAPTER 53

As he squeezed in beside me, I glanced at his shirt. It was a shade or two lighter than before. "Hey, is that a new shirt?"

"Forget the shirt." He frowned. "Where's Bianca?"

"Forget Bianca," I said. "What happened with Rango?"

"Not much," he said. "We had a nice chat in the parking lot, and he agreed to move on. Problem solved."

I gave him a dubious look. "You were gone a long time."

"Not that long."

"And you had to change your shirt."

He shrugged. "Sometimes, conversations get messy."

I narrowed my gaze. "How messy?"

"Messy enough." He glanced around. "Now you tell me, where's Bianca?"

"She's in the ladies room."

His jaw tightened. "She was supposed to stick around."

"As my baby sitter?"

"No," he said, "to keep a watch out."

"For what?" As I talked, I reached down to pull out my cell phone. I checked the time. It was almost midnight. Recalling what Jake had said earlier, I lowered my voice. "The fight you mentioned, that's done with, right?"

Jake leaned back against his chair. "If it is, no one told me."

My heart sank. "So it wasn't the thing with Rango?"

He grinned. "Sorry."

I made a sound of frustration. "So who are you fighting?"

"Why? Worried I'll get my ass kicked?"

At something in his expression, I couldn't help but laugh. "Should I be worried?"

Just then, Bianca appeared at the entrance to the balcony. She glared over at me. "*There* you are."

"Yes," I said. "Here I am."

She was frowning now. "You were supposed to meet me in the ladies room."

"I was not," I said.

"You were too," she insisted. "And I waited there for like a half-hour."

"You are such a fibber," I said. "You weren't even gone a half-hour."

Her lips pursed. "Well it sure *seemed* like a half-hour."

Jake turned toward Bianca. "You were supposed to stick around. Remember?"

I made a sound of frustration. "Oh for Pete's sake. I don't need a babysitter."

"See?" Bianca said. "She didn't want me here." She gave me a look. "Go ahead. Tell him."

I turned to Jake. "I didn't want her here."

"See what I've been putting up with?" Bianca said.

Jake gave her a no-nonsense look. "You're being paid to put up with it. So come on. Tell me what we've got."

With a long-suffering sigh, Bianca claimed a chair opposite us and said, "I confirmed with Trey. He's good to go."

I looked around. I hadn't seen Trey. "Good to go where?" I asked.

Jake turned to me. "If you want to hit the ladies room, this would be a good time."

Even for Jake, something about this whole thing seemed off somehow. I narrowed my gaze. "What's going on?"

"Just a favor-trade," he said. "Not a big deal."

"What kind of favor-trade?" I asked.

"A fight for a fight." He grinned. "Don't worry. I've got this."

"I'm not worried," I lied. "But I'm not going anywhere either."

Jake blew out a long breath. "Alright. You wanna stay? Just promise me two things."

"What?" I asked.

"One – that you remember something." He leaned his forehead against mine. "You're the only girl I want."

I felt myself swallow. "I am?"

"You know you are," he said. "And anything else? It's just bullshit. You know that, right?"

In spite of the tender sentiment, I felt my eyebrows furrow. "What's the second thing?"

"That you'll sit tight and don't move. At least not 'til I get back."

"Back from where?"

"You'll see."

"I'll see what?"

He reached out to stroke the side of my face. "Now come on. Just say it. Two simple words. 'I promise.'" His voice became a caress. "You know you want to."

Like I could deny him anything. I gave a dramatic eye-roll. "Oh fine. I promise."

Jake turned to Bianca. "If she moves," he said, "I'm holding you responsible."

"Me?" Bianca said. "Why me?"

"Because you know the drill," Jake said. "She doesn't."

"What drill?" I asked.

"You'll see," he said.

"Will you stop saying that?" I asked.

He grinned over at me. "You got it."

Almost before I could process what was happening, he pushed back from his chair and strode out of our balcony.

I turned to Bianca. "Where's he going?"

She didn't answer, which as it turned out, wasn't such a big deal.. Because it took like five seconds for me to see exactly where Jake was headed. It wasn't far. But it wasn't good either. □

CHAPTER 54

Almost before I could process what was happening, Jake was standing just inside Tank's private balcony.

Oh my God. I whirled toward Bianca. "Don't tell me the fight's with Tank?"

Bianca reached into her handbag and pulled a small, black electronic device. "Okay," she said.

I gave her an exasperated look. "Okay what?"

"Okay, I won't tell you."

"Well that was helpful," I muttered as I turned back toward Tank's balcony. So far, things looked relatively friendly. In fact, Tank was smiling. That was a good sign, wasn't it? Maybe there wouldn't be a fight after all.

Glass half-full, right?

But then, Jake said something that I couldn't quite make out. Tank's smile faltered. Around the table, the rest of his group became oddly still. The two guys exchanged a nervous look.

Confused, I turned toward Bianca and felt my gaze narrow. She was holding that electronic thing up to her ear.

"What's that?" I asked.

She put a finger to her lips and whispered, "Audio."

"Of what?"

With a subtle motion, she pointed toward Tank's table.

"So you can hear them?" I asked.

She gave me an irritated look. "Not if you keep yammering."

I leaned toward her and positioned my head close to hers. Sure enough, I could hear their voices loud and clear – louder, in fact, than when they'd been practically yelling earlier. Fearful of missing a single thing, I dragged my chair closer and squashed my head tight against Bianca's.

She made a sound of annoyance. "Do you mind?"

"No," I said. "Do you?"

"You know what?" she said. "You two deserve each other."

"Thanks." I said. "Now, be quiet. I want to hear this." I shifted my gaze toward Tank's table, listening as I watched.

Jake gave Tank another friendly smile. "Oh c'mon," Jake said. "I'm your biggest fan. Be a sport, will ya?"

For someone who was just complimented, Tank looked decidedly displeased. "Go fuck yourself," Tank said. "I'm not gonna sign your ass."

I pulled away to give Bianca a questioning look.

She waved me off with a quiet, "Shhh!"

I lowered my voice to just a whisper. "But I didn't say anything."

"Yeah, but you're distracting me," she hissed. "I'm trying to work here."

Silently, I leaned my heard toward Bianca's and returned my gaze to Tank's table, where things were becoming more tense by the moment. Jake was grinning at the blonde who was still cozied up to Tank.

"How about you?" Jake asked. "*You* wanna sign my ass?"

She giggled. "But I don't have a pen."

Tank turned to glare at her.

She bit her lip and cozied up tighter against him. In a move that looked way too practiced, she tossed a long, blonde strand over her shoulder. "It doesn't matter," she said in a voice that was hardly convincing, "because I've got *all* I need right here."

Tank sat straighter in his seat. "Got that right."

"Bummer," Jake said, turning to the brunette. "How about you?

Are *you* getting everything you need?"

At this, I felt a wave of conflicting emotions – confusion, amusement, and in spite of his earlier comments, maybe just a little jealousy. Was this why he didn't want me to watch?

The brunette gazed up at Jake. "Aren't you that Jake guy?" she said. "I just love your videos." She gave him a sultry smile. "Hey, can I see your abs?"

"I dunno," Jake said. "Can I see yours?"

Suddenly, Tank slammed his fist down onto the table. Glassware rattled, and one of the girl's purses tumbled to the floor.

Still seated, Tank glared up at Jake. "Mother fucker!" Tank said. "I don't care who you are. You think you're tough? You think you're funny? Well fuck you, you fuckin' fuck."

Jake flashed the brunette a smile. "I guess he fuckin' told me."

A snort of laughter escaped the brunette's lips.

When Tank turned to glare at her, she clamped her lips shut and looked away.

Seated across from Tank, the two other guys exchanged a nervous glance. One of them said to Tank, "Hey Tank, you, uh, want me to get rid of this guy?"

Jake turned to give the guy a good, long look. "You can try," Jake said.

The guy reached up to tug at his own collar. "I wasn't talking to you," the guy stammered. "I was, uh, talking to Tank."

"Yeah?" Jake said. "Then you might want to use smaller words."

At this, both girls burst into laughter.

Tank jumped to his feet. With one sweeping motion, he upended the table, sending drinks flying toward the guys sitting opposite him. The guys scrambled backward amidst fallen chairs and tumbled glassware.

On one guy's pants, I spotted a long wet streak that started just above his hip and ended near his right knee. The guy looked down at his pants, and then whirled toward Jake. "You asshole!" he said.

"Me?" Jake said. "Not my fault you pissed yourself."

With a sound that wasn't quite human, the guy started shoving his way forward.

"Kip!" Tank said. "Sit the fuck down."

Kip looked toward his chair, the only one that hadn't toppled over. "But—" He gave Tank a pleading look. "My chair's all wet."

With one meaty hand, Tank reached across the upended table. He gave Kip a shove. Kip tumbled backward and landed wide of the chair. His ass hit the floor near a couple of fallen drink glasses lying amidst ice cubes and slices of lime. When the guy pushed himself back up, a giant wet spot covered most of his ass.

"Shit!" the guy said. "My pants!"

"Screw your pants," Tank said.

"But they're dry-clean only," Kip said.

"Shut up!" Tank roared. His nostrils were flaring, and his fists were clenched. Slowly, he turned toward Jake and said in a dangerously low voice, "Get the hell out of here."

Jake held up both hands, palms out. "Hey, no problem, buddy."

Through clenched teeth, Tank said, "Buddy?"

"Buddy, Buckaroo, whatever. I'm going, alright?"

Tank was practically quivering now. "You'd better."

Jake flashed the girls a smile. "Hey, you girls wanna come with me?"

"Mother fucker!" Tank roared, and then charged.

I stifled a gasp.

Tank was on Jake in an instant. With two meaty arms, Tank grabbed Jake and picked him up in a bear hug. He slammed Jake onto the floor and dove on top of him. Tank's fist flew back and slammed against Jake's face.

"Oh my God," I breathed.

Tank was going absolutely nuts. "Not so funny now, are you now, mother fucker?"

On instinct, I pushed myself upward. Bianca grabbed my elbow.

I yanked against her. "Let me go!"

She gave my elbow a good, hard yank. "You go over there now," she hissed, "and you're gonna ruin everything. Remember, you promised."

Frantically, I glanced toward Jake. A crowd of gawkers had formed between us, making it maddeningly hard to see what was going on. But what I did see was enough to scare me half to death. Jake was on the ground, and Tank was standing over him, with a foot on either side of Jake's waist. Tank leaned down and grabbed Jake's shirt. He yanked Jake upward until their faces were just inches from each other.

Jake's face was bloody, but he was still grinning.

Tank wasn't. "You think you're funny, mother fucker?" He gave Jake a hard shake and giant shove backward. Jake slammed against the rails behind him. He stumbled sideways, hit the ground, and rolled over onto his stomach.

Watching, I jumped to my feet. Again, Bianca grabbed my elbow. "Wait," she said.

"How long?" I said. "'Til he's dead?"

She rolled her eyes. "Oh, he's gonna *love* hearing that." Her gaze shifted toward Jake. "Look," she said. "It's almost over."

"What?" I said. "How do you know?"

"Just watch," she said.

CHAPTER 55

Slowly, Jake got to his feet. His nose was bloodied, and his shirt was torn. He reached up to rub a streak of blood off his face. He wiped it onto the front of his shirt.

Around him, the crowd grew quiet as if holding its combined breath.

Was Jake okay? He looked okay. But was he really?

No. Obviously, he wasn't. Because for some stupid reason, he gave Tank a cocky grin and said, "So that's a 'no' on the ass-signing?"

With a roar of defiance, Tank lowered his head and charged. When he reached striking distance, he let loose with a wild punch. Faster than fast, Jake slapped it down with his left hand and struck out with his right, punching Tank in the jaw.

Tank's head snapped backward, but he lurched forward for another wild swing. Jake bobbed his head to the left, and the punch went airborne, sending Tank stumbling off-balance. With guttural curse, Tank swung again. Dodging the blow, Jake turned sideways, striking out with a fast punch to Tank's stomach. Tank doubled over, stumbled backward a couple of steps, and then charged again.

The scene was repeated over and over again as Tank charged, punched, missed, and took another blow – some to the stomach, some to his face, and even one to his forehead. The crowd was going crazy now, some yelling, some screaming, and some placing what I guessed were bets along the side.

I looked around, spotting absolutely no sign of security. How was that even possible?

Finally, Tank staggered backwards, stumbled, and then flopped face-up onto the floor. Grunting, he twisted himself onto his stomach and pushed himself up to his hands and knees. He turned toward his companions and groaned, "What are you waiting for? Get him!"

His two friends exchanged glances, and then Kip plunged forward, heading straight for Jake. He'd gotten barely within arm's reach when Jake's fist shot out, catching the guy square on the chin. Kip staggered backward, tripped over a fallen chair, and crashed into a cocktail waitress holding a tray full of drinks.

The tray tipped, sending glassware and liquid tumbling over the guy's shoulders. "Son-of-a-bitch!" Kip yelled, shoving at the surrounding crowd as he tried to pull himself back up.

A few feet away, the second guy sprang forward. Within striking distance, he swung out with his right fist. Jake bobbed his head to the side and then reached out with both hands to grab the guy's shoulders. Jake pulled the guy toward him, kneed him in the gut, and sent him flying with a wicked upper-cut.

A couple of feet from where the guy landed, Tank was shoving himself off the floor. He staggered to his feet, glared at the crowd, and zeroed in on Jake. With a low, growling noise, Tank moved toward him as the crowd went absolutely insane.

Just then, two huge guys wearing black T-shirts muscled their way into the mix. They'd barely reached the middle when the crowd began to boo. And I knew exactly why. Security. Or at least that's what it said on the backs of their shirts.

"Show's over," one the security guys yelled. "Now move it. You're causing a fire hazard."

Some unseen girl near the back started chanting, "Let them fight! Let them fight!"

To me, the chant seemed pointless. I mean, the fight was mostly over anyway, wasn't it?

Apparently, the crowd didn't see it that way, because soon, the call was taken up by the rest of the gawkers, and ended only when the security guys, one on each side, grabbed Jake by the elbows and started dragging him off to who-knows-where.

Tank, his stance wide and his look defiant, called out, "You're just lucky they showed up when they did, asshole."

I felt my gaze narrow. Where were they taking him? Without thinking, I made a move to follow. Bianca grabbed for my elbow. I shook off her grip and pushed away from the table. As they hustled Jake away to who-knows-where, I followed alongside them, trying to make them stop.

Finally, we reached a large set of double-doors that led into a private hallway. Halfway down the hallway, I gave Jake a desperate look. "You need me to bail you out or something?" I asked.

Before he could even begin to answer, I felt a hard yank on my elbow. I whirled to see Bianca, looking like a girl on a mission.

"Sorry," she told the bouncers. "My friend has had an awful lot to drink. She doesn't know what she's doing."

"I do too," I said.

"No," she said through clenched teeth. "You don't." She leaned closer and gave my elbow another yank. "Now, come on!"

I was getting a little tired of this whole yanking business. I whirled to face her. "Will you stop that?"

"No, *you* stop it," she said.

Fearful that Jake and his captors were getting away, I turned back, surprised to see that all three guys had stopped moving. The two bouncers, who'd looked so fierce just moments earlier, were grinning stupidly at us.

"What?" I demanded.

"Nothin'" one of them said.

I glanced at Jake, and I swear I saw him smile.

Something about this whole scene wasn't making any sense.

"What's going on?" I asked.

Jake scratched his chin. "They're waiting for the fight."

"What fight?" I asked.

"Cat-fight," one of the guys said.

"Oh for God's sake," I said. "We're not gonna fight."

"Speak for yourself," Bianca muttered.

Jake turned to the bouncer on his right. "Fifty bucks, my girl kicks her ass."

His girl? My heart gave a little flutter until the full sentence hit home. I gave him a dirty look. "Are you serious?"

"Nah." He shook his head. "Anyone lays a hand on you, they're gonna be sorry."

Was he joking? I couldn't be sure.

Next to me, Bianca gave a little stomp of her foot. "You know what?" she said. "I've had it!"

"Hey, don't go nowhere," one of the guys said. "I mean, I think we've got a mud-pit someplace."

"Screw you, pervert," Bianca said, turning on her heels. "I'm outta here." With that, she turned away, stomped down the hall, and disappeared out the large double doors.

"Damn," one of the guys said. "I was really hopin' they'd go at each other. You know?"

I whirled around to face them. Slowly, something occurred to me. For two guys dragging Jake off to who-knows-where, this whole scene was surprisingly friendly all of a sudden. My gaze narrowed. I looked to the closest bouncer and said, "So where exactly are you taking him?"

"To see the boss," he said.

"Who's that?" I asked.

The two bouncers exchanged a look. But it was Jake who spoke. "The boss," he said, "is Rango's dad. Wanna meet him?" □

CHAPTER 56

From behind a big old-fashioned desk, the squat, balding man looked from me to Jake. He scratched his chin and asked Jake, "So, this the girl?"

My gaze drifted to Jake. He was sitting with his long legs stretched out in front of him, holding a cold beer to his bloody face. "Not just any girl. *My* girl."

I felt myself smile. Jake and I were sitting in two wooden office chairs opposite the guy. The bouncers had left the instant we sat down, leaving only the three of us until one of the bouncers had returned to toss Jake the beer and leave almost immediately. I had been offered a beer too. I declined. The last thing I needed was a distraction of any kind.

The guy looked at Jake with hooded eyes. "Your girl. So you keep saying. Family, huh?"

My smile faltered. It was true that Jake and I would soon be related by marriage, but I still didn't like the idea of him referring me as family. It implied all sorts of relationships that weren't exactly legal, considering the things I wanted to do to him.

The guy turned his gaze on me. "I hear Randall's been giving you some trouble."

I squinted at him. "Randall?"

"Randall, Rango," the guy said. "Whatever the punk goes by these days."

What did someone say to that? Stalling for time, I studied the guy's desk. It had nothing on it except for a highball glass, half-filled with big ice cubes and who-knows-what drink. There was no coaster, and condensation slid down the glass. It eased onto the wood to form a soggy circle around the drink. Funny too, because Rango was so picky about that sort of thing.

Before I could stop myself, I asked, "Are you really Rango's dad?"

"Hell no." The guy made a sound of disgust. "That kid didn't spring from *my* loins."

"Oh," I said. "I thought—"

The guy held up a hand. "He's the *wife's* crotch-fruit. Not mine."

I shook my head. "Uh, crotch fruit?"

"Crotch-fruit, kid, devil spawn..." The guy shrugged. "The kid's a shitload of trouble."

"Oh," I said. "So you're his, uh *step* dad?"

He grimaced. "Yeah. But you can call me Lou."

I leaned forward. "Is his name *really* Randall?"

Lou chuckled. "You like that, huh?"

"Honestly?" I felt my lips twitch. "Yeah."

Lou was nodding. "Get this. When I meet his Mom, the kid's like seventeen. And he's not in my house two weeks when he decides his name is gonna be what? Rango." The guy gave a wheezy laugh. "What an asswipe."

I couldn't help it. I laughed too. Rango *was* an asswipe. Too bad I hadn't figured it out earlier. It would've saved me a whole lot of trouble.

"If you ask me," Lou continued, "you get a name, you should stick with it."

I felt color rise to my cheeks. Nearby, I heard Jake give a chuckle, which I chose to ignore.

Eager to change the subject, I said, "But about Jake...?" I gave Jake a sideways glance. "He's not in any trouble, is he?"

"Jake?" Lou said. "The way I hear it, he's always in trouble."

Well, there *was* that.

I cleared my throat. "Actually, what I mean is *here.*" I winced. "For the fight. You're not gonna call the police on him or anything, are you?"

At this, Lou almost bust a gut laughing. He looked to Jake. "Yeah, she's a real card, isn't she?"

Somehow, I knew he was making fun of me, but I couldn't quite my finger on why. I looked to Jake for some clue. His gaze held amusement, but no mockery.

"Lou isn't prone to calling the police," Jake said.

"Yeah," Lou said. "I like to solve my own problems."

Something about that statement seemed vaguely ominous. I recalled the things that Trey had mentioned in the job-trailer, something about Rango's dad being someone you don't mess with. At the time, I figured he was spinning tales to stall me. Now, I wasn't so sure.

Again, I looked to Jake. He looked fearless as usual. But in truth, that didn't offer a whole lot of comfort. How did you gauge something like this when nothing scared the guy?

I turned back to Lou. "But he's not in trouble with you, or the club, or anything, is he?"

Next to me, Jake spoke. "Luna, don't worry. We're good. If we weren't, you wouldn't be here."

I didn't know what he meant by that, but for some reason, I didn't like it. If things were bad, where would I be? Hiding out and letting him solve things alone? That didn't seem quite right.

In front of me, Lou spoke. "Jake and me, we're square." He gave a slow nod. "That fight? Pure gold."

"So you saw it?" I asked. "And you're okay with it?"

"That ass-kicking?" Lou's voice hardened. "The fucker deserved it."

Like I was going to argue.

Lou leaned forward. "Let me tell you something. I've got a handful of clubs – a couple in the suburbs, one in Chicago, and a new one we're putting up in Vegas. Tank, he's a V.I.P. at all of them. When he shows up, it's good for business." Lou frowned. "Not so good for my people."

I knew exactly what people he meant. "You mean the waitresses?"

"And more," Lou said. "The guy's an asshole. Runs the help ragged, tips for shit too."

Given what I'd seen with my own eyes, that wasn't terribly surprising. Still, I recalled what Bianca had said earlier about Tank getting an appearance fee to be here. "But, wasn't he invited tonight, or something?" I asked.

Lou grinned. "Not just invited. I *paid* him to be here."

I couldn't help but ask, "Why?"

"Payback." Lou's grin widened. "And publicity." Lou flicked his head toward Jake. "That fight you saw? By tomorrow, it'll be all over the news. And I'm not talking local only. I'm talking national. Shit, maybe international."

I almost laughed. "So you set Tank up? Does he know this?"

"Shit no," Lou said. "Far as Tank knows, Jake's getting tossed out on his ass. Better publicity that way."

I turned to Jake. "So *that's* why we were here tonight?"

Jake leaned forward. "One of the reasons." He reached into his pants pocket and pulled out Rango's little black book, which I had returned to him just a few hours earlier. Jake placed it on Lou's desk and said, "and there's the other reason."

Lou reached out and picked it up. He leafed through the pages and looked up, turning his attention to me. "I heard you had some fun with this."

In spite of his friendly tone, I knew enough to be careful. "Just with Rango's stuff," I said. "I didn't even look at the rest of it."

"Rango's stuff," Lou said as he reached down to open his top drawer. "I've got some of his 'stuff' right here."

Lou pulled out a stack of printouts. I had no idea what they were until he read from the top sheet in a clear, deadpan voice.

"Whoops, I crapped my pants." He looked up, as if waiting for me to say something.

I cleared my throat. "It was a joke. I mean, he didn't *really* do that." Under my breath, I added, "That I know of."

Lou's mouth twitched. "His mom will be glad to hear that." He shuffled to the next page. "I pee sitting down. Is that weird?" He shuffled through a few more papers. "And my personal favorite," he said. "Need to know...Can you get V.D. from a goat?"

Oh my God. I'd forgotten about that one. Color shot to my face. "I guess I was a little miffed," I admitted.

"Gee, I'd hate to see you pissed off," Lou said.

"I've seen it," Jake said. "It's not pretty."

I turned toward him. "Hey!"

He grinned over at me. "And I wouldn't have it any other way." □

CHAPTER 57

Five minutes later, we were outside, heading toward Jake's car. I couldn't decide what, exactly, I was feeling – relief, anger, happiness, all of the above. This was vintage Jake. No matter what he did, I ended up feeling all crazy and mixed up inside.

Walking fast, I said, "You could've warned me, you know."

"Warned you against what?" he asked. "Following me in there?"

There was so much more to it than that, but why quibble? I stopped moving and turned to face him. "Well, yes, actually."

Standing on the sidewalk, he pulled me into his arms. "Like you would've listened."

I felt myself frown. It was true. I wouldn't have listened. "Okay, fine, but still…"

He extended his arms out to grin down at me. "Still what?"

I was feeling weird and sulky. There was still so much that I didn't know, and he was so maddening when it came to giving answers. "Did you and Rango really fight?"

"It was something like that," Jake said. "And just so you know, it was sanctioned by Lou, so you don't have to worry."

"Sanctioned?"

"A fight for a fight. Remember?"

I did remember, and now, I actually understood. By agreeing to fight Tank, Jake was cleared to fight Rango too. It made sense in a Jake sort of way.

"About Rango," I said. "On the dance floor, what'd you tell him?"

"You don't want know."

"Why not?"

"Because it's a secret."

"A secret?" That was the lamest excuse, ever. I made a sound of frustration. I loved him. And I wanted him. But I was *so* over this sort of thing. I felt my chin jut out. "Jake, seriously. I *do* want to know. And I don't like it when you give me the brush-off." I gave him a pleading look. "Okay?"

He pulled me close and said into my hair. "It's no brush-off."

"It is, too," I insisted. For some reason, it suddenly seemed very important to push the issue. I mean, if I didn't start insisting on answers now, would I ever? "And I don't like it," I told him.

He hesitated a long moment before saying, "You really wanna know what I said?"

I nodded against him.

"I told him," Jake said, "that if he ever fucked with my future wife again, I'd fuckin' kill him."

I gulped. "Uh, what? So, were you joking, or, uh?"

"I love you," he said. "It's no joke."

Suddenly, I could hardly breathe. I pushed back to meet his gaze. "I love you too."

"Good," he said, "because I need a favor."

At that moment, I could have promised him anything. "What?"

"Sometime in the next month or so, when we happen to be out someplace, can you pretend we never had this conversation?"

I felt my brow wrinkle. "Why?"

He brushed a stray lock of hair from my forehead. "Because, you deserve better."

"Better than what?" I asked.

"Better than a passing mention on a cold sidewalk."

I knew exactly what he was getting at, and I loved him all the more for it. "I already have the best," I told him with a smile. "I have you."

"Just promise me. Alright?"

Like I could deny him anything. And to be honest, this was a promise I was glad to keep, because it sounded just like the unlikely fairy tale I had always imagined for us. "I promise," I told him.

His lips curved into a smile. "You remember the day we met?"

How could I forget? I'd been twelve years old. He'd rescued me from bullies double my age. He'd been my hero. And then, when I grew older, he'd been my fantasy. Now, standing here in the cool night air, he was real. And he was mine. It almost seemed too good to be true.

I met his gaze. "I remember."

He glanced down. "The way you looked at me..."

I had to laugh. At the time, I felt older than my years, practically a teenager, or so I'd thought. "Yeah," I said, feeling my cheeks grow warm as I tried to make a joke of it. "I thought you were dreamy, like a movie star."

"I'm not talking about that," he said.

"Then what?"

"There was something about your look, I could tell, you thought I was one of the good guys."

"You *were* one of the good guys." I smiled at the memory. "My knight in shining armor."

"That's not me," he said, pulling me close. "But for you? I wanna be."

And somehow, as I lost myself in his steady embrace, I just knew he would be, no matter what.

THE END

Other Books by Sabrina Stark

Unbelonging (Unbelonging Book 1)

Rebelonging (Unbelonging, Book 2)

Illegal Fortunes

Jaked (Jake, Book 1)

ABOUT THE AUTHOR

Sabrina Stark writes edgy romances featuring plucky girls and the bad boys who capture their hearts.

She's worked as a fortune-teller, barista, game-show contestant, and media writer in the aerospace industry. She has a journalism degree from Central Michigan University and is married with one son and two kittens. She currently makes her home in Northern Alabama.

ON THE WEB

Learn About New Releases & Exclusive Offers
www.SabrinaStark.com

Follow Sabrina Stark on Twitter at
http://twitter.com/StarkWrites

44501225R00186

Made in the USA
Lexington, KY
01 September 2015